HIS TOY

WARLORD'S CAPTIVE DUET
BOOK ONE

SINISTRE ANGE

GTB PUBLISHING

 GTB PUBLISHING

Cover by Covers by Sophie

ISBN: 978-1964736129

PROLOGUE

When the Wolf first emerged from the criminal underworld on Earth and clawed his way to the top of the heap, the wealthy families who had relocated to the first-class living installations on the Moon didn't pay much attention. Those who had dealings with Earth were used to the changing regimes of the crime families that now reigned supreme behind the politicians left there. For the Moon Families, their planet of origin was no longer of much concern. They considered it a teaching tool—an entire planet-sized museum of the past—but their focus was on the future and the stars.

Then the Wolf became a household name, and Earth a testing ground, for a certain generation among the Moon Families. They wanted the taste of danger, the thrill of escape, for the Wolf would occasionally select one or two of the young men and women who would visit Earth for schooling or leisure, and they would disappear. Those who spent the shortest amount of time with the Wolf returned with wild stories of orgies and incredible sex, of pain and pleasure, and the adrenaline rush that could only come with the fear of death.

Perhaps not surprisingly, their peers immediately began to make trips to Earth in droves, secure in the knowledge they most likely would not be taken ... but wanting to tempt fate. Their entire lives had been safe, stale ... and so far, none of those the Wolf had taken had ever failed to return.

Of course, there were those who disappeared for months. When they were returned to their families they never spoke of their ordeal. The only way it was known they had spent time with the Wolf was when they were recognized by those who had returned after only a matter of days and were bragging about the experience.

The Wolf's following and power were such that the press was only able to obtain a few photos and little information. Most knowledge of the Wolf came through those few he'd taken or the intermediaries on Earth who transacted other business with the Moon.

The tourist trade on Earth swelled as the wealthy denizens of the Moon continued to court danger, never knowing who might be taken next.

1

Bella woke slowly, feeling groggy. The inside of her mouth tasted awful. The inside of her head felt even worse. She moaned, shifting a bit, and wondered why she was lying on something so hard and uncomfortable.

"Bella," a familiar voice whispered urgently. "Bella, are you awake? Are you okay?"

"Alex?" Her voice came out as a hoarse croak. She forced her eyes open, blinking and squinting as the light blinded her for a moment. "Alex, what's going on?"

There was a muffled whimpering sob behind her, and Bella tried to turn to see who was there, only to be pulled short by the bindings around her wrist, secured to a pole. She stared at the cording, horrified, before blinking and looking in the direction of Alex's voice.

He was sitting up, leaning against another pole where his wrists were tied.

What kind of sick joke was this?

Memories swirled. Bella and her boyfriend Ken had come on vacation to Earth with his best friend, Alex, and Alex's girlfriend Lisa. They'd only had a few days left before going home when she and Alex had gone out to a museum that neither Ken nor Lisa were interested in. Bella and Alex had come back early from the museum, feeling bad about deserting their partners, to find that Ken and Lisa hadn't missed them at all.

Bella had been horrified. Alex had been angry. They'd both packed up their stuff immediately, ignoring the pleas from Ken and Lisa, and gotten in a taxi. She'd been so glad Alex had been there; Bella knew she was a bit of a pushover and, if it hadn't been for Alex's righteous anger, she wasn't sure she would have been able to resist Ken's manipulations and explanations. Not to mention her family had been incredibly approving of their relationship: Ken's father was very influential when it came to assigning space in the housing installations. It had been Alex who had helped her realize she had every right to break up with Ken; that it wasn't her fault he'd cheated on her, and that she needed to get away. Now.

But what the hell had happened after they'd gotten in the taxi? She remembered crying on Alex's shoulder and then ... nothing.

"I'm sorry, Bella, I'm so, so sorry," Alex said miserably.

"What's going on?" she asked again, her voice becoming a bit shrill.

"Shhh." He did his best to be soothing, although it was obvious from the tension in his body he suppressed his own amount of panic. "Stay quiet." There was enough of a forceful demand in his voice that she pushed down the scream that wanted to bubble up out of her throat.

Another whimper behind her had her scooting toward the pole so she could sit up the way Alex was and look around. A fragile-looking young woman was also tied to a nearby pole, although separated from Bella and Alex by about ten feet. With her big crystal-blue eyes, white-blonde hair, and slight figure, the young woman looked like a captured pixie.

"What's going on?" Bella asked again, unable to completely keep the panic out of her whisper.

"I'm so sorry," Alex repeated, looking even more miserable. "We should have never come to Earth ... never gotten into that taxi ..."

Slowly, the hazy memories coalesced. She remembered Alex asking the driver why he was descending into the city when they should have been ascending to head to the space port ... The sickly sweet smell that had filled her nose and mouth, and Alex shouting ...

"Oh my god ..."

"Bella, it's okay, be calm."

"Calm? Be calm? How can you say that?" Her voice rose to a shriek, which cut off when metal scraped against concrete. All three of them turned toward the sound, and Bella's breath strangled in her throat.

The biggest and most dangerous looking man she'd ever seen in her life filled the doorway. The room they were in felt much smaller than it had a moment ago. His cold gaze swept over all three of them but lingered on the little blonde, who whimpered again as his lips hooked up in a cruel smile. The man had the same white-blonde hair as the young woman, although his was barely half an inch long, cut very close to his head, and his eyes were a vacant, sinister grey. Bella didn't blame the other woman for whimpering—she felt like doing so herself, and he'd only looked at her for a moment. There was something about him, the way he held himself maybe, that screamed violence and danger. This was the kind of man who would never be approved for immigration to the Moon, based on that alone.

With his dark pants and their many, bulging pockets, a grey t-shirt, and a vest that also looked to have filled pockets, the first word that went through Bella's mind was '*Mercenary.*'

"Good. You're all awake."

The cruel smile widened in anticipation, and Bella finally understood why her roommates had wanted her to be quiet.

———

After roping them together and hobbling their ankles by cuffing them with a short metal bar between the cuffs, Jordan—as he'd introduced himself—took Bella, Alex and the other young woman down the hall to a large, tiled room with a drain in the middle of the floor. It took every ounce of Bella's willpower not to start screaming. It would make no sense for Jordan to wake them up and *then* kill them, but if that's what he intended to do, this room would be the ideal place for it.

He removed the cords that joined them together and then grabbed Alex's bound wrists. For a moment, Alex tensed, and Bella worried he would try to fight. Although Alex was a couple inches over six feet, Jordan was slightly taller than that, and had a lot more muscle. Alex wasn't exactly weak-looking, but his muscles came from the body-conditioning every young person went through on the Moon. Jordan had obviously built his through far less reputable activities. Like beating people until they stopped making noises.

They didn't know where they were, what other

guards might be around, and Alex's feet were hobbled along with his wrists. As much as Bella wanted to get out of here, now wasn't their chance.

Fortunately, Alex knew that, too, because he relaxed and allowed Jordan to attach his wrists to a chain that hung down from the ceiling.

"Smart boy," was Jordan's only comment.

The little tic in Alex's jaw indicated his rage. She'd seen that same tic when Lisa had tried to tell him she'd only fucked Ken because she thought he'd like it—after all, hadn't they joked about swinging on the trip?

A moment later, Jordan had strung up Bella and the young blonde woman in the same manner. The young woman was even shorter than Bella had realized—her head barely came up to Jordan's chest. Next to the huge man, she looked even smaller than before. Bella hated the little part of her that was relieved the giant was obviously more fascinated with the blonde than he was with Bella. When he'd put Bella's wrists above her head, it had been with as little fanfare as he'd made with Alex.

While Jordan seemed to be gentler with the blonde, who cried silent tears down her porcelain cheeks, he also ran his hands over her body. Which, of course, just made her cry harder.

And what was wrong with her that she was wondering *why* he didn't have that interest, as long as he didn't?

Then Jordan pulled out a knife.

Now Bella couldn't stop the tears either, and the other young woman started bawling outright. Alex began to struggle against the cords, yelling at Jordan to leave 'the women' alone.

"Quiet," Jordan shouted. They all fell silent as he

glared at them. "You're all perfectly safe. Understood?" Bella nodded, Alex glared, and the young woman just cried some more. Jordan gave her a glance and ran his free hand along her cheek. "Quiet down, little one," he said, firmly. Bella stared at him in surprise: he'd sounded almost tender.

Quickly, efficiently, he cut off the young woman's clothes. She was tried valiantly to stifle her sobs, but had trouble with it, considering her body was stretched out and now exposed. She was a slight little thing, her breasts tipped with pink, pointed nipples like pencil erasers. Jordan tutted over the pale blonde hair between her legs. His hands ran over her body again, almost possessively, before he turned away from her and moved toward Bella.

Cold, slate eyes swept over her, taking in her tears. Unlike the blonde, Bella didn't get any reassurance, but he also didn't run his hands over her. Just the swift motions of the knife, a sharp smack to her bottom that made her cry out when he'd grasped her panties and she tried to twist away, and then he was done and moving on.

———

Geezus ... Alex wasn't going to look at Bella. *he wasn't going to look at Bella* ...

Alex snapped his eyes closed to keep from looking at Bella. It was so ridiculously wrong of him to even consider it in this situation. Sure, he'd always thought she was too good for Ken—whom he'd known was a bit of a dog even if they had been best friends—but Alex had never tried to picture her naked. The fact that she was dating his best friend meant Bella was off limits. Too bad his best friend hadn't felt that way about Alex's girlfriend.

He'd known he and Lisa were having problems, and they'd talked on occasion about swinging or threesomes, but he'd always thought they'd been mostly joking. Having her decide to fuck his best friend behind his back was not something he'd ever expected to have to worry about. And now he'd dragged Bella into those problems, too. Dammit, why couldn't he have just gotten a different room in the hotel? Or joined Bella in hers where they could have cried on each other's shoulders, rather than letting his pride get the better of him and insist on storming out and ending the vacation early?

Then they wouldn't be in this mess.

Were they being taken hostage? Everyone knew young people from the Moon had supremely wealthy families, and it did happen every now and then. Or was this something worse? He'd always discounted the idea that the Wolf might actually take someone like him. The Wolf usually dealt in couples traveling alone or young men or women who were in a large group but were unattached. The whole point of traveling with Ken and Bella had been to ensure a kind of safety-in-numbers strategy.

Finished with Bella, Jordan stepped in front of Alex, jolting him from the whirling chaos in his mind. His thoughts were spinning round and round, distracting him, until he was forced back to the present by Jordan's attention.

Jordan sliced the clothes from Alex's body with the same brutal efficiency with which he'd eradicated Bella's. Bella, with her fantastic curves and those beautiful, dark-pink nipples, that little strip of dark hair on her mound—

Dammit, stop it!

He tasted bile in the back of his throat. It didn't matter how beautiful Bella was or how fantastic she looked naked; he was just as much of a dog as Ken to be thinking about that right now. Hell, he was worse than Ken.

"Don't try to be a big man or you'll just get yourself and those girls hurt," Jordan murmured, his voice low enough that Alex knew it was for his ears only.

Then the other man moved away again.

Jordan's indifferent hands washed all three prisoners down with lukewarm water and soap. Well, indifferent to Alex and Bella; he lingered over Trish.

Alex had managed to exchange a few words with her when he'd first woken up, so he knew she was a scholarship exchange student in her second semester of college abroad. The little whimpering cries she made as Jordan washed her had Alex yelling again, but the big man ignored it. Bella was crying too. Alex hated himself for watching the tears dripping onto her breasts, especially when he felt a stirring in his groin as he looked at the creamy mounds with their pretty pink nipples.

Afterward, they were given mouthwash to rinse out the taste of their drugged sleep. It was strange how little things like a wash and a clean mouth could make his brain less fuzzy. Or maybe he was just finally waking up.

The three prisoners were hobbled with a bar that attached to their ankles, wrists tied behind their backs, and marched down a hall. The buzzing sounds of muffled voices came from a door at the end of it, and the muscles in Alex's stomach tightened with tension. He couldn't imagine how the girls must be feeling, considering their naked and vulnerable position and the abundance of lower, masculine voices coming from the end of the hall.

The stories of the Wolf rippled through his mind; the rumors and interviews with the released victims. The ones who had been willing to be interviewed had worn their time in captivity like a badge of honor. The others had returned to as normal of lives as they could without ever talking about what had happened to them. Alex prayed they had been taken by the Wolf, and that he would only be interested in them for a few days. Orgies and deviant sex for a couple days didn't sound so bad. Much better than some of the possible alternatives, and it was a well-known fact the young men and women taken by the Wolf were always returned in good physical health —even the ones that were kept for months.

Horrible to know Alex hoped for them to be put in a position where they would be unwilling sexual participants in some seriously kinky shit, but that was better than being dead or maimed, right? Especially when they knew they would eventually be released, intact and basically unharmed.

He hoped.

———

The room Jordan led them into was almost empty, despite being large enough to hold a multitude of people. It reminded Bella of her history lessons, when they'd studied ancient Earth and the royalty who had ruled over the time period. There was even a slightly raised platform on which there was a table. Chairs were scattered around the table, six in all, but only one man currently sat there. Despite the feeling of being before a throne, the starkness of the room, the bright overhead lights illuminating every corner, the lack of luxury, made everything feel all the more threatening. This was not a place of leisure or comfort – it was a threat.

Not a king, but a despot sat on the hard silver throne before them.

There were other men standing against the wall, guards perhaps, but they all faded into the background compared to him.

Bella's breath caught in her throat. No one had ever seen a picture of the Wolf. No one even knew his real name or where he originated, but everyone knew the description. Tall, dark hair that he'd allowed to go silver at the temples—shocking in an age where almost no one retained their true hair color past the age of forty, preferring to use the various applications that were available to keep the appearance of youth— a muscular body, bright, piercing, green eyes that were hard as jade, a long Roman nose, and cruel lips. She'd always wondered how lips could be described as 'cruel,' but seeing this man she understood. They were thin, mobile, and the smile upon them was threateningly cold.

She shivered, and not just because of the chill in the room or because she was naked. Bella had almost forgotten her nude state, she'd been so ensnared by the powerful man at the end of the room. Now she shivered again and hunched her shoulders forward, all too aware of the ropes that kept her hands behind her, of the hobbles that kept her from fleeing.

Beside her, Alex growled under his breath. She flicked a glance at him, trying desperately not to look anywhere below his shoulders. Beyond her boyfriend—now ex— Bella didn't have a whole lot of experience with men, so she hadn't seen a lot of penises. The urge to look at one swinging so close to her was nearly overwhelming, but it felt way too intrusive. It wasn't like Alex was unclothed by choice, and she could tell he'd been doing his best not to look at her or the other woman.

Jordan was leading them forward with the blonde in front, his hand wrapped possessively around her upper arm, towering over her in a way that might have been protective in another situation. Bella didn't know what to think of it. She really didn't know what to think of anything... Her head rang with the words "We should have stayed at the hotel" over and over again, but it wasn't like hindsight was any help to them now.

"Jordan." The man behind the desk stood as they approached, his gaze flicking over each one of them in turn. It was a quick visual inspection, but it felt very thorough.

Bella quailed and automatically leaned toward Alex for comfort. He was already chafing at the bit, angling himself forward so she was slightly behind him. The sharp, jade eyes noted his movement. Had Alex's obvious protectiveness just helped or hurt them?

The smile across the Wolf's face—it had to be the Wolf—wasn't at all reassuring. "So, what have you brought me today, Jordan? A present?"

His voice was low, gravelly, and hypnotically seductive. Bella stared, shocked to hear such an appealing sound coming from the mouth of a man who was completely physically intimidating.

"You did say you wanted a replacement for Abby soon," Jordan said, his voice indifferent. The big man didn't seem at all intimidated by the Wolf, although something about Jordan's stance said he respected the other man a great deal and he would follow where the Wolf led.

Abby...

Bella remembered the name and the face: a young woman with coppery-red hair and big grey eyes, assumed to have been taken by the Wolf while on holiday on Earth in Old Europa. Her picture and information had been on the newsfeed for months—not because people were worried about her return— once a young man who had been taken for a couple days had confirmed her where-abouts, but because everyone was so fascinated by the Wolf and his ... predilections.

"Mmmm ... I could be persuaded to take a blonde. It would make a contrast from Abby." The Wolf's face was serious, athough Bella got the impression he was teasing Jordan. It was obvious where the big blonde man's inter-ests lay. When he didn't get a reaction, the Wolf contin-ued. "Then again, it has been a while since I've had a couple."

"We're not a couple!" Bella blurted without thinking. Her only coherent instinct was to find some way to get out of this situation, and if the Wolf wanted a couple ... Then, she was horrified as the blonde's face turned to her with an expression of shock and despair. Had Bella just thrown the other woman under the bus? Would she really do such a thing to save herself?

"Not ... a couple ..." the Wolf said slowly, lingering over the words as if tasting them to see how he liked them. Examining her and Alex more closely now, he leaned forward, his sharp gaze obviously taking note of Alex's protective stance and the way she huddled against him for support. Bella's cheeks flushed as that intense gaze traveled over her body again. Her nipples had hardened in the cool air of the room, and she prayed the man didn't read anything into it. She kept her mouth clamped shut.

Maybe it was too late for the blonde, especially with the way Jordan had been acting, but Bella wasn't going to do anything further to push the other woman to her fate. Bella wasn't—wouldn't be—that kind of person.

"Driver said there was another couple following them out of the hotel, begging for a second chance." Jordan sounded both amused and smug. "From what I understand, these two caught their partners together. I thought you might find the dynamic intriguing."

God … had it really only been earlier today when she and Alex had discovered Ken and Lisa together? It felt like ages and ages ago. It also felt small and insignificant compared to what they were facing now, although at the time, it had felt like the end of the world.

Bella blinked. The Wolf now looked at her and Alex with an increasingly arrested expression, his feigned interest in Jordan completely abandoned. A sick feeling rose in her gut as she realized Jordan had known exactly what would cause the Wolf to lose interest in the other young woman. And that Bella's own words had confirmed Jordan's supposition.

"You may have the blonde," the Wolf said, waving his hand at the young woman, his cat-like eyes roving over Bella and Alex, very much like a large and dangerous predator.

Beside her, Alex growled "Trish!" and tried to move. The blonde's name must be Trish. Immediately, several men who had been standing on the sidelines—practically unnoticed compared to the Wolf's overwhelming presence, and to a lesser extent, Jordan's—converged on him.

One of them grabbed Bella's ropes and held her in place as well, while the Wolf came down off the dais to examine her and Alex more closely. Alex struggled, and the three men who held him forced him to his knees.

Next to them, Jordan pulled Trish away and lowered his head to whisper in her ear. He held her against his chest in an almost comforting manner, only belied by the way his hand traveled down her naked back to caress her ass. The young woman started sobbing again, but Bella couldn't focus on that. Not with the Wolf walking toward her.

Up close, he was even more intimidating. The grace with which he moved was elegant while giving off the impression of being deadly. The comparison to a large cat-like predator wasn't far off. Strange that they called him the Wolf, really, although she knew it was more for his behavior than his looks. In appearance, in the way he moved, he was more like the holo-vids she'd seen of panthers, before they'd become extinct.

Her breathing shallowed, panted, as he circled her to look over every inch of her naked body. She closed her eyes and tried to pretend she was ... well, anywhere but here, really. Anywhere else in the entire universe.

"Quite nice."

Bella's eyes flew open, and she squeaked as two hands hefted her breasts and caused her to look directly into the Wolf's amused, emerald eyes. Beside her, Alex shouted to leave her alone. She would have cringed back, but the man holding her ropes had shifted behind her, making it impossible for her to move away from the Wolf's explorations.

"I do enjoy a curvy woman." The Wolf smiled down at her in approval. Her mouth was so dry, she couldn't have answered even if she'd thought of anything to say. The moment he'd touched her, her mind had completely blanked and, as he gently squeezed her breasts to see her reaction, all she could do was whimper.

The gentle caress of his thumbs over her nipples made Bella shiver, and she inwardly cursed herself for the tingles that shot through her body.

This isn't me. It's not what I want. It's not my fault. It's just biology.

Maybe a little bit of the Wolf's natural charisma had rubbed off on her, too. In another time, another place, she might have been incredibly attracted to him.

"Stop touching her," Alex rasped from beside them, still struggling against both his restraints and the men holding him.

"Wait your turn, toy." The Wolf didn't look at Alex. His eyes were still on Bella's face as he pinched her nipples and brought her attention back to him. The slight bite of pain and pleasure zinged through her, straight to her clit. "I'm playing with pet right now."

Her insides chilled. These were his terms for them, his names for them. Pet and toy. He fondled her expertly and kept her eyes glued to his, and Bella wanted to moan in protest from the heat kindling inside her belly. It was so, so very wrong, and yet her body responded anyway, regardless of what she wanted.

"What's your name, pet?

She licked her dry lips and forced herself to answer. "Bella."

"And what's toy's name?"

Alex growled, but she didn't look at him. Looking away from the Wolf probably wouldn't be treated so lightly a second time. "Alex."

"Bella and Alex. Pet and Toy. I like it." The smile he gave her was not at all reassuring.

Then he slid one hand down her stomach, and Bella moaned. Not because it felt good, but because she knew what he would find when he probed between her pussy lips, and she had no doubts that's where his fingers were headed. With his other hand still on her breast, squeezing and kneading and teasing her nipple, the Wolf moved his hand between her legs. Her muscles strained as she automatically tried to press her legs together, tried to stop him from touching her, but the bar Jordan had secured as a hobble had more than one purpose.

When the Wolf's fingers came away wet, coated in glossy fluid, Bella closed her eyes again. She couldn't look. The Wolf laughed, and something slick spread over her lips. The smell of her musk filled her nose, and she felt sick with the humiliation.

"Pet's wet, Toy." The Wolf moved away from her. Bella opened her eyes to find him advancing on Alex, holding his fingers in front of him with the evidence of her arousal. "She's such a very good pet already, I think we should reward her."

"Sir."

A deep voice from the end of the room caught everyone's attention. Bella craned her neck to see who was speaking. Another man came forward with a redhead by his side. She was naked, her hands behind her back, and her head bowed so Bella couldn't see her face. Jewelry jingled on her nipples, and flashes of gold shone from between her legs, indicating something there, as well.

"Ah." The Wolf sounded satisfied. "Slave. I have good news. You've been replaced. You were a very good slave, and you can now go home to your family." He said it with all the joviality of a man bestowing a great privilege.

The woman's head came up sharply, and Bella recognized Abby from the holos. Her eyes were wide as she took in the scene before her, and the most astonishing array of expressions flashed over her face—relief, disappointment, hope, and finally sympathy as she looked at Alex and Bella.

"Thank you, Master."

"I'm not your Master anymore. Go and have a good life." He waved his hand and turned back to his newest playthings. Bella caught one more glimpse of Abby's face, and the relief was back, as well as the strangest impression the Wolf had somehow hurt the young woman's feelings. And then she was turning, led away by the man who had brought her in.

Bella knew the drill from the news vids. At some point today or tomorrow, Abby would arrive at the shuttleport, safe and sound. She'd be hounded by reporters the moment they realized who she was. Her family would be notified. They'd probably be there to greet her the moment she landed on the Moon and to do whatever they needed to maneuver through the social minefield that was part of being a returned "guest" of the Wolf's. While many of the younger members of their Society saw it as a point of interest, or even a badge of honor, there were just as many who saw the returned persons as damaged goods. Not that they'd say anything so insensitive in public, of course, but the stigma as well as the fascination, was there.

Bella had always been fascinated. And she hadn't blamed the victims. Although she hadn't thought she'd ever be in their place, either.

"So, Toy, what do you think we should reward Pet with?" the Wolf asked as if he hadn't just released a young woman back to her real life after months of keeping her in a position of sexual slavery.

"Freedom. Let her go."

Bella stared at Alex, astonished. Would he really try to send her away at the cost to himself? How could she leave him here, even if the Wolf agreed? She'd never forgive herself.

The Wolf laughed uproariously, so she knew it wouldn't happen anyway. But at least he found them amusing right now. She'd gotten the impression he enjoyed toying with them, playing with them, but if they bored him, he'd find other ways to make them interesting. And Bella really didn't think she wanted to know what those other ways might be.

"Oh, I do like spirit." The Wolf's eyes glowed as he looked down at Alex with the same speculation and interest with which he'd examined Bella. "You two are going to be quite delightful. In fact ... I know." He turned back to Bella and rested one hand on Alex's head. Alex tried to toss it off, but the Wolf just gripped his hair tightly and jerked his head upright hard enough that Alex grunted with pain. "Bella, Pet—you get a choice. Do you want me to fuck you right now? Or do you want Toy to fuck you?"

2

Oh, god ... Bella's head whirled. Have sex with him or have sex with Alex?

Really, it was no choice at all.

"Toy. I mean, Alex." Horror struck through her as she realized what she'd said first.

"Bella no!" Alex strained against the Wolf's hand in his hair, the men who were holding him on his knees. "You don't have to do this!" He glared up at the Wolf. "Let her go."

"You're getting repetitive. Boring." The Wolf's green eyes glinted in a way that belied his words, and he reached into his pocket, ignoring Bella's pleas to leave Alex alone, that she'd made her choice. He pulled out an object and popped it into Alex's mouth, and then wrapped the straps around his head. A gag.

Panting from the fear that coursed through her, Bella almost dropped to her knees. Just because the Wolf was known for letting people go unharmed didn't mean he wouldn't change that now. One of the most common things his former victims had stressed was how unpredictable he was.

"So, Pet." The Wolf dropped Alex's head now that he'd hushed the younger man and walked back toward Bella. "You'd rather fuck Toy than me? He doesn't seem very willing. I certainly am."

His hand reached down to grope his cock through his pants, and Bella gasped as she saw the sizable bulge there.

"No," she whispered. This time she did fall to her knees, nearly making the man holding the ropes behind her stumble. "Alex..." Her voice grew in strength as she looked across the short distance between them. "Alex, you have to fuck me. Please."

The Wolf sighed. "I suppose I should feel insulted... but after all, it's not like we know each other yet, so I'll let it slide this time, Pet." His voice became crueler as he spoke, and he reached out and tweaked her nipple before caressing her head, the way he might pet a dog. Then he snapped his fingers at the man behind her. "Release her ropes. I'm going to let you beg Toy, Pet. And if he doesn't agree to fuck you in the next two minutes... then I will."

The restraints around her wrists were cut, as was the hobble around her legs. She forced herself to her feet and stumbled over the few steps it took to get to Alex. Bella ignored the men behind him, ignored the chuckling and the snide remarks all around her, and she reached out and took Alex's face in her hands.

"Alex please, you have to do this. He's going to rape me, you know he will. He's not bluffing. Just nod your head. Just nod your head and say you'll fuck me."

God, what had she come to ... This morning she'd been incensed that her boyfriend and Alex's girlfriend had cheated on them. Now she was having to beg Alex to fuck her. And he was looking at her with the most tormented expression on his face, his eyes begging her to do something—anything other than ask him to do this.

"It's not rape, Alex—I'm choosing you," she pleaded. Except they both knew, given a real choice, she wouldn't be having sex with anyone. Her voice dropped down to a strained whisper again. "Please … Alex … you have to save me."

———

Alex wanted to scream with frustration. Didn't Bella see? By giving in, by playing this sick game, they were already losing to the Wolf. And at the same time... he didn't doubt that the man meant every word he said. If Alex didn't have sex with Bella, the Wolf would.

But what was to stop him from doing so anyway, afterward?

He could see Bella wasn't thinking about that. Her pupils were huge, dilated from fear—all she could think about was getting past this first obstacle, this first terror.

And he couldn't blame her. That same terror pulsed inside him. The gag the Wolf had put in his mouth wasn't huge, but it was large enough that he couldn't spit it out. It filled the inside of his mouth, made of some material that shaped itself to block as much noise as possible and pressed down on his tongue.

A grating sound made both him and Bella turn their heads. There was a hole opening up in the middle of the room's huge floor, a platform rising out of it. On the platform was a huge bed, its canopy and corners festooned with chains and restraints. Several wooden structures surrounded it, all looking threatening as Alex imagined the various ways a human body could be secured to them. A sick feeling rose in his stomach. He couldn't leave Bella to the Wolf's mercies.

Even knowing the Wolf could still do whatever he wanted to them afterward. Alex just couldn't make the choice that would leave him unaffected and condemn Bella.

Besides, a faint hope inside him whispered, maybe the Wolf just wanted a show right now. He was unpredictable, right? Maybe he just wanted a show and then he'd let them go.

Alex nodded, and Bella nearly sobbed with relief.

"Too bad. Only a few more seconds, and I could have played with Pet." The Wolf glanced at his watch. He nodded to the men behind Alex. "Release Toy." The man stepped closer as Alex's ropes were undone, his face completely serious, and stared straight into Alex's eyes. "Don't even think about trying to escape. There is no way you'll make it out of this room, and if you try to, I will tie up Pet, and I will tie up Jordan's new blonde, and I will let every single one of my men come and fuck both of them while you watch." A cruel smile glinted across his lips. "And I have a lot of men under my command."

The frightened sob Bella let out as she snuggled closer to Alex made his heart break. His arms were free now, and he immediately pulled her to him while trying to ignore how soft and silky her skin felt against his. When he reached up to remove the gag, the Wolf slapped his hand away.

"The gag stays in, for now." The Wolf stepped back. He gestured grandly at the platform that had been raised in the center of the room. It reminded Alex a bit of the ancient gladiator arenas, where emperors put on spectacles for their underlings. He had no doubt this particular stage served a similar purpose. At least there weren't too many people in the room. "Choose your pleasure."

When Alex hesitated, Bella grabbed his hand and started dragging him toward the platform, headed straight for the bed. Alex let Bella lead him and tried to focus on her and not on their surroundings. It was surprisingly easy to push the other men in the room to the back of his mind and focus solely on her naked curves, the way her bottom wobbled as she hurried them both along. Bella was a beautiful woman; he'd always thought so. He just hadn't thought he'd ever be in a position to see her completely naked, much less do something about it.

It was shameful how his body reacted—how it had been reacting. Being chosen over the Wolf wasn't exactly a commendation, but Alex would do his best to make this ... if not pleasant, then at least not awful for Bella.

He wanted to tell her that, to whisper in her ear that everything would be okay—even if it wasn't a promise he could keep—but the gag meant all their communication was one way.

When they reached the bed, she looked up at him with troubled, frightened, hazel eyes. "I'm sorry," she whispered. "I'm so sorry ... and thank you."

Alex nodded, hoping his eyes showed his own apologies, his own unhappiness at the situation, even while his cock strained toward her. The generous curves of her breasts and hips were more than enough to make any red-blooded male stand up and pay attention. The hard pink nipples tipping her generous breasts would have made his mouth water if he hadn't been gagged.

They looked at each other for a long moment, wordless communication passing between them. They were in this together. Partners. And they would support each other through this.

"Better hurry, you two, before I decide it would be more fun to join you than watch you." The Wolf's voice purred but it was heavy with threat.

Bella's eyes widened, and then she grabbed Alex's hand and squeezed her eyes shut as she brought it to her breast. A wave of dismay swept over him. He'd never slept with a woman who wasn't one hundred percent willing. How was he supposed to do this when she couldn't even look at him touching her? And yet, they didn't have a choice, did they?

The heavy weight of her breast was soft and warm in his hand, and he groaned as her nipple pressed against his palm, his fingers automatically closing around the offering of flesh. How incredibly horrifying to discover his cock throbbed even harder, not caring that this wasn't his or Bella's choice.

Aware of the surrounding eyes and doing his best to ignore them, Alex reached up to cup both her breasts in his hands. To his surprise, Bella let out a breathy little moan as he gently squeezed. It soothed his feelings somewhat to know his touch wasn't completely repellent. Unless, of course, she was pretending he was Ken. Which he would kind of understand, even if it was still a little lowering to think she might be imagining her cheating ex.

But if that's what it took, then that's what it took. He certainly wasn't going to blame her for doing whatever she could.

Still ... Alex had no need to think of Lisa. All he had to

do was forget the other people in the room, forget the gag in his mouth, forget the room itself, and focus on Bella, and his cock was hard as a rock. Warm, soft, sweet curves, her skin like silk under his hands. Another time, another place ... So, he did his best to pretend.

He plucked at her nipples and watched her face closely to see the muscles relax there as he gently caressed her. After seeing the Wolf's rougher handling, he wanted to be as gentle as possible while he fondled her.

"Good. Now lift her up onto the bed."

Alex's jaw clenched, making it ache even more around the gag, as he felt Bella shiver in response to the Wolf's command. Couldn't the damn man just let them be? Just for a few minutes?

But he couldn't risk disobedience—not with Bella so vulnerable. They were surrounded on every side by the Wolf's men, Bella was frightened and exhausted, and Alex wasn't much better. With the Wolf's threats hanging over their heads, it would be stupid to attempt even the tiniest bit of disobedience. If Alex didn't follow the Wolf's orders, it could very well be Bella who paid the price.

His eyes slid over to the side, where Jordan sat with Trish on his lap. The tiny blonde was crying, her eyes closed, with Jordan's arms wrapped around her, one large hand fondling her small breast. There was more than just Alex and Bella's fate riding on his obedience.

He slid his hands down to Bella's hourglass waist and gently lifted her up the few inches to the bed before scooting her back so all her weight was on the mattress. Those big, serious, hazel eyes gazed up at him through thick lashes. At least she wasn't crying anymore, even though her eyes were red-rimmed and her lips swollen from the crying she'd been doing earlier. Alex touched her cheek, sweeping back some of her hair that was stuck to the dried tears.

"Lie down, Pet." The Wolf was watching them with hunger in his eyes.

———

With her legs hanging off the bed, Bella closed her eyes again and obeyed. Everything felt so surreal. Alex's lips stretched around that awful gag and made his expressions distorted, but she could see the worry in his eyes.

Mostly, she had been worried he wouldn't be able to go through with it. And she would so much rather him than the Wolf.

She wouldn't have chosen to have sex with Alex if she hadn't been forced into the situation, but it was less of a violation. At least she knew Alex; had talked with him, trusted him.

Laid out in front of him, Bella felt much more vulnerable. Having his big, muscled body so close to hers earlier had made her at least *feel* more protected even though it had been an illusion. It was obvious Alex wanted to protect her and would do whatever he had to. Even have sex with her.

Bella understood his reluctance, but she'd felt strangely rejected when he'd hesitated. He wasn't really rejecting *her*, just the situation. It was stupid to feel otherwise. The fact that he was obviously hard, now, was both reassuring and a little frightening. Looking up at him, she could see both hesitation and desire in his eyes.

She did her best to focus on just him but couldn't help seeing the Wolf standing just a few feet away, to the side of Alex, watching them with need in his eyes. It made her heart pound faster as her body tensed, the desire to flee welling up inside her.

"Fuck her, toy."

Alex grimaced and closed his eyes at the crudeness of the Wolf's demand. Bella did her best to block out the words, to concentrate on the gentle way Alex ran his hands down her body and pulled her legs up to drape them over his arms and spread her thighs wide for him. The wetness that had begun when the Wolf had played with her breasts hadn't gone away, and now that Alex was touching her, she felt free to enjoy it without shame.

The head of his cock pressed up against the soft, wet lips of her pussy, and Bella gasped. When she met Alex's eyes, she was shocked by the desire she saw there, even though it was tinged with guilt. Even if he was angry at the situation and protective, he still wanted to fuck her. The hard cock at the entrance to her body wasn't just a reaction to being around a naked woman—that was real desire in his eyes.

Bella didn't know how to react to that, and she didn't get a chance to before he was pushing into her. She gasped, and her body arched as the thick rod of his erection pushed into her, stretching her open.

She'd been avoiding looking at his nakedness and hadn't focused on the size of his penis. It was bigger than she'd realized, and her pussy muscles clamped down around him in shock at both the breach and size of him. Thick, hot and hard; he made a strangled noise, and when she looked up at him again she realized that he'd groaned in pleasure, but it had been muffled by the gag. His warm, hazel eyes were half-lidded now, the muscles of his body tense against hers.

With a little whimper, Bella dug her hands into the

sheets, unsure where else to put them. Bella didn't want the Wolf to think she was encouraging any of this. She didn't want him to know it felt good.

It was all she could do not to moan when Alex drew his hips back and plunged forward again to sink deeper inside her. The rounded head of his cock burrowed straight into her body, the ridged portion dragging against her inner flesh as he pulled away and thrust hard again. He was so very thick, and stretched her muscles more than any man she'd been with before, making her gasp and cry out in shock as he split her wide open. With her thighs draped over his arms, she was completely spread and vulnerable, with no way to halt or even slow the advance.

No way to stop him from burying himself inside her, his muscled body leaning forward so she bent almost double at the waist, her pussy stuffed full of his cock, and the hard bone of his pelvis pressed against her swollen clit. Bella gripped the mattress even tighter and tossed her had back and forth, closing her eyes as she concentrated on not rubbing herself against him. The press of his hot body against her sensitive pussy lips, which felt stretched and tight, was incredibly erotic. The sensation of him so deeply embedded inside her, even the eyes of their watchers tickling over her skin—all of it was both frightening and exciting.

She hated the part of her that found some kind of sick satisfaction in what was happening. Maybe it was because she'd never quite measured up to the standards of beauty on the Moon. She'd never considered herself very desirable, and some demented part of her found the arrested gazes of the Wolf—of his men, of Alex— somehow flattering. After all, the Wolf could have any woman he wanted, couldn't he? He didn't have to make do with leftovers.

And, while he might be getting twisted satisfaction out of her and Alex not being a couple, Bella couldn't deny the real desire she saw in the Wolf's intensely bright eyes. It was too disturbing to look at him while Alex was deep inside her, panting with long, deep breaths as if he were trying to hold back his pleasure even though it was impossible.

It was also too disturbing to look at Alex. The mixed emotions swarming over Bella were becoming all raveled up in the pleasure growing deep in her core. If only he would move hard and fast, do it quickly and get it over with … But he seemed to be struggling with himself, his long strokes in and out of her lingering, and she couldn't stop the feelings of pleasure burgeoning inside her.

Closing her eyes didn't help because then it was all too easy to forget where they were, what was happening, and to become lost in the pleasure of Alex's thrusts between her legs. Her thighs tightened, trying to squeeze him, but his arms were much stronger and kept her spread wide and open.

Bella let out a little moan and opened her eyes again, trying to remind herself where she was.

She turned her head to the side, away from the Wolf, and found herself looking straight at the blonde—Trish. The young woman sat on Jordan's lap, facing away from the huge man, who had one muscular arm wrapped around her and across her body to squeeze her breast. He'd positioned her so her legs were on either side of his and then he'd spread his own thighs, forcing her to spread her legs even wider. His other hand covered the pink flesh between, his fingers were very, very busy. Tears streamed down from the woman's blue eyes, but her nipples were hard, and the fleeting look of shame as she met Bella's gaze said she was reluctantly enjoying Jordan's caresses just as Bella did with Alex fucking her.

The big man had his face buried in Trish's shoulder, obviously kissing and suckling on her neck. The blonde woman stared at Bella and Alex with a kind of horrified fascination—the same way Bella stared at Trish and Jordan. It was like watching a train wreck that was somehow erotic; she couldn't look away, no matter what she wanted.

Her pussy became wetter and made sloppy noises as Alex pushed in and out, his thrusts coming harder and faster at just the right time to force her body to respond with pleasure. Watching Jordan's glistening fingers stroke Trish's folds, Bella knew the other woman faced the same dilemma. And for some sick reason, it was all turning Bella on.

She moaned and dragged her gaze away, horrified at her reactions, only to find herself staring into the Wolf's glittering eyes. He'd moved closer, so he was almost touching Alex, his lips parted with anticipation as he watched her. Somehow, he knew ... He knew she was close, that she would orgasm while Alex fucked her, even though she didn't want to.

It should have dampened her response, it should have made the pleasure subside, but Alex rubbed against her swollen clit, and Bella cried out, her hips lifting as she stared into the Wolf's triumphant green eyes. The shameful ecstasy burst out of her core, her body rippling and shaking with as she clenched down on Alex's cock.

A ragged groan tore from his throat, muffled by the gag but clearly audible, as her pussy convulsed around him. His hands tightened on her waist as he pounded faster, harder, and Bella clutched at the bed beneath her as the ecstasy spiraled wildly out of control. Tears leaked from her eyes, and she squeezed them shut as a defense against the Wolf's eager gaze.

Alex's cock pulsed inside her, and, as he groaned again, she realized he was coming. Hot liquid sprayed her insides, and she gasped as her pussy milked him, eagerly accepting the offering as it set off another wave of rapture that rippled through her body.

Then he slumped over her, his muscular chest heaving, and bent her completely in half as the strength and fight went out of him. She didn't even whimper a protest —thanks to her fitness training she was very flexible— and completely understood why he was so spent. Every single one of her muscles felt languid, as if her climax had also relieved her body of all the stress and tension it had been carrying since she'd woken up in that awful cell.

Behind Alex, the Wolf sighed; a deep, satisfied sound. "You two are going to give me so much pleasure. And now it's my turn."

3

The Wolf's words pinged through Alex's brain, but he couldn't make sense of them. His mind felt fuzzy, hazy, as if all his ability to think had been sucked right out of his cock along with his jizz. Bella's orgasm had ripped the last shreds of his self-control away, a battle he'd already been losing thanks to how hot and wet she'd been.

What had the Wolf meant, when he'd said it was 'his turn?'

Alex struggled to push himself upright, ready to defend Bella.

A heavy hand pushed Alex back down, and Bella let out a small cry as his weight came down hard and bent her body in half again.

Alex growled behind his gag and tried to push himself back off her, but he had gravity working against him, and his arms were tangled in her long legs. The pressure on his back moved—two men were on either side of him, both holding him down on top of Bella. His cock was still lodged inside her, slowly shrinking but quite firmly planted. The weight of his body and the men pressing down seemed to do something pleasurable to her because she gasped, and her pussy tightened around him again. It was too much for the sensitive surface of his cock, and he felt himself jerk inside her as he spasmed.

Behind him, the Wolf chuckled. "Ah ... Toy ... I'll be interested to see how you enjoy this."

Something slick and hard pressed against Alex's anus, and he howled behind the gag as the Wolf's finger began to invade him.

The Moon families didn't mind experimentation as long as there was at least one child in each family who would create a new generation. When he'd first been declared an adult, Alex had experimented with some of his male friends. He'd decided it wasn't for him; he preferred the soft curves of women, their musky scents and slick pussies. And while he'd enjoyed anal sex when it was his cock doing the breaching, he'd found he hadn't enjoyed receiving nearly as much. In fact, he'd only tried it a couple times before ending his experimentation, and that had been years ago.

The Wolf's finger burrowed into him, stretching the nearly virgin orifice, and Alex began to struggle in earnest. It was only the squeaking cries from Bella that caused him to freeze again as he realized his struggles were hurting her.

"I'm sorry," she whispered, looking up at him with tear-filled brown eyes. She must have realized what was happening. "I'm so sorry."

He wanted to tell her it wasn't her fault, he didn't blame her. How could he? What was she supposed to have done—chosen the Wolf? It wasn't like either of them could have predicted the outcome.

He couldn't help trying to squirm away, trying to

push up while the Wolf had his finger buried inside him. Alex groaned as the intruder probed and twisted, greasing up his channel with lubrication. The stroking tip found a spot inside him that made his body clench and blood surge to his dick.

No. No, no, no, no, no.

Alex shook his head and gritted his teeth against the rubbery gag. Maybe he couldn't fight back, maybe he couldn't run away, but he'd be damned if he'd enjoy this.

A sudden gripping thought nearly slayed him: was this how Bella had felt as she'd creamed herself all over his cock? It made him feel a lot less good about making the sex pleasurable for her.

He couldn't look at her any longer, couldn't see the guilt and pity in her eyes—especially with his own guilt nearly suffocating him now—and Alex buried his face into Bella's shoulder. The Wolf pulled his finger out and then came thrusting back, this time with two fingers to stretch Alex's sphincter. The worst part was it didn't entirely hurt. It burned slightly as his muscle stretched and spasmed, but the Wolf's questing fingers also pressed against his prostate as they plunged in, and Alex's cock stiffened slightly in the hot grasp of Bella's pussy.

The fingers twisted, plunging in and then retreating again, making Alex writhe uncontrollably against Bella's softness, though he did his best to keep still, if only to avoid hurting her further.

They were trapped together, their bodies still interconnected, while the Wolf continued his torment.

Was this her fault? If Bella hadn't chosen Alex earlier, would he be suffering like this now?

The idea that she'd saved her own skin, only to sacrifice his, even unintentionally, was horrifying.

Bella couldn't tell exactly what the Wolf was doing to Alex but she could guess.

The idea of anal sex had always horrified Bella. It seemed so dirty and undignified. With Alex's big body on top of her, his broad shoulders blocking out her vision, she couldn't see the Wolf at all, but it was obvious he didn't feel the same way.

Alex shifted on top of her again, and it was all Bella could do not to moan. His pelvis pressed against her splayed pussy lips, and his pubic bone still ground against her clit every time he moved—and that whole area was super-sensitive after her shameful orgasm. She was thankful to be flexible enough that being bent in half, even for a length of time, was only uncomfortable rather than painful. Unfortunately, being merely uncomfortable didn't do anything to decrease the pleasure that sparked every time Alex's body rubbed against hers.

He made a groaning noise behind his gag, muffled and pleading. When she looked up at him, his eyes were closed and his forehead was wrinkled as if he were in pain or, at least, extreme discomfort. That or …

The sudden pressure deep within her told Bella his cock grew inside her, hardening and pushing its length back into the depths of her pussy.

"Oh!" She writhed beneath him again and tightened around the hardening shaft.

Was Alex aroused by what the Wolf was doing? And was he enjoying it, or was it the same as when her body had responded without her mind's consent? Bella didn't doubt the Wolf was a master at eliciting the physical responses he desired.

But there was nothing she could do to help Alex. Bella was more trapped than he was, pinned beneath him like a bug on a stick. The analogy would have made her giggle if the situation weren't so awful.

Something bounced on the bed beside them, and Bella looked over and gasped when she saw Trish's face only a foot away from hers. The young blonde was bent over the bed, her wrists still tied behind her back, and Jordan stood behind her, fisting a huge, angry-looking, red cock. He saw Bella watching and winked at her, and then positioned himself.

Trish's cry as Jordan began to push into her made Bella want to close her eyes but, just as before, she couldn't look away. The contrast between Trish's humiliated and degraded expression and Jordan's look of abject pleasure was striking. The young woman closed her eyes and bit her lip as the big man behind her began to pump back and forth, fucking her with long, hard strokes.

To Bella's horror, as before, Trish's ravishing made her own pussy spasm in sympathetic response, bringing her unwanted pleasure.

———

Bella's body tightened around Alex's cock as the Wolf fingered his ass. He chanted 'No, no, no, no, no' behind his gag, but, of course, no one could hear it—and he doubted the Wolf would stop even if he could hear Alex's pleas. Bella was mostly quiet, other than the occasional squeal or moan, but Alex didn't blame her for not drawing further attention to herself. He was glad she didn't. At the very least, his current position protected her from molestation by the Wolf or his men. Even if it wasn't by his choice, at least he could feel like he was doing something for her.

Unfortunately, there wasn't anything he could do for Trish. At least it looked like Jordan was being fairly gentle with her. Alex wasn't sure if he had a hope for that, himself.

The Wolf's fingers were relentless, pushing and stretching the tight ring of muscle, spreading the lubricant liberally in Alex's spasming channel. He could only groan and try to relax, try to make the burn lessen. He remembered that much from when he'd experimented before.

Then the fingers withdrew entirely, and Alex's body relaxed and left him panting for breath. He hadn't realized how tense his muscles had become while the Wolf had violated him.

"Hold him still."

Hands came down on his shoulders and wrists from either side, and Alex began to struggle again. Bella's hands tightened on his shoulders as she clung to him and squeaked with dismay, but he couldn't help it.

Something hot and hard and much thicker pressed against his anus and began to push in. The pressure was immense, and Alex found himself panting and groaning, unable to do anything as one of the Wolf's hands rubbed his lower back. The man was speaking, but Alex couldn't hear any of the words. There was a roaring in his ears, and all he could do was squeeze his eyes shut and fight against the overwhelming sensation of being unbearably stretched. If the Wolf's fingers had burned, his cock was like a searing brand.

A fear tears leaked from Alex's face, and Bella's hands rubbed his chest as if to try to make him feel better, as the Wolf's cock stretched him wider and wider. When the crown popped in past his sphincter, Alex groaned with the minor relief.

The Wolf sank deeper into him, thrusting inch by inch, and made Alex spasm when the head of the Wolf's cock pressed against his prostate. His own cock, still firmly lodged inside Bella, had started to soften again but, with the stimulation against that sensitive spot, it began to swell.

Noooooooooooooooooo ...

Alex's protest was lost behind his gag as the Wolf began to rock on the spot, rubbing his cock over that sensitive portion of Alex's interior over and over again. All the blood in his body seemed to start rushing into his dick, which was all too happy to grow thicker and longer in the warm confines of Bella's body. Alex grunted and strained; there was nothing he could do with the Wolf's men pressing him down on either side. Beneath him, Bella squirmed and gasped, her movements only adding to the pleasure that began to mix with the burning discomfort of his nerves.

Jordan paid them no attention and ran his hands down Trish's sides as he continued to fuck her. If Alex hadn't been able to see her tear-stained face, it would have looked like a regular couple having sex. With her, as well, he could see the same struggle not to enjoy what was happening.

The Wolf and his men were masters at coaxing a

response from even the most reluctant of their victims. There was nothing Alex could do. He'd always been strong but, right now, he was overpowered and outnumbered.

When he gave up and told himself it was only for the moment, Alex's body relaxed.

"Good Toy … let me into that tight ass."

The Wolf retreated and plunged in, deeper than ever, and his cock slid, burning … burning … until his hips pressed against the curve of Alex's ass. They were now linked together, the Wolf filling Alex as Alex filled Bella.

The Wolf wrapped his fingers in a bruising grip around Alex's hips and began to move.

Each time he pulled away, he dragged Alex partially with him, which meant each time he plunged forward, the momentum and weight of his body caused Alex to sink back into Bella. It was as if he fucked both of them at once, Alex's cock a mere extension of the Wolf's depraved machinations.

It was awful.

It was wonderful.

Alex had never experienced the like before. His insides burned as the Wolf stretched him, over and over again, but his cock was in the wet haven of Bella's pussy. Every drag of the Wolf's cock across Alex's prostate made his dick jerk as his asshole tightened in response. Somehow the burn, the discomfort, the strange feeling of fullness began to intermingle with the more pleasant sensations of Bella's soft body beneath his and her rippling pussy clenching around him.

The pain and pleasure were shocking in their intensity. Alex felt like he was having an out-of-body experience: half of him brutally used by an infamous criminal, the other half in heaven as he wallowed in Bella's soft-ness. It seemed so wrong to take any pleasure in the expe-rience at all, but he couldn't help it. The tight wetness of her sheath was killing him by inches, even if his move-ments weren't under his control this time.

The Wolf's thrusts came harder and faster as Alex's tight tunnel submitted and adjusted to the rough intru-sion. Bella's hips moved and met his thrusts, and her eyes were closed—turned away from Jordan and Trish, turned away from *him*. He couldn't help but wonder where she had gone in her mind, but Alex was glad this wasn't entirely awful for her. The soft little 'ohs' that dropped from her lips made the blood pump through his veins even harder.

He could almost lose himself in the hazy burn of plea-sure like Bella had—God knew he wanted to—but he resisted because that was the only thing he had left. The only thing he could control. Not that it made a difference to his body: he could feel his orgasm approaching as the Wolf pounded into his ass and forced him to enjoy Bella's sloppy pussy for the second time.

It was wrong, and he fought it. Uselessly. The rubbing head of the Wolf's cock found his prostate with every prod, Bella's body moving under his, her soft moans of pleasure—it was all too much.

Alex shouted behind his gag in despair and ecstasy as he began to orgasm. Beneath him, Bella arched and her pussy rubbed against his body as she tightened around him in sympathetic rapture.

Behind him, the Wolf kept pumping and forcing his body to keep moving and thrusting into Bella, even as his cock began to spew cum into her pussy for the second time in less than an hour. The stimulating friction against his cock was too much to bear, and he cried out behind the gag as it became painful for his shaft to continue fucking her.

When the Wolf groaned and shoved deep, filling him completely, it was a relief. Alex slumped over Bella's body, and she shuddered beneath him in the final throes of her own orgasm. Spurts of cum pressed pass the tight ring of his sphincter and shot deep into his body. It was utterly degrading.

Alex had never felt so useless, so helpless in his entire life. This wasn't him.

Was it?

———

The Wolf sighed with satisfaction as he pulled away, and Bella opened her eyes when she realized that it was over.

To her left, Trish's eyes were closed, but the flush on her cheeks and Jordan's triumphant shout as he slammed hard into her made it clear he'd manipulated her body in the same way the Wolf had Bella's and Alex's. More tears trickled from underneath Trish's eyelashes, and when she opened her eyes, Bella could see her own shame mirrored back at her.

Bella felt awful. Sick. How could she have orgasmed —not once, but twice! And the second time, while Alex was being forcibly fucked, as well. Yet the tingling state of her pussy, the hypersensitivity of those soft folds against Alex's body, made it impossible for Bella to lie to herself.

The men who had been holding Alex down pulled him upright and supported him as he stumbled back. Her legs fell down from the crook of his arms, and she moaned with relief as her body unfolded. Her thighs landed well apart, so as not to put any pressure on her sore pussy lips, which were decidedly battered, by now.

The Wolf's gaze swept over Bella and Alex, his eyes taking in the cum seeping from Bella's red, swollen pussy, the sticky juices covering Alex's crotch, and he smiled. The way he looked at them ... It was almost triumphant.

"Very good. You both have pleased me." Relief and hope swept through her at the Wolf's words, but he firmly crushed them with his next. "I look forward to doing ... so much more with both of you. But for now, I have work to do. Dr. Margolis, Nurse Roche, come and take care of my Pet and Toy." He turned toward Jordan and raised one dark eyebrow. "I assume you'd like to go through the procedures for your blonde yourself?"

"Yes, Sir."

Bella looked over at Trish, who looked frightened but resigned. Her nipples were still hard and dark pink from the pinching abuse Jordan had put them through, and the blonde thatch of hair between her legs was matted with their combined juices. Jordan's proprietary arm about her said he'd rather not have anyone else touching Trish at all.

As a man and a woman came forward, Bella found herself shivering. She didn't want more strangers touching her—not even a doctor and a nurse. It was rare that such medical professionals were needed on the Moon; the families were always healthy, and any defects or internally occurring illnesses rarely needed the human touch. Computers and automated constructs did everything for them. To her increasing horror, she realized the doctor was headed toward her, and the nurse toward Alex.

The doctor was a thin man, younger than the Wolf,

with sharp, narrow features and a cruel cast to his smile. Dark eyes looked Bella up and down, an aura of anticipation hanging about him.

"Please, no," she whispered and hugged herself as she sat on the bed, her legs coming together to protect her most sensitive areas, even though it put pressure on her swollen pussy lips.

"Now now, be good, Pet." The Wolf came forward and stroked her hair in a propriety manner. Out of the corner of her eye, Bella saw Alex try to come toward her, despite how exhausted he must be, only to have the two men who held him drag him away and follow the nurse out of the room. "Dr. Margolis is only going to do some necessary things for processing. At the moment, he doesn't have permission for more than that, but if you're bad, then I'll let him do a great deal more."

As frightening as the Wolf was, his almost kindly demeanor made him seem a lot less threatening than the Doctor, who smiled at her in an increasingly unsettling manner. It seemed that he liked her fear, which only made Bella more afraid. But if there was one thing she trusted, it was that no one here would go against the Wolf's orders.

And she certainly didn't want to get in trouble and have the Doctor given *carte blanche* to do with her what he would.

Trembling, she nodded and got up.

"Good Pet."

The Wolf grasped her around the waist and patted her bottom to send Bella on her way. To dismiss her. One of his men followed as she walked on trembling legs toward Dr. Margolis. The doctor smirked and waved his hand for her to follow, before he turned and walked off in the same direction they'd taken Alex. Bella glanced over her shoulder: the man following her—obviously a soldier —smirked, too. Behind him, the Wolf settled back down at his desk and got back to work as if nothing had happened.

4

Dr. Margolis led Bella to a large room, where the walls and floor were tiled and white. Steel cabinets lined one wall, their gleaming surfaces giving no hint as to what horrors they might be conceal. There was a drain in the center of the room, which Bella stared at with a sinking feeling. In the far-right corner, there was a shower stall with nothing to obscure the view of anyone inside it, and in the center of the room was the kind of table she had seen on her rare visits to the doctor. Well. Almost.

It was made of padded black leather and steel, and had stirrups attached to one end and a multitude of straps hanging from the rest of it. A person could be secured to it in far too many ways.

"Come, come," Dr. Margolis said impatiently. "Get on the table and put your feet in the stirrups."

Bella turned at the end of the table and put her hands on it to hoist herself up. The soldier took up a post by the door and it was a strange thing, a relief to have another man there to see her naked body and witness whatever Dr. Margolis planned to do, but she was glad not to be alone with the doctor. That Alex had been taken to a completely different room made her feel more alone and vulnerable than ever. She'd take an extra pair of eyes on the doctor any day. Especially since she hoped the presence of the soldier would keep the doctor from exceeding the Wolf's orders.

"Feet in the stirrups."

Bella whimpered slightly and stared at the floor as she did what he asked. She hated the spread position of her legs and the way her pussy lips seemed to stick together for a moment. Her inner thighs were slick with Alex's cum, which had been dripping out of her all the way down the hall and had just trickled past her knees. Since she'd been following the Doctor, Bella hadn't had a chance to wipe herself off.

"Now lie back."

"Please—"

"Quiet!" The doctor snapped at her and reached out to grasp one of her nipples and pinch it, hard. Bella shrieked, and her hands came up to bat his fingers away to no avail; he just pinched harder. "Put your hands down and lie down."

Tears rolled down her face as she forced herself to put her hands down and lie back. Her nipple throbbed in the strong grip of his fingers, and Bella whimpered as she inadvertently tugged the little bud as she lay back. Once she was on her back, Dr. Margolis released her nipple, watching her face intently. Her fear of him spiked again as she realized the soldier in the doorway hadn't batted an eye, and the Wolf's words came back to her.

She needed to be good and do as he said if she wanted to avoid punishment, and obviously the doctor was allowed to mete it out. Perhaps the soldier would stop him; perhaps he wouldn't.

And right now, the doctor wanted her to be quiet and lie still. So, Bella forced her fears down and lay there, quiescent, as he strapped her down to the table. Straps went around her ankles to fixing them to the stirrups. One went across her lower belly, another across her chest, just under her armpits and above her breasts. Her arms were stretched out over her head and strapped down, and another band went across her forehead, immobilizing her and leaving her completely helpless in front of the sadistic doctor.

Moving back down to her feet, Dr. Margolis grasped each of her ankles and forced them even wider apart, making Bella cry out at the sudden movement and stretch of her muscles, which were already sore. Her pussy was splayed wide open and felt like it was splitting apart—there wasn't a single centimeter hidden from the doctor's lascivious eyes.

Not that he was looking there. He watched her face, obviously enjoying her fear and helplessness, aroused by his control. He locked the stirrups into place and went to one of the cabinets. Because of the strap across her forehead, Bella couldn't turn to see what he was doing, but she could hear the clinking of metallic objects. Not knowing what he was gathering only made her anxiety worse.

Bella closed her eyes and forced herself to breathe deeply, to try to calm down. With her eyes closed and nothing to distract her, she could feel her heartbeat pounding in her ears.

The screech of wheels and rattling of metal instruments had her opening her eyes again. As the doctor came into view, her breathing accelerated. The gleam in his eyes and grin on his face said whatever was about to happen, she wouldn't enjoy it.

"First things first," he said conversationally, holding up what looked like a gun with a long needle attached. The doctor smiled at her, reveling in the terror on her face. He walked around to her side and wiped a small area on the meat of her bicep with a wet pad, and then pressed the needle to the spot. "This will just pinch for a moment."

Bella cried out as the needle slid inside her but held as still as possible to keep it from moving around in her flesh. It stung on entry, and she felt sick feeling it probe down into her. There was a small noise, and it pinched before he pulled the needle away and wiped the spot again. This time, it burned a bit when he ran the pad over it, and the astringent smell rising up to her nostrils told her the pad had some kind of disinfectant on it.

"I just inserted a tracker into your arm." Dr. Margolis ran his finger over Bella's cheek as he grinned down at her. "Anywhere you go, anywhere on Earth, the Wolf will be able to find you. Although, right now it has a double duty: it's not just a tracker, but if you try to leave the compound at all, it will begin to release an electric charge through your body. It won't kill you, but it will be excessively painful."

He said that last with a kind of relish that stabbed fear through Bella's heart. Just when she thought she couldn't be any more afraid of the doctor he would say something that sent her to another level she'd never known existed.

"Now then, let's clean you up a bit."

Returning to her spread legs, the doctor methodically

cleaned all the residue of cum—now dried—from her thighs and pussy lips. He wasn't gentle about it either, and pinched her labia between his fingers to pull the tender flesh away from her body as he cleaned it, running the wipe between every single fold. Bella winced and bit back her pleas. It wouldn't matter, and she didn't want to give the sadistic man the slightest excuse to punish her. If this was his normal treatment, she hated to think what else he might do to her if he was allowed.

"Now to clean your insides." The doctor's grin spread.

Bella couldn't keep quiet. She had no idea what his words meant, and that made them even more threatening, She moaned and squirmed against the restraints. Of course, they'd been tightened far too well for her to do more than wiggle, which caused her breasts to sway back and forth.

The doctor picked up what looked like a hose with a long, metal tube at the end of it. On the other end, the hose attached to a machine. The tube was as thick as a finger and had little holes all over it. Bella gasped as the doctor stepped between her legs, where he pressed the cold metal to her hole and pushed it inward. She could hear the sloppy, sloshing sound as he inserted its cold length into her vagina, pushing out some of the cum.

"This is called a douche, my dear." Dr. Margolis pushed the nozzle deeper.

Bella winced and moaned as the metal tube was completely inflexible against her soft walls.

"We'll start with a nice hot one for you."

Bella screamed as her insides were pummeled with burning-hot water. It felt as though molten lava cleansed her insides.

As she pulled and wriggled against the restraints,

crying out and begging for him to stop, hoping the soldier would intervene, the Doctor pressed another button, and the spray stopped. When he pulled the hose from her tight channel, a mix of water and cum sprayed outward with enough force to get some on his jacket. Not that he noticed. The rest of it trickled down the drain next to the table.

"Please, please not again," Bella begged as he reinserted the metal into her pussy, where her walls were even more sensitive than before the hot torture. "Please, I can't take it."

"Well, you don't really have a choice now, do you?" The doctor smiled unpleasantly as he pushed the button again.

Ice water sprayed her insides at high velocity, making Bella scream and writhe again. It burned, but in an entirely different way, and the chill felt like it sank into her very bones. Crying and pleading had no effect, but she couldn't stop as the icy water froze her overheated insides, the extreme difference in temperature making it all the more painful.

When the doctor finally removed the thing from her pussy, Bella was crying incoherently, shivering with the shock.

"Mmm ... you look a bit cold, my dear." The doctor slid the wand back into her frozen pussy. "Let me heat you up."

"No! Please!"

The combination of heat and ice inside her caused Bella's body to bow against the restraints, but there was nowhere for her to go. Her screams echoed around the room; the water felt even hotter because the walls of her cunt were so cold from the ice water she was sure it was boiling her insides.

When the doctor pulled the machine from her pussy, it was again followed by that spray of water that quickly reduced to a dribble. As Bella panted and sobbed, he leaned close to inspect the swollen, angry folds.

"Hmmm ... Too much hair here."

Bella barely heard what he was saying. She barely registered it as he spread something over her abused pussy and mound. She didn't care that he was permanently removing her pubic hair—at least it didn't hurt. As he scraped the hair away and left her pussy bald and smooth, the prominent pout of her swollen lips became even more pronounced. The doctor pulled and tugged at the abused folds, and she squealed a bit as he inspected for stray hairs, but after the pain of the hot and cold douches, a few pinches were bearable even if they were to a sensitive and sore area.

"Now that you're all clean, it's time to take a look inside," the doctor said cheerfully and pulled over a large stool to sit on.

Bella could barely make out his head between her legs, his face only inches from her pussy, and she moaned, sure that whatever was to come would be some awful torment.

Something cool and slick pushed into her pussy. It was unyielding and uncomfortable, but it wasn't painful, and she breathed a sigh of relief. Then she heard something click and click again, and suddenly there was a great amount of pressure inside her pussy, as if the walls were being forced apart.

"What are you doing?" She was too exhausted to do more than wriggle a little.

The doctor smacked the top of her freshly bared mound, and Bella squealed.

"Be silent."

But she couldn't stop herself from moaning as there was another clicking noise and her pussy stretched again. The doctor didn't seem to mind noises in response to what he was doing: screams and pleas didn't provoke any sort of reaction other than sadistic pleasure—it was only questions that brought retaliation.

Another click, and she was having trouble breathing, her pussy felt so hugely stretched.

"Oh please ... please stop ... It's too much."

The doctor ignored her and clicked his instrument another setting higher, and her pussy gaped even further. But he didn't punish her for speaking; it just didn't do her any good.

Tears leaked down the side of her face, tears of humiliation, of degradation. She wasn't sure what kind of instrument he had inside her, but she was quite sure the doctor was looking into the most private area of her body.

When the pressure eased, she gave a sigh of relief, and her breath came easier, as well. The instrument slid easily from her body.

Then the doctor made a few more movements, and his finger, slick with lubricant, prodded her anus. Bella tensed and tried to clench her butt cheeks together, though the wide spread of her legs made it impossible.

"Don't! Stop!"

The doctor chuckled and increased the pressure on her anus, wedging the tip of his finger into the wrinkled hole as Bella let out an outraged cry.

"Don't enjoy anal, my dear? Don't worry, you'll have ample opportunity to get over that."

"I've never done it!" Bella snapped back at him, still trying to move her body away.

The doctor had frozen. He stood between her legs, looking down at her helpless body.

"You mean that? You've never had anal sex?" The doctor looked amazed at her confession.

Bella saw his excitement and pressed her lips together. The doctor scowled and smacked her pussy lips with his open palm. After all the abuse her poor privates had taken in the past few hours, it hurt more than she could have ever imagined. Bella howled, and her muscles strained to close her legs, but, of course, the restraints were too strong. As if to emphasize her helplessness and the need to cooperate, the doctor spanked her pussy again before repeating the question.

Tears in her eyes, Bella gave in. "No. Never."

"Have you ever had anyone play with your anus?"

"No."

The smile that spread across the man's face had Bella's heart sinking further. She hadn't known it could go any lower.

"Well, this is unexpected ... Unprecedented, in fact." The doctor leered at her. "You, my dear, are the very first anal virgin that the Wolf has ever taken."

The first? Surely, that couldn't be true ... Some of Bella's friends thought she was a bit of a prude, and she hadn't experimented with sex as much as a lot of them had, but she hadn't thought she was truly all that unique. Had Ken cheated on her with Lisa was because Bella had always refused to let him even touch her there? Or touch him there? It was a well-known, common perversion, but had never been one that appealed to her.

"Dr. Margolis," the soldier by the door said, giving a short cough. "You can't ..."

"I won't," said the doctor sharply, obviously resenting the soldier's presence and reminder. For a moment, Bella thought she'd gotten a bit of a reprieve, but the doctor leered at her again. "But there are certain things that I *can* do."

This time, he stood right where he was so he could watch her face as he pressed his lubricated fingertip back against her anus and began to steadily push in. Knowing how much he liked her reactions, Bella screwed her eyes shut and tried to show as little as possible on her face, although she wasn't entirely succeeding.

The doctor's finger pushed in rudely, slowly, as if he was enjoying making a leisurely invasion of her virgin hole. The sensation wasn't wholly unpleasant, but it was extremely uncomfortable, and it just felt *wrong*. Bella couldn't imagine how Alex had managed to take the Wolf's cock in his asshole—just the doctor's finger felt huge, like it was too big to fit. She couldn't help moaning as he pumped it back and forth inside of her, forcing her tight sphincter over the ridges of his knuckles again and again. It felt dirty and nauseating, and yet there was something about it that felt a little good, too, and she really, really hated that part.

She didn't know how long the doctor frigged her ass, although she could well imagine how lewd and awful it looked to the witnessing soldier. When he finally stopped, she sighed with relief and opened her eyes, only to find the doctor smirking at her.

"Time for the plug, my dear," he said. "Trust me, you'll thank me later." He held up the plug, and—while it wasn't very large— it still looked way too big to go in her asshole. It was at least as long as his finger and tapered to a point. The thick bulge before the narrow neck that attached it to the base was definitely bigger around than his finger.

Without putting any extra lubricant on the rubber probe, the doctor pressed it against her anus, which was already fairly well lubricated from his intensive fingering. Bella groaned and mewled as the plug began to push in. Without any extra lubricant, it wasn't an easy passage, and she began panting as the doctor slid it back and forth, stretching her anus a little wider every time. When it came to the fattest part of the plug, she let out a cry and squirmed to get way as her sphincter protested the invasion, the burning discomfort that almost became an ache.

Then it was past and inside her, and Bella moaned with relief. Uncomfortable, yes, but at least it wasn't painful.

The doctor toyed with her for a few more minutes, and she whimpered as he twisted and pulled on the plug. Whenever he did the latter, it felt like she was about to go to the bathroom, and sweat broke out on her forehead. It was only when the soldier in the doorway shifted, and the movement caught Dr. Margolis's eye, that he sighed and desisted.

The doctor looked a bit sour and came back up to her head, holding a tube of something. "Open your mouth."

For a moment, she considered resisting, but she was too battered at this point. Did she want to give him an excuse to make whatever was about to happen embarrassing and painful as well?

She opened her mouth.

To her relief, the doctor didn't do more than squeeze something out of the tube and into her mouth. It felt like cool gel and tasted like mint. So far, it was the least unpleasant part of her day.

"Swallow it."

She did as he said, and it tingled and soothed all the way down the back of her throat. Until now, she hadn't realized quite how much the inside of her throat hurt from all the crying, yelling, and begging she'd been doing, but the gel made it feel much better.

Dr. Margolis smiled at her. "That should take care of your gag reflex for at least a month, my dear. That pretty mouth is going to become very well used, and it wouldn't do to have you gagging or vomiting."

The coolness in her throat now sent a chill through her entire body as she realized what he meant.

But it was over. The doctor began unstrapping her from the table. As she sat up, her head spun dizzily, and the soldier came forward to steady her and help her stand. Which she was exceedingly grateful for, as she didn't want Dr. Margolis to touch her any more than necessary. He made her skin crawl. The soldier might be the lesser of two evils, but she'd take him in a heartbeat over the doctor.

"Looking forward to seeing you again, my dear." The doctor leered again.

The way his tongue flicked out over his lips reminded her of a snake, and Bella shuddered. Worse, she knew he liked seeing that kind of reaction, but she couldn't stop it, anyway.

The soldier let her lean on his arm as they walked out the door and into the hall. Her body felt strange, as if it wasn't really hers. The fat, battered lips of her pussy were incredibly sore; between them and the plug in her bottom, she had to walk awkwardly with her thighs apart so it was more of a waddle. The soldier was patient and walked at a pace she could manage.

For the first time, she really looked at him. He had plain, brown hair and ordinary features, enough muscles to make it clear he was a fighter, but, mostly, he looked like a perfectly normal guy, just a bit older than she was.

"Careful there." He caught her as she stumbled, and Bella nearly burst into tears just because he was being kind. Well, 'kind' compared to everyone else today.

"Please," she said, clutching his arm. "Help me."

He smiled and patted her hand comfortingly. "You'll be okay. The Wolf always lets his toys go eventually. It's hardest at the beginning, but everyone adjusts. Some of them end up not wanting to leave. Just do your best not to get in trouble. Don't remove the plug until you're told to, don't argue when you're given an order, and don't try to fight back or escape. The real troublemakers usually get sent to Dr. Margolis until they're ready to behave."

Not the most comforting words in the world, but Bella took what reassurance she could. Who wouldn't want to leave this awfulness? Even the other girl, Abby, had seemed relieved her ordeal was over with, and she'd called him Master. All Bella knew for sure was—no matter what—she would do whatever it took to stay away from Dr. Margolis.

As the soldier continued to help her down the hallway, she wondered where Alex was and what was happening to him.

5

After being dragged away from Bella, the gag still firmly in his mouth and his asshole burning from the Wolf's hard use, Alex allowed himself to slump in his guards' hands and forced them to drag him. He picked up his feet to keep the skin from being scraped off, but he didn't make their job easy.

Ahead of him, Nurse Roche stopped, turned around, and raised her eyebrows. "Well, if he can't walk, then carry him," she said briskly, and then turned back and continued.

The bigger soldier shrugged and picked Alex up over his shoulder, which was humiliating. Alex had always considered himself a fairly big guy—definitely strong—but this soldier had about twice his mass. The only sop to Alex's pride was that the soldier didn't seem to be having an easy time carrying him. He could wait for the soldier to tire out and then try to struggle and escape ... but there was the other soldier to consider. Not to mention Alex had no idea where Bella was. And Trish was with Jordan. She wasn't Alex's responsibility, but he couldn't handle the idea of leaving her here—but going up against Jordan would be a suicide mission. So, he just hung there like a piece of meat, feeling even lower about himself.

Fluid trickled down the back of his thigh, and Alex shuddered. His focus on escape was a way to help him ignore everything that had just happened.

The second time, in some ways, had felt even better, which made everything worse. Alex didn't like anal sex. He'd experimented with other men because it had seemed expected at his school, not because he'd been interested, and he'd stopped as soon as he could without looking like a prig. The mitigating factor must have been that he was already inside Bella's soft, warm pussy while the Wolf was fucking his ass, but it still didn't make Alex feel better. He shouldn't have gotten hard at all, much less been able to come.

Ahead of them, he heard a door opening and then they passed through a doorway into what looked like a medical exam room. In the center of the room there was a large frame with wooden slats and bars running horizontally across it.

"Secure him, please," Nurse Roche said.

Alex's body tensed, but he forced himself to relax again. There was no point in fighting back right now. He'd only lose and probably be in a worse position than before.

The soldier carrying him set Alex down in front of the frame, and the other one stepped forward to grab Alex's wrist and push it above his head. They attached him to the cuffs on the frame so his limbs formed the shape of an X, and shortened the length of the cuffs' chains so there was no slack for him to move. Then they put two slats on the frame, one in front of his chest and the other behind his back, at about the same level. The reason became clear a moment later when the soldiers bent the frame in half, and it forced Alex to bend forward at the waist.

The wooden slats across his chest and back kept his body from sagging and forced his ass up in the air, and Alex had a moment of panic as his vulnerability was reemphasized. The panic only subsided when both of the male soldiers stepped back and took up positions by the door. They were obviously there to guard him or in case Nurse Roche needed them, not to inflict further indignities on his leaking asshole.

He made a noise behind his gag, wanting the nurse to remove it. Alex turned his head he and looked at her, pleading. She smiled at him and patted his cheek.

"I think it's best if the gag stays in, Toy. That way no one will be subjected to any useless pleading."

Alex groaned. His jaw was aching from the gag, and he constantly had to swallow to keep from drooling. It was not at all comfortable. Then again, neither was any other part of his body, so why should this be any different? Maybe because Nurse Roche hadn't seemed that intimidating. Maybe because she was treating him with more caution than the Wolf had. After all, if it wasn't for his restraints and the two soldiers in the room, he could easily overpower her, even exhausted as he was.

The nurse injected him with a tracker, smiling when she informed him of what it was. Every time he looked up at Nurse Roche, she gave him a little smile that began to look more and more like a smirk. As if she enjoyed having a big, brawny man at her mercy. Alex looked away.

She ran her hands over his back, massaging his muscles and he couldn't help but groan. It felt good to have the tension smoothed away somewhat. Then her hands moved down to his lower back and onto his buttocks, and he tensed all over again as she moved behind him.

Gentle fingers massaged the rim of his anus, and he gritted his teeth around the gag at the reminder as her fingers made a sloppy, wet sound from the Wolf's cum.

"Looks like we're going to need to clean you out back here," she said, cheerfully.

Alex's stomach dropped. He didn't understand what she meant, but his imagination couldn't come up with anything pleasant. And there was nothing he could do, although he automatically jerked at the restraints. The frame rattled but didn't give in the slightest.

He couldn't see what was happening, although he could hear all sorts of strange sounds, but Nurse Roche was pulling a hose up from a special floorboard and attaching a long nozzle to the end of it. The nozzle was about four inches long and slightly tapered, made of a special material that had been specifically designed for the use it was about to be put to.

All Alex knew was something hard pressed against his anal hole, too stiff and unyielding to be denied. With his legs far apart and attached to the frame, he couldn't clench his buttocks closed, anyway. There was nothing he could do but pull uselessly at his restraints as Nurse Roche fed the tube into his asshole. Once it was firmly lodged inside, she pressed a button on the hose, and the base of the nozzle, just inside Alex's opening, expanded into a little round ball, making it impossible for him to expel. He groaned at the sudden change in the nozzle as that part of his tunnel stretched and protested.

"Good boy." Nurse Roche patted his ass, and Alex rattled the frame again. Her patronization was getting to him. He wasn't doing anything to be good; he just didn't have the option of doing anything else.

A gush of fluid into his rectum, distracted Alex from his growing frustration and anger. The fluid was warm, almost soothing if it wasn't for the location, and that just made Alex all the more uncomfortable. If whatever the nurse was doing had led to something painful, he would have preferred that. Painful he could resist, could fight against. This almost-pleasurable feeling of warmth in his belly was harder to be angered by.

The flow of warmth continued, filling him, until he was uncomfortable, and his body started to strain against the restraints. Which was exactly when the nurse stopped it.

"Almost done," she said cheerfully and pushed another button. The nozzle expanded and pressed against the walls of his body, and the water began to flow out of him, cleaning out his bowels before being sucked down through the hose and into the wastepipes of the building. "A good enema is just what you needed. No more mess. It's a lovely little system."

Her chirpy tone, as if what she was doing was normal, really grated. Alex tried to concentrate on his annoyance, rather than the feeling of pleasurable relief that swept through him as the fluid rushed back out. The nozzle shrank inside him, including the little bulb that created a plug, and then it was withdrawn. He sagged in relief and hated himself for doing so. Not that he'd ever expected to be in this kind of situation, but any time he'd ever imagined himself captured at the hands of enemies—What little boy didn't?—he'd thought he would do better than he had so far.

· · ·

Nurse Roche wiped around his anus with a cloth, cleaning the last remnants from the abused hole, and then the frame began to move, bringing him back to an upright, standing position.

Alex closed his eyes as she cleaned the sticky mess of his sperm and Bella's juices from his groin, hating the reminder of what he'd done before coming to this room. So far, his actions had not been those of the hero he'd always pictured himself as. He didn't know what else he could have done under the circumstances, but being cleaned of the aftermath filled him with shame and guilt and fury.

"Alright, Moon Boy, let's get you measured." The term sounded like an insult, but he ignored it.

Measured for what?

The nurse came around to the front of him and knelt down in front of his soft cock. He had a moment of disdain as he looked down at her. Would she try to get him hard to measure the length of his dick? Even if he wasn't completely disgusted by the situation, he'd just come twice. Getting him hard again when he wasn't remotely aroused wouldn't be easy, and it seemed stupid for her to want to measure his cock.

But she didn't seem at all interested in trying to get him hard. She had a soft ring made of a stretchy-looking material—possibly similar to the material from the enema nozzle—and she pushed his balls through it, one at a time, before pulling his limp dick through, as well. The ring rested snugly against his groin and around his entire cock and balls, and made his dick feel strange. The sensation of his pulse flowing through that entire area was amplified.

"Hmmm ..." The nurse fiddled with a remote in her

hand, and the ring tightened, although not uncomfortably. Just snugly, as if it were hugging the base of his cock and balls. "That should do it, but let's make sure."

She leaned forward and took his cock between her lips, and his hips surged forward in shock. Her hot, wet mouth around his dick seemed more intense than he'd ever felt—maybe an effect of the ring. He clamped his jaw around the gag and resisted the trickles of pleasure that tingled through him as her tongue flicked against his pee-hole and she sucked gently on his flaccid dick.

Alex tried to think of everything he could to keep himself from getting hard. The Moon. His family. Finding Ken and Lisa in bed together. Bella—no, that was a bad idea. The Wolf. How sore his asshole was.

None of it did any good. Slowly but surely, his dick began to harden as the nurse skillfully fellated him. Alex felt the same sense of shame and humiliation he had when he'd first looked at Bella's naked body and hadn't been able to control his reaction. Jerking hard at the frame did nothing but make the soldiers in the doorway smirk, and even looking at them did nothing to halt the slow rise of his cock.

Even though the things going through his mind should have deflated him immediately, it was like his cock couldn't get smaller, like it could only get bigger and harder. The nurse's fingers tickled his balls, which were exquisitely sensitive as his cock grew and the ring snugged against his body grew tighter.

Nurse Roche was obviously skilled at giving oral sex —she was able to take the entire length of his cock down her throat. His cock hardened no matter what he did to try slowing the process. He didn't give in though, and when she finally pulled her lips from the angry red organ, he growled at her through the gag.

She ignored him, putting her hand around the shaft and pumping it. "Very nice …" she said approvingly. "I think you might be the biggest Moon Boy we've had here." A wicked smile crossed her face. "In fact … I think I might even like to play with you a bit, Toy."

The frame he was on began to tilt backward, and Nurse Roche stepped out of the way until it held his body completely parallel with the floor, at which point it began to lower. The entire time, his cock ached and grew even harder, despite the cessation of stimulation. Alex didn't know how, but he knew it was because of the ring she'd placed around him.

Once he was on the floor, Nurse Roche stood over him, lifting up her skirts as she straddled his waist. Alex had plenty of experience with women, including older ones. He loved women and, while he was always faithful when he was in a relationship, he'd had a fair number of sexual partners in his life. But he'd never had an experience like this, where he was completely out of control of the situation. He'd never had a woman hike up her skirts and point his cock to the ceiling so she could lower herself onto it without any participation or cooperation from him.

Despite the fact that her pussy was slick and tight, he couldn't let go and enjoy what was happening.

Not that she seemed to care. Neither did the soldiers in the doorway. They watched impassively as Nurse Roche, her skirt bunched around her hips, started to bounce up and down on top of his cock. It felt fantastic, physically. His cock was so hard, so engorged, and the wet haven of her pussy fit snugly around it. But his head was not engaged, and he felt sick and ashamed that he couldn't force his traitorous organ back down.

The nurse's moans filled his ears and churned his stomach as she bounced and gyrated on top of him. He truly did feel like a toy; a sex toy she was using for her own gratification. As her pussy squeezed and slid up and down his shaft, his orgasm began to build, the physical stimulation overriding his mind.

Part of him felt relieved: it would be over soon.

But the tight ring around his balls and dick had done something. The sensation built and continued to build, far past the point of comfort, and yet the tight ring held his physical reaction in check. Alex groaned, his body straining to cum now, the intense need completely over-whelming as Nurse Roche continued her self-pleasure ride on his cock. Tears welled in his eyes as the discom-fort became almost painful, like a blockage within his body, and the pressure was building up and up behind it ...

The nurse threw back her head and screamed out her orgasm, and the ring around his balls and dick loosened just the tiniest increment ...

Alex's orgasm slammed into him like a freight train. It was heaven and hell, for the second time that day, as he pumped seed into her squeezing pussy. She ground down on top of him for all she was worth, rubbing her pussy over his groin as she spasmed with ecstasy.

When the nurse was done with him, the ring around his cock and balls loosened again, just enough to be snug without being constrictive. Alex breathed hard through his nose as Nurse Roche sighed happily and lifted herself back up. She thoroughly cleaned off his cock and balls again before returning the frame to its standing position.

The last thing she did was remove the gag and have him swallow a soothing, cool gel that coated the back of his sore throat. Alex glared at her but didn't say anything, even though the gag was removed. He couldn't think of what he wanted to say, his thoughts and emotions were in such upheaval.

The soldiers re-cuffed his wrists in front of him and secured a collar around his neck. It was comfortable enough, not too tight, but it made him even angrier. Like they were marking him as something lower than human. Unfortunately, anger couldn't sustain him. He was practically shaking on his feet, pathetically weak as they led him down the hall.

People passed by them. They all looked at him, some with anticipation, some with desire, and some with something like smug superiority. Alex glared back at all of them. A few looked away when he did that, which was a small balm to his pride.

They stopped at a door and one of the soldiers opened it, the other pushing him through. The door snapped shut behind him.

"Alex!"

"Bella!"

Utter relief swept him as he saw her sit up on the bed in the center of the room. There wasn't much else in the room other than the overly large bed that could probably fit six people. The moment he had the thought, Alex wished he hadn't. Bella was wrapped up in what looked like the sheet, tendrils of her brown hair falling down, her eyes red from crying. And she still looked beautiful.

Jumping up, she ran to him, and he lifted his arms up so she could throw herself at him before wrapping her arms around his waist as she started to sob. Lowering his arms around her, he noticed that she was neither collared nor handcuffed, and he felt a bit of grim satisfaction at that. Someone must think he was a threat, even if he'd been incredibly ineffective so far.

But this ... Hold Bella while she cried—that he could do.

As he did so, pressing her against his body and letting her weep onto his chest, he took quick stock of the room. It was remarkably bare: there was the large bed, a table with some food on it, and what looked like some kind of storage on the far wall.

"It's okay sweetheart ..." he murmured into her hair. "It'll be okay, I promise ... I won't let him beat us. We're going to escape."

Bella pushed back from him, although she couldn't go very far since his hands were cuffed and he couldn't open his arms to release her. To his shock, her expression was one of horror.

"What? No!"

6

As Alex and Bella compared notes, it quickly became apparent to him why Bella was so frightened. She lay on her side on the bed, watching him eat, and the tears had dried on her face, but she still shivered with fear while she told him about the ordeal Dr. Margolis had put her through. It made Alex want to punch his hand through the wall, just hearing her voice shake as she talked about it. To see how scared she was of the doctor.

He felt almost ashamed, feeling that she'd been through much worse than he had.

"It doesn't matter if we obey, don't you see?" He waved the roll of bread he had in his hand. Which was a bit awkward, but he kept forgetting his hands were cuffed together as he tried to gesture with them. "The Wolf still controls everything, he can decide to do whatever he wants to us, no matter whether we do as he says or not."

"I don't want to be punished, Alex." Her bright eyes became even brighter as the sheen of tears covered them.

"Maybe you're stronger than I am ... but I just, I can't take it. The Wolf always lets his victims go, eventually."

"And I don't want to wait around for that. Who knows when or what he'll do to us in the meantime? He could send you back to the doctor just for fun, if that's what he decided to do!" He hated to see the way her face paled, but she had to see what he was saying.

"So it's better to do something that will definitely get us punished? And what about the trackers? I'd rather behave and not make things worse for myself than do something that I know will have awful consequences!"

She sounded just as convinced of her argument as he felt of his own, and, unfortunately, he could see some of the sense of her words. The problem was that he was right, too.

"I don't know, Bella," he said tiredly. "I can't even think straight right now. I don't think we should just passively sit by until he releases us"—he held up his hand to stop her next words—"but I do see your point. I just don't know what to say."

Bella bit her lower lip and then nodded. "I see what you're saying too. I'm just ... I'm scared, Alex. And I hurt. And I don't want to be sent back to the doctor."

Her voice shook, and he inwardly cursed himself for causing her more distress. Going over to the bed, he sat down next to her head and stroked her hair, hoping it might comfort her. While she accepted it, she didn't look at him—the woman seemed lost in her own thoughts.

"By your own admission, Alex, what you went through with Nurse Roche wasn't anything like what Doctor Margolis did to me ... and I could tell he wanted to do more. If we tried to escape and were caught ... Besides which, what about Trish? Can we just leave her here?"

"You're right. And I didn't mean we should escape today … but Bella, I'm not going to stop trying to plan. I'm not going to stop looking for a way to make it work. If I figure out a way that should work for all of us, will you at least listen to it?"

The shudder that went through her wasn't reassuring. Her voice was soft when she spoke again. "I'll listen, Alex, but that's all I can promise."

Sliding onto the bed beside her, Alex hesitated and then relaxed as she rolled over and snuggled into him. It took a moment or two of arranging for them to get comfortable, her head pillowed on his arm, his cuffed wrists around her body. The sheet was still wrapped around her, but he preferred that to having her naked body pressed up against him.

Despite the circumstances, his attraction to her remained.

Her breathing slowed and then steadied, and he was grateful she felt safe enough to fall asleep there with his arms around her. His presence didn't give her any real protection, but she needed to sleep. He did, too. After all, who knew when the Wolf would call for them again, and it wasn't as if they could escape today.

He didn't know where they were in this building, much less where in the world the building was located. And were Jordan and Trish also still in this building? Bella was right on one aspect—there was a lot of planning to do before they could escape.

———

The Wolf's men came for Alex and Bella some time later, and they woke as the door opened with a bang. Bella shrieked and quivered, pressing her face into Alex's chest as if to hide herself from reality. His muscles tensed all over, ready to fight, but he was tangled up in Bella and the sheets. Which was probably a good thing: there were four men, far too many for him to overcome even if his wrists weren't in cuffs, and they all looked like fighters.

"Get up, it's time for dinner," one of them said.

Carefully pulling away from Bella, Alex stood, completely unabashed by his nudity. In stark contrast, Bella tried to stand while still covered in the sheet. One of the men snorted and stepped forward to rip the scant covering away from her. Bella let out a cry of dismay and surprise.

Without thinking, Alex lunged for the man, only to be caught by two of the other men, who chuckled.

"I love it when we get a fighter." Someone smacked Alex on the ass, and he snarled, but there was nothing he could do as they forced him to his knees. One of them placed a hand on the back of his neck, right over his collar, to help hold him in place.

The two other soldiers stood over Bella as she pushed herself upright, her shoulders hunched and her hands trying to cover herself. Her mound had been completely shaved of the soft brunette curls that had been there before her trip to the doctor. She hadn't mentioned it when she'd talked about what the doctor had done to her, and Alex realized she was ashamed.

Her pussy lips looked swollen and red. The doctor's rough handling and douching had irritated them.

"Hands at your side, slut," one of them snapped, giving her a slap on her bottom.

Bella squealed, but her hands fell to her sides. She

looked lost, uncertain, and her fingers twitched and balled into little fists as she tried to figure out what to do with them.

Alex hated himself for the little stirring he felt in his cock as he looked at her, so he looked away.

"Come on," said the soldier with his hand on Alex's neck. "Let's get them back to the Common Room."

———

It was the same room they'd been in before, but now it was filled with tables and people sitting around, eating. Bella shook as both men and women leered at her, some snickering, some pointing at her and Alex. Very few looked sympathetic.

Despite the great number of people in the room, she found her eyes going automatically to the dais, where the Wolf was. He had such a commanding presence that it didn't matter how many people there were in the room— and there had to be at least fifty—eyes were automatically drawn to him. Beside her, Alex muttered under his breath.

She couldn't decide if he was brave or stupid. Maybe a bit of both. She felt cowardly and stupid. He was right: the Wolf didn't need an excuse to punish them. On the other hand, her cowardly self didn't want to give the Wolf an excuse, either.

Looking around for the soldier that had been almost nice to her earlier, she couldn't see him among all the people, but she couldn't see all the way around the room, either, as they were led to the dais where the Wolf was waiting.

Jordan sat at the table up there, Trish perched on his lap. The delicate blonde at least had clothing: a simple blue dress that buttoned down the front. Bella could see underneath the table it was a very short dress, but at least it was something. Trish held her hands stiffly by her sides, much like Bella, and her gaze was firmly planted on the floor. The top buttons around the neckline of her dress were undone, and Jordan had his hand inside, fondling her breast as he spoke to the Wolf.

Did anyone here ever think about anything other than sex?

Then again, she didn't know what they'd done during the afternoon while she'd been sleeping. Whatever it was that kept the Wolf at the top of the food chain on Earth.

Bella felt horribly aware of her puffy, sore pussy lips and the stiff plug in her bottom that made her waddle a little bit, and gave up looking around and just stared at the ground as the soldiers brought them up to the table.

Silence trickled through the room—not immediate, but a slow hushing of voices as if the gathered crowd became aware entertainment was imminent.

Bella peeked through her lashes and saw the Wolf and his men looking over her and Alex, their expressions frankly lascivious. One of them, seeing Bella watching, grinned and rubbed his crotch. She dropped her gaze again. Alex's presence beside her was the only thing that kept her from bursting into tears. He was so strong, and she didn't want to let him down by weeping uselessly, the way she had, earlier. Perhaps some of the shock of their situation was wearing off—her brain didn't feel as fuzzed as it had.

"Well, well, my new Pet and Toy. Don't you two clean up pretty." Even though the Wolf spoke in normal tones, the acoustics of the room meant everyone there could hear every word he said. Snickers rang out behind her and Alex, and she could see his fists clenching. She hoped he would keep quiet. It wasn't like being mocked would harm either of them. "And we have something new ... an anal virgin! My very first!"

Hoots and lewd comments followed this announcement, and Bella felt her cheeks flame brightly. Out of the corner of her eye, she could see Alex turn to stare at her in shock. She closed her eyes. Although she'd told him most of what had happened with Dr. Margolis, she hadn't shared everything. Just the most painful parts. Not the embarrassing ones.

"Get her up on the table so everyone can see that pretty pussy and virgin asshole," the Wolf said.

Bella moaned softly as the two men on either side of her lifted her up. Some of the Wolf's other men were already clearing a space on the table, moving the plates of food to the side so there was plenty of room for them to lay her down on her back, her bottom right at the edge, while the two men held her legs. They bent them at the knee and spread them apart, exposing her pussy and the base of the plug in her virgin asshole to the entire crowd. The cheering grew louder at her humiliation as her swollen, abused pussy lips were shown off.

"Such a good Pet." The Wolf grabbed her wrists and pulled them above her head. He wasn't looking at her face. Reaching down, he fondled one of her breasts, bringing the nipple to a hard little point, which he tugged between his fingers. Bella moaned again, hating herself for the little trickle of pleasure that spurted through her. "Pet's pussy looks pretty sore. I believe we have some balm that can help that." He looked over to the side.

"Doctor Margolis ... please give Toy the balm you've prepared."

She'd felt faint when he first called upon the doctor, and the relief that swept through her when Alex was given the balm almost made her sob. The Wolf still toyed with her breasts, making her nipples hard and achy with his attentions. The pleasure went straight to her pussy, much to her horror.

"Toy ... I think it's up to you to help soothe Pet's pussy."

Alex was allowed to approach, and stood on the other side of the table. The men who guarded him positioned him slightly to Bella's side so he didn't completely block the view of her privates for the rest of the room. The hard, stubborn expression on his face was back as he looked down at the small pot of balm he had in his hand.

"Please Alex," Bella begged, knowing he would need permission from her to touch her. Permission she was happy to give. Her poor pussy ached, and if the Wolf was going to do more to it ... She'd take anything to help it feel better beforehand. Right now, she couldn't bear to be touched there, otherwise. "Please Alex, I need ... I need something ... it hurts so."

Cursing under his breath, Alex dipped two fingers into the balm. Bella moaned with relief when he gently stroked it along the outsides of her inflamed pussy lips. It was soothing, cooling, and the dissipation of the sore ache was more of a relief than she could have ever imagined.

"More, Alex, please!"

Laughter rang out behind them, and his shoulders stiffened. From her position on the dais, her voice could be heard throughout the room because of the damned acoustics, but she didn't care, as long as he didn't stop. His face grim, Alex spread the balm onto her inner pussy lips as the Wolf began to tweak and tug at her nipples again.

Bella moaned. The soothing balm was doing more than just relieving the soreness. It was allowing her body to feel pleasure again. Alex's gentle strokes began to feel teasing—a sharp contrast to the Wolf's rougher handling of her breasts—and to her shame, it aroused her. Was there something wrong with her, that she could be turned on in such a situation? So many people around them, witnessing her humiliation as she was forcibly fondled, and yet her pussy was getting wet.

"Don't forget to get some inside of her," the Wolf said. His voice filled with satisfaction at the scenario he'd arranged. "I've heard that Dr. Margolis' douches are quite painful."

His face not showing any reaction, Alex covered two of his fingers with the balm and pushed them into Bella's pussy. Gasping with the sudden relief, the cessation of the burning of her insides, Bella's hips lifted as Alex's fingers probed her tunnel. The plug in her bottom made his fingers feel even bigger. It felt good. Too good.

Even though her body wanted more, she was glad when he began to withdraw.

"I didn't stay stop," the Wolf snapped. "Use your fingers to spread the balm around inside her cunt."

The two men glared at each other over her body, Alex's fingers still at the entrance of her pussy. Bella bit her lip, her eyes looking up pleadingly at Alex. She hadn't forgotten the doctor was still in the room. The Wolf had her nipples between his fingers, all he would have to do was twist viciously to cause her quite a bit of a pain. And yet, she didn't think she wanted Alex to continue ... it felt too good. And she didn't want it to.

Alex's expression hardened again, and he looked away first, his fingers sliding back into the slick tunnel. She moaned, and her pussy and asshole clenched, tingling around the invaders. The Wolf began to gently tug and play with her nipples again, his big hands squeezing her breast-flesh as his fingers tormented her more specifically.

"Keep spreading the balm until she comes. Otherwise, I'll turn her around on this table and fuck her pussy until she does, so ... it's up to you, Toy."

"Oh nooooo ..." Bella moaned again as Alex's fingers moved inside her. She didn't know what she was saying 'no' to. Both scenarios. Part of her felt guilty, wanting to escape being raped by the Wolf while the Wolf had already fucked Alex. Better to come on Alex's fingers ... but she didn't want to do either.

It was too humiliating, held spread open on the dinner table before a crowd, her pussy being fingered by her friend, her nipples and breasts squeezed and pulled by the Wolf. And yet ... Alex was too good at pleasuring a woman for her body to resist. The tingling of her breasts in the Wolf's hands, Alex's clever fingers, and even the plug in her bottom, which had awakened nerves she hadn't known existed, were just too much for her.

Bella's hips lifted, her legs still held in a firmly spread position by the two men, her moans filling the room from the dais. The room was mostly hushed, watching, waiting to see if the men could coax a climax from her unwilling body.

"Oh no ..." she whispered, her breath coming out in a gush as Alex's thumb brushed over her clit. The little nub was swollen, aching. The sound of his fingers pushing in and out of her sloppy pussy filled her ears, as did the harsh breathing of the Wolf. She looked up and met his startling, green eyes in that handsome face—so at odds with what she thought he should look like. Cold, green eyes. Lustful, but cold.

He squeezed her nipples tightly, and she writhed. Alex's thumb pressed against her clit, and it was like a switch flipped in her body.

"No, no, no, no, no pleeeeeeeeeeeease nooooooo!"

It felt as though her lower body was on fire again, but this time a good kind. Her asshole tightened around the plug, and the full sensation and the way it jerked inside her enhanced the pleasure that began to ripple outward from her pussy. Alex's fingers plunged inside her, his thumb rubbing little circles directly against her clit, and she tugged at the Wolf's grip on her wrists, her legs trying to kick as the ecstasy overwhelmed her.

The men all held her in place, forcing her to remain spread, forcing her to ride out the entire orgasm, until she shuddered and slumped. Only then did Alex remove his fingers, unable to look at her.

Shame filled her, even as the cheers from the room filled her ears. Damn them. And damn her body for making it possible.

The men holding her legs brought them down, bringing her back upright. She swayed slightly. But at least her pussy felt better. The lips were no longer so swollen and, when she peeked down, they still looked puffy but they were pink instead of red. Whatever had been in that balm, it had been high-quality, and she was greatly relieved. Shame was better than pain, right?

Slowly the cheers died down, everyone's attention

still on the dais, and the back of Bella's neck prickled, all the little hairs standing up. Whatever the Wolf had planned, he wasn't done yet.

"I think Toy did a very good job, don't you?" More cheering. "I believe he's earned his dinner for taking such good care of Pet. Of course, Pet still has to earn hers."

7

Seeing the way Bella's cheeks paled at the Wolf's pronouncement that she still had yet to earn her dinner, Alex had to squelch down the urge to leap across the table at the man. Alex was still guarded. And there were a lot more men on the other side of the table, not to mention Trish. Jordan had pulled down the top of her dress completely and was openly fondling her breasts, tugging at the little pink nipples. She sat there, red-eyed, obviously unhappy, but compliant. Because what else was she supposed to do?

Alex knew how she felt. His helplessness was making him crazy. At least Bella's pussy no longer looked so raw. Knowing she felt better, that he'd at least made part of her situation more tenable, was a small sop to his pride.

The men holding him turned him outward so he was facing the crowd. The little ring around his cock and balls was still snug, but not uncomfortably so. His cock had hardened a little while he'd been fingering Bella; he hadn't been able to help it.

He growled as they pushed him to his knees, knowing

whatever was about to happen, he would have to watch. Men brought Bella up to stand beside them, and three more men stepped forward in front of the dais, looking up at them eagerly. Alex's eyes darted around the room, but he couldn't see a clear line of escape even if he knew what lay outside the doors.

A rough hand grabbed his hair, and Alex growled again, stilling slightly as the Wolf came around to their side of the table and was the one holding his hair. Since the Wolf was about to announce whatever it was Bella had to do to earn her dinner, Alex would try his hardest not to do anything to make it worse. Just like she had asked him to.

"Pet ... these men have done particularly good work for me today, and I think they've earned a reward. You're going to provide them with that ... with your mouth."

Bella moaned and whimpered as the men on either side of her pulled her forward and down the dais and pushed her to her knees in front of the man to the far left. He grinned at her and reached out with one hand to grab her hair and the other to loosen his pants. Alex tried to stand, to move forward to help her somehow—he didn't know how—only to be stopped by the grip on his hair. Instinctively, he reached out to hit the Wolf, and then every muscle in his body seized up as a painful electrical current ran through him.

Even his lungs seized so he couldn't cry out, couldn't shout, couldn't even curse.

Just as suddenly, the current released him, and he fell forward on all fours. His hearing returned in a rush: the crowd cheering and laughing, the wet, sloppy sounds of a cock being sucked, and a slight buzzing that seemed to be coming from somewhere inside his head. Every muscle quivered as he gasped for air, the shock fading to a tingling pain that pricked him, but slowly faded.

"Bad Toy," the Wolf's voice rumbled, low and close, right in his ear. The man crouched next to him, close enough to grab if Alex could get his muscles to cooperate. If he didn't get hit with that electrical energy again. Fingers ran along the back of his neck down to his collar. "Did you think this was just for decoration? No. Men like you … you need to be shown from the beginning who's in charge. You act, and sometimes you don't think. You don't think about what I might do to you. Or what I might make Pet do. And so things like this collar …" The finger hooked around the back and pulled slightly, enough to cut off some of his air and Alex jerked backward a bit. "This collar ensures that until you learn to start thinking before you act, I won't have to worry about your behavior."

No, he wouldn't. Alex felt another surge of rage and helplessness run through him. But what else could he do? He looked up.

The man who was being serviced by Bella had turned her to the side, so the crowd could see as he stuffed his cock down her throat. Her hands were on his thighs, tears trickling down her cheeks, as the man fucked her mouth roughly.

"Stop it. Stop them," he gritted out. "Just stop it."

"You can save her," the Wolf said. "All you have to do is take her place."

———

Bella hated being grateful for anything Dr. Margolis had done to her, but as the soldier fucked her mouth with deep, rough strokes, shoving his cock in to the root before pulling it out again, she was very grateful for the gel he'd given her to kill her gag reflex. Otherwise, she'd have probably thrown up by now. He used her roughly and with no concern for her other than to ensure she didn't pass out. She sucked in breath every time he pulled out of her throat, and breathed through her nose frantically. Her pussy still tingled a bit from the orgasm she'd had at Alex's fingertips, but she did her best to ignore it.

The worst part was that this was the soldier who had seemed so nice, the one who had been encouraging when he'd helped her to the room and away from Dr. Margolis. And now he was groaning with pleasure as he raped her mouth, the head of his cock bruising the back of her throat. She could hear the crowd's pleasure at watching, the men who said they hoped to try her out sometime soon, the women who wondered aloud if she was as good a pussy-licker as she was a cock-sucker.

And it slowly faded to just noise as tears streamed down her face and she concentrated on breathing in between the rough thrusts.

"Aaaaaaaaaah fuck!" The soldier threw his head back, his grip tightening on her hair as he pulled her against his crotch. Her lips pressed against his hairy groin, the head of his cock lodged in her throat. Something warm and liquid spurted, and her throat worked convulsively, sucking it down into her stomach without being able to taste it because he was so deeply in her mouth.

The cum settled in her stomach and made her nauseous.

When he pulled away, she moaned and gasped for breath before finding herself being spun around on her knees.

"My turn," the next man said, grinning down at her. Bella blinked up at him. She could barely see him through the tears that clung to her lashes. Her throat was raw and sore, and she whimpered.

"Wait." The Wolf's voice rang out from the dais, and Bella's heart rose in uncertain hope. She looked over to see him standing next to Alex, who knelt beside him. The expression on Alex's face was one of uncertainty. The Wolf looked down at him. "Toy, would you like to take over for Pet?"

Oh, no ...

Bella tried to speak, but her mouth was too dry. She couldn't allow Alex to protect her at the expense of himself, could she? But she could see him steel himself to answer in the affirmative.

"Apparently not." The Wolf nodded his head at the man standing beside her. "Take her."

"No!" Alex shouted as the second man grabbed her hair and turned her to face his crotch, where his thick cock stood out, already aiming for her lips. "I'll do it, I'll take her place!"

"You'll get another chance, and perhaps you won't think so long about your decision," said the Wolf, sounding bored. "Pet, suck him."

"And you're going to have to do a bit more of the work," the man said, bringing her lips to the head of his cock. "Lick it."

Just do it and get it over with.

Part of her was devastated that Alex felt the need to debase himself to take her place and protect her; another part was even more despairing that he hadn't done so in enough time to save her from this. She swallowed to renew the moisture in her mouth and took a deep breath and licked the swollen crown of the man's cock.

He tasted slightly different from the soldier who had seemed so nice originally, although it was still that fleshy taste of man and musk. It filled her mouth as she licked all around the fat head and down the length of his shaft, and he moved her head and his dick around to his satisfaction. There was something hypnotic about it, and the sounds of the crowd merged into a constant buzz that filled her ears but didn't make any sense. She preferred it that way.

"Good." The man's voice stood out from the blended voices. "Now suck it."

The tip pushed into her mouth, and Bella flicked her tongue over it, finding the pee-hole and toying with it. The man grunted his approval, one hand reaching down to begin casually fondling her breast. His hand was big and warm and surprisingly gentle as he squeezed and kneaded the soft flesh. The nipple began to harden as he rubbed his thumb over it, and Bella found herself rhythmically sucking and moving her mouth up and down his shaft without any force from him.

She paused in her movement—shouldn't she at least put up some kind of token resistance? Rather than so easily participating in the rape of her own mouth?

Displeased with the cessation of her movements, the man pinched her nipple hard, and Bella squeaked. She began sucking again, pulling his cock deep into her mouth.

To her horror, the flash of pain that went through her at his pinch was tinged with more than a bit of pleasure. Her pussy clenched, and she wanted to cry when she realized she was becoming wet again. What was wrong with her? The gentle manipulation of her nipple now that she was sucking his dick again made her shudder.

Bella tried to focus on her cock-sucking, to distract herself from the responses of her body. It was surprisingly easy to forget that her gag reflex was gone, and difficult to make herself slide her lips all the way down his cock to the base. When she did that, his hips jerked, and he groaned his approval, his hand becoming slightly rougher on her breast with the increase of his enjoyment.

Her throat spasmed, protesting because it was sore from the first soldier's abuse, and Bella let her head pull back while she took a deep breath through her nose. The man pressed down on her head, taking more control as he forced her fully back down on his cock. The pinching, tugging of his fingers on her nipple made her shudder as wetness began to trickle from her pussy, his thrusts into her mouth slow and steady.

For the most part, he seemed content to allow her to set her own pace, as long as she didn't take too long. Bella began to move faster, working her tongue over the underside of his length. She just wanted this to be over with, and the only way that was going to happen was if she made him come. If she continued to be slow, reluctant, it would only extend the proceedings.

Ignoring the people watching, ignoring how she must look as she began to bob her head up and down his shaft, sucking hard, Bella focused on getting him to come.

The man began thrusting back even more, still squeezing her breast as the head of his cock battered the back of her throat. It hurt, especially after the first man had been so rough with her, but she could tell from his groans he was close to coming, and she forced herself to keep sucking hard through it. The slurping wet sound filled her ears over the hum of the crowd and his encouraging groans.

Her stomach began to churn, as if her body sensed his oncoming orgasm, and then he grunted and released her breast to grasp the back of her head. He shouted his pleasure and continued thrusting as his cock began to pulse. Bella did gag now, when the bittersweet jets of cum coated her tongue and the back of her throat as he fucked her mouth through his orgasm. Unlike the first soldier, he seemed to have no inclination to bury himself completely while he came, and her mouth filled with salty fluid as she struggled to swallow.

Little drops leaked out past her lips and dribbled down her chin as he continued to forcefully thrust and batter her mouth and throat. Nausea rose as her stomach wanted to reject the fluid, but she had to swallow what she could or else she wouldn't be able to breathe.

The man now pulled her face against his stomach, burying her nose in his pubic hair as he sent the last spurts jetting straight down her throat. His cock began to soften and shrink, but it meant she was forced to swallow every drop of his cum still in her mouth. Very little found its way down her chin.

Bella wasn't sure she would be able to eat now. Her stomach felt strange and sloshy with the two hot loads she'd swallowed. It made her want to go to the bathroom and throw up—not eat dinner.

The man pulled away, and she wiped her chin and swollen lips with the back of her hand, panting for breath and wishing she had something that would wipe the taste of him from her mouth.

"Well, Toy? Are you going to take Pet's place?" Out of the corner of her eye, Bella saw Alex stand and move toward the third man without saying anything. He clenched his fists at his sides, and his face held a look of absolute determination.

She wanted to tell him no; she wanted to tell him not to save her at his own expense ... but she couldn't get the air into her lungs. Tears stung her eyes and slid down her cheeks as Alex knelt in front of the third man, shameful relief washing through her that she was done.

———

It had been years since Alex had done this. The man in front of him didn't seem to care whose mouth he was putting his cock into; his facial expression hadn't changed at all as he went from watching Bella to thrusting his cock into Alex's mouth. The man had obviously been excited by the show and was eager for his own turn.

Alex knelt in front of him and kept his fists clenched at his sides as he opened his lips, and the man shoved his cock into his mouth. The warm, salty, fleshy taste brought back memories of his days of experimentation when he'd discovered he had a decided preference for women. The hot, hard rod dragged over his tongue.

He didn't resist, but he didn't participate, either. Although it was instinct to explore with his tongue, to taste, to do what he'd done in the past, Alex forced his tongue to remain still and he didn't suck or do anything to help.

Not that the man cared.

As he began to fuck Alex's mouth, Alex heard the Wolf

ordering Bella to crawl to him. His fists clenched even tighter. The Wolf had better not have her do anything more. She'd looked pathetically exhausted, her eyes reddened from tears, lips swollen, and every inch of her body weary and defeated. Alex hadn't saved her just to allow the Wolf to abuse her more.

To his relief and shame, all the Wolf seemed to require was that she watch Alex take her place. He really wished she wouldn't. The Wolf had her sitting beside him, her head leaning against his leg so he could stroke her hair as if she truly were a pet. So she had to watch. But that was better than some of the alternatives.

Alex closed his eyes and tried to forget where he was. The man fucking his mouth didn't require any effort from him. When the head of the man's cock hit the back of Alex's throat, he had a moment of panic ... but he didn't gag at all. Neither had Bella, but Alex had thought it might be a natural talent of hers—and had been even more aroused by the idea. Seeing her having to service the other men and the misery on her face had fortunately kept him from becoming fully erect.

Now he was completely soft as the man in front of him began forcing his cock down Alex's throat. Alex had never been able to deep-throat. The gel Nurse Roche had made him swallow must have had something to do with it. It was the only thing he could think of.

While it was a relief he wouldn't throw up in front of everyone, Alex hated the feeling of the man's cock blocking his airway, the sensation of being so fully invaded. It seemed to go on forever: the man fucking him like his mouth was just a convenient hole to use, his throat beginning to burn as thick meat shoved into it again and again.

He was glad he'd kept Bella from having to do this. He'd managed to intervene in time, this time.

The man shoved deep, catching Alex off guard, and he sputtered as cum filled his throat. The sudden lack of air surprised him, and he tried to pull away. The sickly-sweet taste of semen filled his mouth as a spurt erupted directly over his tongue, and then the cock was out, and jets of cum spattered across his face.

The crowd cheered as he took another two spurts in the face, and the white, sticky fluid dripped down onto his chest. He reached up to wipe it away.

"Stop. Hold still, Toy." The Wolf's voice rang out from the dais, and Alex dropped his hand, gritting his teeth. The feel of the warm cum on his skin only emphasized his humiliation. His throat burned from rough usage—how had Bella managed to get through two of the men? "Pet, go clean Toy off with that sweet mouth of yours. And crawl."

Alex tried not to look as Bella crawled toward him, her brown hair hanging down on either side of her face, not quite long enough to cover the swaying breasts underneath her body. She was unconsciously seductive, and it made him want to cover her up so no one else could see. She probably didn't realize how many of the men and women in the room were salivating from watching her crawl. Those on the dais with the Wolf stared with appreciation of the view from behind.

Alex was naked and couldn't hide any arousal. He focused on the cum on his face and chest, the soreness of his throat, and his anger at everyone around them. All the people who were watching, who were allowing this to happen and not even trying to stop the Wolf. Did any of them think it was wrong? Or were they just cattle, following the Wolf's lead?

When Bella reached him, Alex gave her a little smile and mouthed, 'I'm sorry.'

'Me too,' she mouthed back before gently placing her hands on his shoulders and leaning forward to lick his chest with her soft, pink tongue.

A shudder went through him at the touch of her hands and mouth, the way her tongue lapped and tickled his skin. His balls tightened, and his cock surged slightly as she dragged her tongue over his nipple, cleaning the cum from it. The tiny bud hardened, and Alex gritted his teeth as he tried to imagine whatever he needed to keep from becoming erect.

It was easier when she reached his face and licked him clean. Until her breasts brushed against his chest.

By the time she finished, his dick was at half-mast, although at least he'd managed to keep from becoming entirely hard. They both looked up at the Wolf—Bella first, and then Alex's gaze following hers—and waited for their next order. Alex's fists tightened as he realized it.

The Wolf smiled at them. His cock made an impressive tent in his pants, but the man nodded and waved at someone on the side of the room. The focus of the room changed, no longer trained on them; everyone knew the entertainment was over.

Bella and Alex found themselves seated on the floor of the dais, in front of the table and in full view of the room as they ate, but neither of them cared that they didn't have true seats or that everyone could see them. They didn't talk to each other. Alex didn't know what to say or whether their position meant the entire room would hear.

They both sat, Alex consumed with his own thoughts. He worried about the Wolf's restraint, his decision not to indulge himself, and what that might mean for the rest of their evening.

8

To Alex and Bella's surprise, after they ate, they were both escorted back out of the room—this time by new soldiers, who must be the night guard. One of them caught Alex eyeing them and smirked, giving a meaningful look at Alex's collar. He understood the message: they had the same control over its effects as the Wolf had. It was something to keep in mind.

Bella didn't agree with him about trying to escape, but there had to be a way. If only they'd been able to talk to Trish at some point ... But she'd been kept firmly planted on Jordan's lap throughout the entire dinner, and when Alex and Bella had left, she'd still been there. Alex wasn't sure how to deal with that little wrinkle—neither he nor Bella would feel right about escaping and leaving someone behind.

When it came down to it, if he had to make the decision, he would. Hell, if he had to knock Bella out when the time came, he would. That might not be a bad idea anyway; he wasn't sure how deep Dr. Margolis and Nurse

Roche had planted the trackers, but it wouldn't be as easy to get them out as it had been to put them in.

As these thoughts whirred through his head, he tried to pay attention to the hallways they went through. They seemed to be returning to the bedroom, following the same route they'd taken to get to the large hall. His supposition was confirmed when they were shown back into the room.

So, he knew where the bedroom was in relation to the main hall. At least that was something.

———

Bella lay curled up on her side, wrapped in her sheet, and watched Alex pace the room. He tugged at the collar around his neck a couple times, irritably. Neither action was anything new: he'd been doing both for a while now. When they'd first gotten back to the room, she'd tried to take the collar off at his request, a useless exercise that had resulted in both receiving a sharp, electrical shock. Nothing debilitating—it was like a very strong, static build-up that stung her fingers—but it wasn't something either of them wanted to repeat immediately.

After that, Alex sat on the bed with her for a bit, and held her, but Bella could almost hear him thinking, and then, eventually, he'd gotten up to pace. And mutter. And pace some more. She knew he was still thinking of escape.

Part of her wished he would come up with a viable plan, although she couldn't help thinking of everything that could go wrong, too. And the repercussions that would come with it.

"Maybe we could cut it off," she said, watching him tug at the collar again.

"What?"

She gestured to her neck. "Maybe we could try to cut it off."

Alex shook his head. "I don't think we'll be allowed anything sharp enough. And I think the Wolf, and maybe even some of his men, have a remote that controls the current in it. If we can just get our hands on one of the remotes, we can turn it off and it should be easy to take off."

"How do you know that?"

"The Wolf ah … used it on me earlier this evening." Alex didn't look at her. Bella felt chilled. Had Alex tried to do something before the Wolf had given him the option of taking her place? And been punished for it?

She would never have known if he hadn't told her.

His pacing reminded her of the animals that they'd seen at the zoo when they'd first arrived on Earth. Majestic beasts that had been caged and yearned to run free, that paced the walls of their cage just like he was doing now. Eventually, they'd be freed, and she held to that thought. She would do whatever it took to survive to that day.

Would Alex? He seemed so intent on escape, on being the author of his own freedom. But what if they couldn't escape? He was so strong. She knew he thought her fear of trying to escape made her weak, but what if she was better equipped for this situation than he was? Bella could bend, she could adapt … but if Alex couldn't escape, would his strength mean he'd break before he bent?

———

There wasn't much to do in the room. Alex paced. Bella watched him. Eventually she brought up Ken and Lisa and their families, wondering if anyone realized they were missing yet. It hit Alex in the gut that they had probably been missing for about twenty-four hours, now—and in such a short span of time, his world had turned on its head.

He'd broken up with his long-term girlfriend, been kidnapped, ravaged by a warlord of Earth, been forced to have sex with one of his friends—and now that he'd seen her as a sexual object, he was having a hard time unseeing her. Bella was beautiful. Even with her pink-rimmed eyes, slightly swollen from all the crying she'd done, wrapped up in a sheet, and exhausted, she was gorgeous. And he had to wonder what was wrong with him to notice, given the situation.

At least the ring around his cock and balls wasn't too tight. When he started to stiffen, he could still go down again by thinking about something else.

Eventually, he lay down on the bed on his back, and Bella scooted up to lay near him. He offered out his arm, and she snuggled into the crook of it, her body pressed against his. The sheet over her did nothing to reduce the effect of the warmth of her body or her soft curves, and he gritted his teeth as he willed his dick to stay down. Bella didn't need to deal with that kind of shit from him, considering everything else they were going through. He didn't want her to have to worry about him, just because he didn't have his physical responses under control.

She didn't seem to notice or, if she did, she trusted him. She stayed snugged up against him and sighed. The tension seeped out of her body.

He didn't feel tired lying there, but he must have

fallen asleep because the next thing he knew, something was being wrapped around his wrists and ankles, and Bella was being pulled away. Alex cursed and, in a surge of movement, tried to grab at Bella and lash out at whoever was touching them.

Laughter surrounded them from every side as they were pulled apart on the huge bed, Alex's wrists and ankles attached to the head and footboards, despite his struggles. He was too swamped by sleepy confusion to effectively fight back. Secured to the bed, he turned to see Bella struggling against the Wolf and a woman in uniform. They attached her wrists and ankles to the bed. as well, with one key difference—her legs were spread.

"Leave her alone," he snarled as Bella slumped in her bonds and looked up at the Wolf with wide, fearful eyes.

"Gag him," the Wolf said, not looking up from his scrutiny of Bella's lush curves. Alex snarled again, but was forced to open his mouth when one of the soldiers held his nose and cut off his air to get the gag in. Jerking his head around did nothing but get his hair pulled. Once the gag was in his mouth, his head was released, and he was able to look back to see the Wolf fondling Bella's breasts.

But those bright green eyes were looking straight back at Alex. Waiting for his reaction.

And that was the only reason Alex managed to hold still instead of straining uselessly against his restraints again. Instead, he glared back, knowing he didn't look at all threatening when he was tied up and gagged, but putting all his fury and frustration into his gaze anyway.

Just give me five minutes, loose and able to fight.

It was as if the Wolf knew what he was thinking, and the older man grinned as he squeezed Bella's breasts a little harder. She whimpered, and Alex growled into his gag, tugging once again at the restraints ... just to check.

"Leave us," the Wolf said, and Alex became aware of the others in the room again. They all looked disappointed at the order but they left.

The dynamic in the room became more intense and more dangerous. Which made no sense at all—shouldn't the presence of multiple people have been more intimidating? But this was the first time they'd been completely alone with the Wolf—a man known for his unpredictability—with no audience. Would it turn out the audience spurred him or helped restrict him?

His presence dominated the room as he loomed over them, kneeling on the bed, his hands on Bella's breasts, pinching at her tight, pink nipples. Alex couldn't watch, so he looked away.

"Bad Toy," the Wolf said, his voice silkily threatening. "You have to watch ... or I'll hurt her."

Alex's head whipped back around just in time to see the Wolf's hand come down hard between Bella's legs. She let out a loud cry and her hips jerked. There was no way she could have protected herself, with her legs cuffed and spread, and even though Alex didn't want to play more of the Wolf's games tonight, he knew he wouldn't look away again. Because the Wolf might be unpredictable, but he would follow through on his threats.

The throbbing sting of her pussy awakened the unhappy nerves. The salve Alex had spread on her before dinner had done a remarkable job of soothing the soreness, both inside and out, but that entire area remained very sensitive.

The strangest part was the Wolf didn't seem to be paying much attention to her, even as he fondled her breast and pulled at her nipples—awakening more unwelcome sensations in her groin. He was staring straight at Alex. And from the corner of her eye, she could see Alex glaring back. Watching because, if he didn't, the Wolf would hurt her again.

Bella quivered with fear. It was all too easy to imagine how she could quickly become a tool, rather than a 'pet,' used to prod Alex. The Wolf seemed to enjoy the dynamic between then two of them; perhaps especially because they weren't a romantic couple. She got the impression that the Wolf was as aroused by messing with their heads as he was messing with their bodies.

Focusing his attention on her sensitive nipples, he lowered his head and took one into his mouth. Bella fought back a moan, biting her lip and hating that it still felt good even though she didn't want it. The entire time, the Wolf kept staring at Alex.

She turned her head away from Alex, not wanting him to see if even the smallest flash of pleasure crossed her face. Not wanting him to see her humiliation at being fondled and played with just to get to him. Was the Wolf even sexually interested in her? Or was he only interested in how she related to Alex?

Feeling Alex's eyes on her made her skin tingle. She felt ashamed that he was watching, and yet slightly comforted by his presence—even though he couldn't do anything. Maybe it was because she wasn't going through this alone.

The Wolf's hands left her, and she looked up, frightened of what might happen next.

He began stripping without looking at either of them, as if they weren't in the room at all; as if he hadn't just been touching Bella. And Bella couldn't help looking at him as he took off each piece of clothing and kicked it into the corner. He was older but still impressively muscled, with scars on his chest and back—one large one on his thigh, and what looked like an old burn on the back of his hip. This was not a man who sat back while his men did all the dirty work; it was obvious he'd seen action.

Bella couldn't help but stare, fascinated by the markings all over his body. It was unusual for anyone on the Moon to have any kind of scars. Very few people were ever hurt, and when they were injured, they always had the scars removed. Imperfections were looked down on; no one would casually wear them the way the Wolf did. And yet, somehow, it added to that charismatic appeal he exuded; the utter confidence with which he shucked off his clothes and showed them his body.

Once he was naked, his erection jutting out from the thatch of hair at his groin, he turned back to the bed, his green eyes glittering malevolently. All his attention on Bella. And she immediately wished it wasn't. He did glance at Alex, as if to make sure he was watching, and then the Wolf climbed onto the bed between her legs.

She shuddered and automatically tried to curl in on herself but couldn't.

"Pretty Pet," the Wolf murmured, stroking the insides of her thighs, squeezing the flesh slightly in between the caresses of his fingers. "Pretty Pet has such a pretty pussy now. Look at all this pretty pink flesh ... and this big, fat plug underneath."

As he twisted the plug in her bottom, awakening nerves she'd almost forgotten about, Bella squirmed uncomfortably. With the Wolf playing with the toy, it felt like she had to go to the bathroom.

"Is this the biggest thing you've ever had in your asshole, Pet?" He stared her down with those predatory green eyes. Bella felt her own eyes spark with tears. Alex growled with unhappiness behind his gag.

There was no point in not answering the Wolf's question. All he wanted was information. Even if it was embarrassing information—that was better than a multitude of other things.

"Yes," she whispered. And then cried out as the Wolf pulled, and the fattest part of the plug forced its way past her tight sphincter before it tapered off. The sensation of being completely empty was a relief. But now, she had to worry whether the Wolf would force his cock into her virgin asshole in place of it.

To her shock, he didn't show any immediate interest in the hole he'd just stretched and emptied. He tossed the plug to the side and he knelt over her, leaning down to suck at her nipples while he played with her breasts. Bella shivered as his hands kneaded her soft flesh, and hated her sensitive nipples as they were pinched, tugged, sucked, and nibbled. The Wolf took his time, seeming to enjoy just playing with the sensitive mounds. Occasionally, he would pause to look at Alex, and every time, Alex must have been watching because the Wolf would go right back to enjoying her breasts rather than hurting her.

Wetness began to grow between her thighs, even as

she tried to ignore the pleasurable sensations. The breaks between the Wolf's toying with her breasts, as well as his increased attentions now, took their toll on her control over her body's responses. It felt good. Demoralizing, how the Wolf could do this to her, over and over again, apparently, but even that didn't stop her pussy from getting wet.

As if he could read her thoughts, one of his hands slipped down between her legs and began to stroke the soft folds of her pussy. Bella didn't realize she'd moaned until she heard the sound echoing in her ears. The Wolf chuckled, pleased, and she closed her eyes as her face flushed bright red.

"Such a nice, wet pussy," the Wolf murmured, loudly enough that Alex couldn't miss the words or the implication.

Bella gasped as the Wolf's finger thrust inside her, his thumb sweeping over her clit at the same time. Her hips jerked upwards in response as the Wolf pulled away and moved himself down her body. Then he lowered his mouth to her spread core and slid his finger back out of her pussy to press it into her anus. His tongue licked up the center of her folds.

The finger didn't hurt, and, though her asshole was sore, it had been stretched enough by the plug for the Wolf's thick finger and knuckles to feel only strange, not painful. It might have helped that he was very skillfully eating her pussy, creating a surge of pleasure in that receptive area.

Nooooooo!

Bella clenched her jaw against the word, knowing it wouldn't change anything and not wanting to give the Wolf any extra satisfaction or distress Alex any further.

The sloppy wetness increased as the Wolf continued to lick and suck on her folds, teasing her clit so her muscles tensed and spasmed with need—a need she was determined to ignore. When she looked down at the Wolf to try to fight her body's response by watching exactly who was creating the sensations, she was more than a little disturbed to see his attention had returned to Alex.

And she didn't dare look at the man next to her. Her breath caught in her throat as she realized that the Wolf was just watching, almost daring Alex to look away so the Wolf could punish Bella for it. Even her fear didn't stem her arousal as the Wolf's tongue thrust inside her and then licked up to her clit before he slid back down to fuck her with it again.

When he pulled away, she almost whined. Her entire pussy tingled with the need for satisfaction, even as fear flashed through her again. Both nipples stood out on her chest, hard and tight, even though he hadn't touched them since he'd lowered his mouth between her legs. Bella hated how visible her arousal was, from those tight pink nubbins to the glossiness of the Wolf's lips and chin, which were coated with her juices.

The Wolf wiped his mouth with his hand and casually reached over to spread the juices over Alex's upper lip and the gag. Bella looked away, not wanting to see Alex's expression at her body's betrayal.

"Doesn't Pet smell good?" The Wolf grinned down at Alex. "She tastes good, too. Maybe I'll let you try, sometime."

The image of Alex between her thighs with his mouth on her made Bella shiver and clench. It was something Ken hadn't done very often when they'd been together—

which might be why she'd had such trouble resisting the sensations the Wolf had elicited.

The Wolf raised his eyebrow, watching her reaction, and her entire body flushed.

"Oh my, Toy," the man purred, putting his thumb about a centimeter above her clit and rubbing in a slow circle. She didn't know if he was doing that because he didn't know exactly where her clitoris was located, or because he knew it would be maddeningly teasing. Not that she wanted him to touch her there. Not really … "I think Pet likes that idea. Or maybe she just wants to get back at that cheating boyfriend of hers, what do you think?"

There wasn't any response to that, but Bella knew Alex had looked away when the Wolf's hand came down hard on her pussy again. Her clit was so tormented by having been teased that it almost felt good to have direct contact, and she cursed inwardly even as she prayed Alex wouldn't look away again. He made an incoherent noise beside her—the Wolf's abuse of her tender flesh had angered him. Bella didn't know whether that made her feel better or worse.

The Wolf stared at Alex, and Bella turned her head away as he lined up his cock with her pussy. Her entire body was trembling non-stop now. This was it—the Wolf was really going to fuck her. And he would force Alex to watch while he did it.

The hard, thick crown of his cock nudged into the entrance of her body, not quite roughly but not gently either. Bella couldn't stifle the whimper that worked its way up out of her throat. Despite the salve that Alex had spread on her, she wasn't prepared for this. It wasn't like she'd had a lot of sexual partners, and her body had never been invaded, tortured, and used the way it had been today.

The slickness that had come while the Wolf had played with her wasn't enough to make for an easy entry, and she whimpered and squirmed, tears sparking at her eyes as he began to rock his hips back and forth, thrusting a little deeper each time. The low, guttural groans of pleasure he made sickened her, though she knew they were as much for Alex's benefit as anything else. The mattress beneath her moved as Alex pulled at his restraints.

There was nothing she could do but lie there as the Wolf shoved his cock in deep, and Bella whimpered as her body split apart from how large he was. Just as big as Alex, just as hard, and just as hot inside her. The weight of him rested against her lower body as he looked over at Alex, triumphant and fully buried inside her.

Then he began to move.

The friction felt horribly good, especially as he angled himself so his groin rasped against her swollen clit with every thrust. He took his time, with long smooth strokes in and out of her body that made her sensitive nerve-endings tingle. If he hadn't eaten her out beforehand, hadn't teased her, she would have been alright. But her pussy was much more sensitive than usual, and, with her rectum emptied of the plug, there was nothing to distract from the thick cock filling her over and over again.

"Noooooo ..." Bella moaned, not at the Wolf—because that would have been useless—but at herself.

She writhed beneath him, trying to move away, trying to angle her body so he didn't hit all the right spots, but the restraints were too tight, and his weight was too heavy.

"That's it, Pet," he murmured into her ear, softly

enough Bella was sure Alex couldn't hear what he was saying. Another form of mental torment, probably. "It feels good, doesn't it? You're so tight around my cock, I can feel how much you like it every time I do ... this ..."

And the head of his cock ran over her g-spot right before his body pressed against her clit and Bella arched beneath him, hating herself for the involuntary response. It did feel good. Not that she would admit it.

But even she could hear her breathing picking up, turning into rhythmic panting as he fucked her, pleasuring her against her will. All the while, constantly checking to make sure Alex was watching.

———

Even if he wanted to look away now, Alex wasn't sure he could—although the Wolf's demand gave him unhappy permission to watch.

If he could look away, would his cock not react?

He was half-hard from looking at her naked body and smelling the juices the Wolf had smeared under his nose; half-hard from hearing her sexy little moans and knowing she was aroused. It wasn't too hard to tell what made her uncomfortable and what made her feel good. Bella was an open book, which only made her easy prey for the Wolf.

Alex didn't blame her. It was obvious the Wolf was practiced in pleasuring a woman. He knew exactly what to do, what to look for, and could exploit it to the extreme. What Alex hated was his reaction to watching it. The cock ring gripped him tightly as he struggled to keep his mind on his anger, his rage, rather than the stunning sight of Bella writhing on the edge of orgasm.

The Wolf's green eyes bored into his own, arrogantly triumphant, taunting him for his helplessness.

The man groaned with pleasure often as his cock sank into Bella's body with a hot, wet sound. The masculine groans grated on Alex's nerves, rousing his fury every time. By now, he would have thought he'd be past being prodded, but the Wolf kept finding new ways to anger him, and forcing Bella to pleasure was one of them.

Watching every thrust, every grinding movement of the Wolf's body against hers was utter torture. Especially as Bella began to whisper "no, no, no" while her body spasmed and convulsed. She was fighting herself, a battle he watched her lose as her back arched and she thrust her breasts up to rub against the Wolf's chest while she cried out.

Tears trickled down her cheeks as she squirmed and moaned, and the noises made his cock finally stand fully at attention. Alex watched as she came, achingly beautiful and seductive in her pleasure.

The Wolf rode out her orgasm, allowing her to ride the full wave of her pleasure. As soon as it was done, he began to pound into her, hard and merciless.

Alex fought his restraints again as Bella cried out, this time in pain as the Wolf slammed into her body. He no longer watched Alex's reaction, no longer tried to make Bella's body betray itself. The Wolf wasn't interested in anything but his own pleasure. His groans were much quieter, much more natural as he pummeled Bella's pink pussy, which turned pinker by the minute as the Wolf's body slapped it.

Her thighs quivered as she tried to close her legs against the assault, and her head shook back and forth. Her back arched upward again, a last-ditch attempt to pull away. The Wolf grimaced as he threw back his head and groaned loudly; his hips pressed against Bella's body, and Alex knew that the man was coming.

Bella slumped beneath him, breathing heavily, tears still on her cheeks as she let out a little moan of relief. Alex could practically hear his pulse pounding in his ears.

When the Wolf looked over at him, Alex glared and then flushed as the Wolf's gaze lowered to his erect cock. Still planted firmly inside Bella, the Wolf laughed.

"It looks as though Toy enjoyed the show, Pet. Good job."

She made a little mewling sound and didn't look at Alex. Alex hoped she realized it was mostly the effect of the cock-ring, which wouldn't allow his dick to deflate once he was aroused by anything, and that he hadn't been aroused by watching the majority of what had happened. He was just aroused by her.

The Wolf put his weight on one arm, his body still over and inside Bella's, and reached over to take Alex's cock in his hand. There was nothing Alex could do as the Wolf pumped him, hard and long, his thumb expertly sweeping over the weeping slit in the tip. It felt incredible. Alex groaned against the gag as his body shuddered and released jets of white cum up onto his chest.

Fuck.

His cock jerked in the Wolf's hand with the last few spurts of cum.

Shamed, Alex looked away. He hated that he'd come by the man's hand while the Wolf was still inside Bella.

The Wolf grunted his satisfaction, and Alex could hear him moving around. He left the cum drying on Alex's chest and stomach, but the chains on his restraints were loosened to where he could bend his elbows enough to rest his head and sleep. The Wolf also removed his gag. Maybe Alex should have felt grateful for that, but mostly he felt sick and angry. He didn't say anything though, just worked his jaw with relief that the thing was out.

The Wolf released Bella from her restraints entirely and then pulled her up with her back against his front, a heavy arm around her waist. The Wolf slapped the wall next to the bed, and a panel opened. When he hit one of the buttons, the lights went out and left them in blackness.

Alex knew Bella and the Wolf were close by, but he couldn't see them anymore. There was nothing more he could do now except try to rest and save his strength for when he had a better plan. Would the Wolf leave Bella unrestrained every night? If he did, maybe Alex could use that. He'd need to learn what each of those buttons on the panel did.

His mind was whirled with plans again, maybe to keep him from thinking about what he and Bella had been through, but his exhausted body sucked him down into sleep anyway.

9

When Bella woke the next morning, she and Alex were alone in the room, and he was still asleep. She'd spent a troubled night trying to fall asleep with the Wolf's big body around her. Being held in Alex's arms made her feel secure and comfortable, but having the Wolf wrapped around her was like being held by ... well by a wolf. One that had decided not to eat her yet, but she wasn't sure when she might be its next meal.

Which only reminded her of how he *had* eaten her last night.

Bella shuddered and forced her mind away from that. The restraints had been removed from Alex's wrists and ankles, just like hers had, but when? Had the Wolf done it, or had others been in here? It disturbed her to think she'd slept through the Wolf's exit from the room, no matter how exhausted she'd been.

"Alex," she whispered, reaching out to touch his arm. "Alex, wake up."

He came to with a jerk, and she snatched her hand back, just in case. Brown eyes looked around the room warily before they came to rest on her and softened. He blinked a couple times before he realized he was free. Alex reached out to touch her, but then his hand stalled, unsure of its reception.

"Are you okay?" he asked, worriedly.

Her heart went out to him. Poor Alex. There was something of an ancient knight in his soul—a protector—and he was unable to protect her right now. The few times he had been able had been when the Wolf had wanted to play some twisted game. Every time, it had been an assault on Alex's pride. Yet his first thought had always been for her, not for himself.

"I'm fine," she said, which was mostly true. Her pussy ached a little, but a night of rest had helped. She'd been more than a bit worried about what the Wolf might want with her in the morning; it was a relief he wasn't here, but also rather worrisome. The man's unpredictability was anxiety-inducing. "Are you okay?"

Alex's face hardened for a moment and then softened again. "I'm fine sweetheart, you don't need to worry about me." He reached out and pulled her into his arms. She snuggled in immediately, the sheets still between them. Flaking dried bits of his cum still clung to his chest, but Bella didn't care. Just having him hold her felt nice. Reassuring, which she needed even if it was false reassurance.

They were only like that for a few minutes when the door opened. Bella's entire body tensed, and she looked up to see Jordan entering the room, holding Trish's hand and pulling the petite young woman along. Today, she was in a white dress that made her look especially innocent, and her long, white-blonde hair hung loose down her back and over her shoulders. She looked at

Bella and Alex with wide eyes but didn't seem unduly frightened or anxious, which helped Bella relax just a little bit.

"Up." Jordan was the same as he'd been yesterday: curt, mercenary, and intimidating.

To Bella's surprise, Alex got up quickly, but, as he positioned himself between Bella and Jordan, she realized he hadn't been doing it out of obedience. Unlike Bella, he hadn't relaxed at all. His back muscles were tense, and his hands were fisted at his sides. Bella couldn't see his face, but she was sure his expression was anything but cooperative. She slid off the bed behind him, nervous about the rising tension in the air.

Jordan just laughed. "Go ahead and try something, boy," he drawled, deliberately insulting. "I don't need that collar to keep you in line."

Bella touched the back of Alex's shoulder. He flinched, but the soft touch seemed to help him remember himself. He glanced over his shoulder and down at her, his face hard and set. Bella looked back at him and tried to put her desire for him to not make any trouble into her eyes.

"She's smarter than you, you know," Jordan said, amused by the interchange.

Alex's head swung back around, and Bella reached out to grab his hand. He hadn't made a move toward Jordan, but just in case.

"Come on. Shower, then breakfast, and then you'll get a chance to be outside for a bit if you behave."

That didn't sound too awful, as long as there were no surprises. Bella squeezed Alex's hand, and he squeezed it back. She was able to fully relax then. Jordan turned and walked out of the room, not waiting to see if they followed, pulling Trish behind him. She shot a fleeting look over her shoulder at Bella and Alex, too quick for either of them to read her expression.

But they followed.

———

The entire morning, Alex spent learning. Maybe he couldn't fight back right now, and Bella was right—they weren't ready to escape—but he could at least learn. Plan.

And they'd seen more of the compound this morning than they had yesterday—and it was definitely a compound. Huge. The entire building looped in a circle around a gigantic outdoor space.

There was an area where soldiers played with a ball and hoops, an old form of sport that was pretty much only played on Earth, now. Sports on the moon tended to be newer variations on old games, played in either low or null gravity. Another area had a large pool. And then there were the gardens.

It was almost enough to make him forget where he was … but not quite. As if he could ever entirely forget with the collar around his neck. Or the one around his dick.

Jordan had taken them to a locker-room-type setup where they all showered together. He'd kept an eye on everyone, although most of his attention had been taken up with washing Trish. Neither Bella nor Alex had been able to get near their fellow captive so far because Jordan had yet to let her more than a foot away from him. Most of the time, he held her hand or had his arm around her. If it wasn't for the slightly panicked and dazed expression on Trish's face, they would have looked like a normal couple.

Jordan didn't seem to have harmed or abused her beyond his sexual attention. In some ways, it appeared as though Jordan was taking good care of her. She just had to put up with his focused, and sexual, attention.

They'd been given food—sandwiches—which they'd taken outside. That was when Alex learned that it was still early in the morning. The sun shone high in the sky but not directly above them, and his internal clock said it was morning, not afternoon. Either the Wolf had left Alex and Bella sometime in the middle of the night, or he awoke infernally early.

After the showers, the food, and now being out in the sunshine, Alex felt deceptively normal. Had Jordan allowed all the activity on purpose, to put them off-kilter? Or perhaps it was a different kind of message: behave, please the Wolf, and this was the kind of treatment they could expect.

Jordan led them to the pool where he grabbed two pairs of goggles from a bin. "Get in. You need to exercise."

Alex shrugged at the man's direction and willingly jumped into the pool. Only once he was fully immersed did he realize he'd tensed in case the water affected his collar—it didn't.

"Come on." He smiled at Bella. She looked at the pool and then back at Jordan, who was helping Trish disrobe. "The water feels good."

They would both need to keep in shape if they were going to escape eventually. Exercise would be essential, plus it would release endorphins that would help keep them from getting depressed. If the Wolf planned on keeping them for a long period of time to continue playing his sick games, perhaps he wanted to ensure his captives were healthy and sane. But that played into what Alex wanted, too, so, for right now, there was no point in fighting.

———

After swimming, Bella and Alex were left to their own devices in the outdoor area until lunch. Bella still wasn't able to get close to Trish. Jordan accompanied all three of them everywhere—even the bathroom—and he barely let go of Trish in all that time. He constantly played with her hair, which was such a similar shade to his own. The possessive hunger in his eyes every time he looked at her was frightening.

When Jordan first herded them back into the compound, Bella didn't know where they were going until he brought them to the same hall the Wolf had been in yesterday. She tensed, though the atmosphere was slightly less fraught than it had been the night before. There were a fair number of people in the room, although not as many as yesterday, and the bed had been raised in the center of the room again.

Alex reached out and put his arm around her and tightened it protectively, but this time it wasn't all that reassuring. She knew far too well he couldn't do anything to protect her.

"Keep moving," Jordan said from behind them, and Bella felt Alex stumble slightly. He muttered a curse and glared over his shoulder; Jordan must have pushed him. Bella moved forward, hoping to distract Alex. His temper would be short now that they were being confronted by yet another one of the Wolf's games. Just the bed ready and waiting for occupants set both Alex and Bella on edge.

"Ah ... Pet, Toy, and Jordan's little girl," the Wolf said from the dais, standing. His eyes glinted with appreciation and swept over their naked bodies as they came in. This time, Trish hadn't been allowed to dress, and his gaze took her in, as well. "Looking all shiny and new. I do hope you're hungry."

They were. It had been hours since Jordan had given them the sandwiches—which hadn't been all that big a meal to start with—and then they'd been swimming and moving around out in the sun. Bella's stomach tightened in anticipation. Whatever everyone was eating, it smelled amazing and made her even hungrier.

"Up on the dais," Jordan ordered, giving Alex a push. Bella started to follow him, but Jordan grabbed her arm. "You're going to the bed, Pet."

Bella started to tremble again. Alex turned around, and Jordan shoved him hard enough to send him stumbling forward several steps before he fell to his knees in front of the dais. Several of the soldiers standing there flanked him before he could stand to ensure he wouldn't be able to interfere. Jordan pushed Bella, more gently, toward the bed, and pulled Trish with him.

"Who wants to see the girls eat?" the Wolf asked loudly. His words were met with a rowdy cheer. He reminded Bella of an ancient Roman emperor, entertaining the masses. Except she wasn't a gladiator, and he didn't want them to fight. The Wolf looked down at the two young women as Jordan led them onto the bed. "All you have to do for lunch, girls, is eat each other first."

Bella and Trish looked at each other. Although Bella had experimented a bit with other women, especially her close friends the look on Trish's face said she didn't have any experience with other women.

"It's okay," Bella whispered to her, ignoring the catcalls coming from all sides. She reached out to take Trish's hand to the sound of even more cheering, which she ignored. Bella squeezed the young woman's hand and attempted to smile. "We can do this."

Trish nodded a little stiffly, her eyes going toward Jordan as if she expected him to step in and intervene, but he had already stepped back and was watching them with a hot look in his eyes. He was just as eager as anyone else to see Trish and Bella perform.

Trish turned back to Bella. "I've never done this before," she whispered, looking a bit stricken. "I don't know how to do this. Oh my god ... everyone's watching!"

"Just follow my lead." Bella leaned forward and kissed Trish on the mouth.

It made her feel strange because Trish was reluctant to kiss her back. She kept her lips tightly clamped against Bella's. Carefully, gently, Bella brought her hands up to cradle Trish's face, hoping to make the kiss look more passionate than it was. If Bella's guess was correct, the Wolf wanted a show more than anything.

———

"Well Toy, don't you want to know how you're going to earn your meal?" The Wolf came alongside Alex. Still on his knees, Alex had to look up at the man, and did his best to ignore the obvious bulge at the front of the Wolf's pants. "It's easy, Toy. All you have to do is willingly suck my cock. And swallow my cum."

The taunting tone in his voice made it obvious he

knew it wouldn't be easy for Alex. He almost immediately said no but then shot a worried look at Bella, who was still kissing Trish. The younger woman was reluctant and not really responding, although Bella was doing her best. Bella already had her work cut out for her; what would happen if Alex didn't suck the Wolf's cock?

As if reading his mind, the Wolf chuckled and reached out to grab Alex's hair and tilted his head back to force him to look up. "Don't worry, Toy. Whatever you choose won't affect Pet. But you're not going to eat until my cum is in your belly."

"Fuck off," Alex said, sneering. He didn't know whether the Wolf told the truth, but it fit right into his sick, twisted games. Alex was hungry but he wasn't that hungry. If what he said wouldn't affect Bella—and he did trust the Wolf on that, for some reason—then he wasn't going to be shy about letting his true feelings be known.

The Wolf laughed. "You might change your mind after a couple of missed meals." Alex shuddered, and the Wolf laughed again.

Sick bastard.

If the Wolf withheld meals until Alex swallowed his cum, he knew he'd give in eventually but he wouldn't cave right away.

The Wolf turned his attention back to the bed, and Alex looked, too. The women still kissed, but it wasn't a very entertaining show. The watching crowd was bored with it, too, and shouted derisive advice.

"Jordan," the Wolf said, "this is boring. See if you can't liven them up a bit. Give Pet a couple stripes with your belt for encouragement."

Bella shrieked and pulled away from Trish to beg for mercy as the blonde looked on, horrified.

"Stop!" Alex shouted, and the soldiers next to him grabbed his shoulders and pressed down to keep him on his knees. "You said my choice wouldn't affect her!"

"Yours doesn't," the Wolf said with a shrug. "But they're taking too long."

The snap of leather against flesh had Alex's head whipping around as Bella shrieked. Trish had curled up on the bed in a ball, her arms around her knees and back against the headboard to watch with wide eyes as Jordan raised his arm again. He had one hand on Bella's back to hold her, bent down, over the bed, and one long, red line already showed across her creamy buttocks.

CRACK!

Bella screamed again, and Alex lunged, only to be drawn back by the soldiers on either side of him. There was nothing he could do as Jordan lifted his arm again.

CRACK!

A third stripe, diagonal to the other two, landed across her ass, and Bella's body jerked as she sobbed out another scream.

"Enough." The Wolf rested his hand on Alex's head. The word stopped Jordan, who lowered the belt and looked back up at the dais. "Let them try again."

———

The burning flames of her bottom made Bella feel like howling, but it wouldn't help. At least it had stopped. At least the Wolf hadn't continued the torture. Bella had been more than willing to make a better effort at putting on a show, even before the Wolf had ordered Jordan to strap her. Now, with her entire bottom on fire, she didn't have any hesitation.

She crawled up on the bed toward Trish, and the pretty blonde was still curled in on herself, big eyes wide. A flash of anger went through Bella. After all, it was Trish who had been hesitating, and yet Trish had gone unpunished.

"Come here," Bella whispered angrily. She wouldn't offer up her ass for Jordan's belt again just because Trish was reluctant.

"I can't …" Trish whimpered, her eyes big, as she looked around at the room. "Everyone's watching … I just … Oh god …"

Shit.

It was up to Bella. Her stomach growled, reminding her she wasn't just doing this for the Wolf's entertainment or to avoid punishment, but for food. While Bella didn't have any particular attraction to Trish, she'd definitely rather put on an erotic show than any of the other options she'd been presented with so far.

She reached out and grabbed Trish's ankle, and dragged the smaller woman into the center of the bed to pull her out of her curled-up position. Cheers erupted around them.

"What are you doing?" Trish stared up at her in shock.

"Saving us."

Pushing herself on top of Trish, in between the other woman's thighs, Bella kissed her hard. She didn't care if Trish opened her mouth now; the fall of her hair would mask what the kiss truly looked like. The important thing was the show.

Beneath her, Trish wriggled and squealed and tried to push Bella off, but Bella was bigger and heavier. Guilt trickled through her for a moment, but what other choice did she have?

"Hold still," she whispered furiously, pulling away from Trish's lips for a moment. "Just do what I do."

To Bella's relief, Trish stopped struggling, though she didn't help, either. She just lay there, limply. That was better than struggling, though. Bella brushed her hair out of the way so the people on the dais—most importantly, the Wolf—would be able to see clearly what she was doing.

Tears rolled down Trish's cheeks as Bella began to move her mouth down the woman's slender neck and collarbone with little kisses and licks of her tongue designed to look more interesting than they probably felt. Bella hadn't done anything quite like this before, but she'd seen plenty of videos and she tried to imitate what she'd seen in those.

When she reached Trish's breasts, the other woman shivered and moaned as Bella squeezed the pert mounds and sucked one nipple into her mouth. Trish's breasts were smaller than Bella's, but her nipples were longer and very sensitive. Trish was obviously humiliated and reluctant about the situation, but her back arched as Bella sucked hard on the little bud.

So far, in captivity, Trish probably hadn't had to do anything but be available for Jordan's passions, but that put her and Bella at a disadvantage right now.

Then the gist of some of the catcalls reached her ears —they liked that Trish was reluctant. As long as Bella put on a good show, it wouldn't matter what Trish did.

Perverts.

But a wave of relief went through her, even as her stomach gurgled hungrily.

Bella attacked Trish's tits with gusto, making her movements as big and obvious as possible while she straddled the younger woman's hips. She sat up and rubbed her pussy lips over Trish's bare mound and continued to play with Trish's breasts.

"Oh noooo ... please stop!" Trish moaned as Bella's fingers pinched her nipples and tugged, elongating them and turning them dark pink. She gripped Bella's wrists, trying to pull them away, but Bella hung on and twisted the tender nibs. Beneath her, Trish bucked, her face reflecting her conflicting emotions.

The rough treatment of her nipples was arousing her, but she didn't want to be aroused, and it looked like it hurt a bit, too. Bella was surprised to find her own pussy becoming wet from rubbing against Trish's bare mound. She felt a bit bad for becoming turned on at all, but the squirming of Trish's body against her sensitive parts felt good.

Instead of responding, Bella leaned over and pulled Trish's nipple into her mouth again, suckling hard and making the young woman's back bow as she thrust her breast up into Bella's mouth. She grabbed the back of Bella's head, but couldn't seem to decide whether to pull Bella closer or push her away. The crowd around them became louder with encouragement.

Inching her lower body down, Bella removed the stimulation of Trish's mound against her pussy and squirmed into a more comfortable position. She moved down Trish's stomach, kissing and licking the soft skin. Out of the corner of her eye she could see Jordan moving to get a better view as she lowered herself between Trish's legs. His eyes were hot with lust and excitement.

"Oh god …" Trish covered her eyes so she couldn't see everyone.

For the first time, Bella wondered if Trish's protected position as Jordan's doll was actually a handicap for their situation. Although Jordan had put parts of her body on display and had fondled and fucked her with others in the room, Trish had so far not been the center of attention. She wasn't handling it well.

Oh well. Too bad. Bella hardened her heart. Her own experiences, in a very short time, had already made her more ruthless. She was driven by two distinct motivations right now: the need for food and the desire to avoid punishment.

Bella pushed Trish's legs wide, thankful the young blonde wasn't fighting her, even if she wasn't helping.

Trish's pussy was wet, shiny with her cream, the pale, pink lips puffy as they split open to reveal her engorged clit. Bending over, sticking her ass up high in the air, and knowing anyone seated behind her would have a good look at her own privates, Bella slid her tongue up the center of Trish's slit and back down again. Trish didn't taste unpleasant—mostly sweet with just a hint of bitter, kind of like a melon, really, with just a hint of rind.

Bella tried to remember everything she could about eating pussy, and also about making it look good. She angled her head so Jordan and the Wolf and the others on the dais could see her tongue sliding up and down Trish's wet lips, and kept her hair out of the way while she did her best to tease Trish's clit as much as possible.

The young blonde moaned as her body responded, and her hips bucked slightly against Bella's mouth. When her thighs tried to tighten around Bella's head, Bella pushed them back apart and started sucking harder on

Trish's pussy lips, before she found the swollen bud of her clit and began to suckle hard on that.

Trish bucked and moaned, her small breasts wobbling as she writhed against Bella's mouth. The woman was going to come, and the cheers around them became even louder at her public humiliation.

"Oh … oooh … oh noooo!" Trish screamed when she came, her sweet juices becoming excessive, coating Bella's chin as she sucked hard on the young woman's clit.

———

Alex was starting to hate his cock. It was rock-hard from watching Bella with Trish. He'd tried to look away, but every small sound had brought his attention right back to the erotic sight. They were gorgeous together, with Bella's darker beauty contrasting Trish's pale features, and watching Trish come on Bella's lips was intensely appealing.

He knew he wasn't the only one to think so, but he hated that Bella would come back to the dais and to see the clear evidence Alex had watched. And enjoyed watching. The cock ring was tight around his balls and dick; even if he tried to put his mind to something else, he would stay hard.

The entire room watched as Bella licked a moaning and quivering Trish, using her tongue to clean the younger woman of her orgasm. Bella crouched between Trish's spread legs with her breasts hanging down and her ass high up in the air. She tried to placate the Wolf with her posturing, but this image would be burned in Alex's brain forever.

"Well, Pet has certainly earned her meal." The Wolf's eyes gleamed as Bella sat up on her heels, looking relieved. She wiped the rest of Trish's juices away from her mouth and only looked at the spent young woman for a moment before looking away. The expression on Bella's face was a combination of guilt and shame. She probably felt a lot of the same emotions he had yesterday after he'd been forced to do the same to her. "Jordan, perhaps you can ensure that your babydoll earns hers. Come here, Pet. Crawl to me."

Some people watched as Bella got off the bed and began to crawl up to the dais toward the Wolf, but most of them were watching Jordan lay down on the bed and put Trish on top of him. His cock looked huge next to her small frame, but he made her straddle his hips and sink down onto it. The subsequent gasping, feminine moans filled the room as he forced her to ride him.

By that time, Bella had joined Alex on the dais, and he pulled her into his arms and let her hide her face in his shoulder.

"It's okay," he murmured, feeling the wetness of her tears against his skin. "You did what you had to do. She knows that. It's okay."

Bella murmured something back, but he couldn't understand what she said. He just held her tighter, whispering reassurances and trying to drown out the sounds of Jordan's groans of pleasure and Trish's gasps as she bounced up and down on his cock. The slap of her wet pussy against his body, the squishing of his dick into that sloppy channel, was mostly buried by the crowd's rowdy catcalls, but some of that leaked through, too.

"Get Pet something to eat," the Wolf said to one of his men.

Bella pushed away slightly and looked up. "What about you?" she whispered to Alex.

The Wolf heard her and laughed, and reached out to stroke her hair. "Toy isn't eating lunch today, Pet." He raised one dark eyebrow at Alex, daring him. "Unless you've changed your mind?"

"Fuck off," Alex reiterated. And then pulled Bella in close to him again, as if he could protect her.

But the Wolf didn't retaliate. He just laughed again and walked back around to the other side of the table.

When Bella's food came, his men kept her and Alex apart so she couldn't share. And his stomach tightened and growled.

10

After being returned to what Bella was starting to think of as 'their' room, she and Alex were in for a surprise. One of the walls had a screen on it that was playing what she recognized as one of the more popular news stations, and her and Alex's pictures were on it.

"Oh my god!" She gasped and ran forward to touch the screen as her weeping parents were shown closing their front door on the cameras after refusing to comment. Alex's parents appeared immediately afterward doing the same. She barely noticed Alex coming up behind her or the soldier closing the door and locking them into the room.

They both recoiled when Ken's face filled the screen.

"Bella is my girlfriend. I love her so much. I can't believe she disappeared on the same day as my best friend. Lisa—Alex's girlfriend—and I, are leaning on each other for support." The camera panned out to show Lisa holding a tissue and standing beside Ken as he reached out to put his arm around her. She dabbed at her eyes, which leaked tears but weren't at all swollen or red. Bella suspected the use of eye drops and then felt a little bad for being so cynical—but come on! "All we can do is hope for their safe return. If someone knows where they are, please contact this number."

A phone number Bella didn't recognize flashed across the screen. It was probably for some kind of investigative authority.

"Are you worried that they were taken by the Wolf?" one of the surrounding reporters shouted. It was always the first question everyone asked when someone was reported missing on Earth. Sometimes something else had happened to them, but everyone was always more interested in stories involving the Wolf.

Lisa sniffed delicately. "We don't know. We haven't received any contact from anyone about them." And she covered her face as she appeared to burst into tears again.

Bella watched dispassionately. Had anyone bought Lisa or Ken's act? She felt incredibly far away from them and their betrayal, as though in the couple days she'd been missing, she'd already become a different person. And wasn't that true? Her priorities, her motivations, and her thinking had realigned to deal with the situation she was in now. Lisa and Ken seemed so very small by comparison.

"Attention whores," Alex said, just behind her, and Bella turned to look up at him.

He didn't look angry, just disdainful. Contemptuous. And that was exactly how Bella felt. While her parents and his waited for some kind of contact, some indication of what had happened to their son and daughter, Ken and Lisa were putting on a show for the masses. One that was patently false.

Although ...

"Maybe they're feeling guilty," Bella said, her voice empty of any sympathy.

Alex snorted. "That's possible. Whatever. So, obviously we've been reported missing." He raised his voice enough to drown out the words coming from the television. Ken was saying something more. Bella decided it wasn't important and turned her back on his face to watch Alex throw himself down on the bed.

"Yeah … How long do you think it will take for them to figure out where we are?"

He shrugged. "I guess it depends on when the Wolf releases that other girl … Abby. She'll be able to tell everyone that she saw us."

Bella approached the bed, hesitant to ask, but she really wanted to know. "What did the Wolf want you to do in exchange for lunch?"

Alex turned his head away from her as she sat down on the edge of the bed. Even though she was naked, for the first time, she didn't bother trying to cover herself. What was the point? And being naked was starting to feel almost natural.

"He wanted me to suck his dick."

"And you didn't."

"No."

There was a long pause while Bella tried to think of what to say next and to block out the news story droning on in the background. The broadcast had moved on to popular analysts, who were talking about all the facts and figures of the disappearances of Moon family members on Earth and how many of them were eventually revealed as captives of the Wolf.

"I'm going to have to eventually," Alex said softly. He

looked back at her, his expression troubled. "He made it clear that I won't get a meal until I do."

"So why didn't you today?"

He shrugged and looked away again. "I don't know. Pride. To show him that I wouldn't just give up immediately. To show him that he can't control everything."

"You need to eat, Alex."

"I know. I will."

Eventually.

He didn't say it, but the word hung in the air. Bella chewed on her lower lip; Alex wouldn't be eating today. He was making some kind of stand that was important to him. And to be honest, Bella wished she could do the same. Salvage something of her pride. But she was also back to worrying that when Alex did finally bend, it would be because he'd been broken.

"Come here, Bella, stop worrying." Alex held out his arm. Bella crawled up beside him and lay down with her head on his shoulder. He was so big and muscled, a firm anchor for her to cling to. Maybe she shouldn't worry about him breaking, but she wasn't afraid of being alone in this situation. "I can hear your thoughts running around your head."

"I'm scared, Alex," she whispered.

"I know, sweetheart. But we can get through this. We can. It's just games. He's playing lots of nasty little games. But we can survive, and we can win by getting free."

With the way she'd pinned down Trish today and how disassociated Bella felt from her former life, would she still like herself by the time the Wolf was done with his nasty little games? Maybe winning wasn't survival;

maybe it was staying true to herself. That's what Alex was doing. That's why he'd gone without lunch today.

And what had she done? She'd forced Trish to orgasm for the entertainment of the Wolf and his soldiers.

Maybe she should stop worrying about Alex and start worrying more about herself.

———

Alex cuddled Bella against him and reviewed what he'd learned so far about the Wolf and the compound they were living in. There had to be a reason the news story had been showing in their prison. To show him and Bella they were being missed? To mess with their heads about their exes? Or just to remind them why they should behave so they could get home?

Bella's breathing evened out as she fell asleep, which didn't surprise him. They'd been woken fairly early, exercised, and then she'd had an emotionally and physically charged interaction in front of a large audience. His stomach growled and tightened. Alex was tired too—not for the same reasons, but because he'd exercised and then not been able to replenish his energy.

Eventually, he would have to eat. His body demanded it. And if he was going to stay in good enough shape to escape, then eating would be necessary. But he wouldn't just give in to the Wolf, either. He'd learned a lot, listening to the men around the dais talking while Bella and Trish had been on the bed.

Like that none of the Wolf's men were particularly concerned about the kidnapping. But their attitudes had been more than indifference. Their tone had conveyed their belief that Alex, Bella, and Trish deserved what was happening to them. Not personally, but in general, because they were from the Moon families.

Why did they feel that way? And how he could use it? If he and Bella were ever going to find an ally to help them—which he wouldn't discount, even if he wasn't going to hope for it—they would have to be someone. So, he needed to find out why these people weren't.

He didn't know when he fell asleep, but he must have because he jerked awake when the door opened to admit three guards. Bella stirred beside him, snuggling even further and pressing her soft curves into his side. Alex shifted to try to push her further behind him, away from the door, not that it mattered. It was just instinct.

He and Bella were escorted to the bathroom to do their necessary business before being taken back to the room where the Wolf held court. That was how Alex was beginning to think of it: a barbarian King with his barbarian court.

Smells assaulted him from every side as he and Bella entered the room, savory and incredibly appealing. He nearly groaned as his stomach rumbled and tightened, completely empty and ravenous. His mouth watered, and he felt light-headed from not having eaten since early that morning. This was the first time in his life he'd ever gone without food for this long, and he'd never felt anything like it.

"Hungry, Moon Boy?" One of the soldiers sneered as Alex's stomach rumbled again. "Must be for the first time in your life, huh?"

The goons laughed as they pushed him forward. Bella shot him little, worried looks. As much as he would have liked to reassure her, the room was too loud for her to hear him if he spoke quietly, and he doubted the soldiers would let him lean in. The derision in their voices was obvious as they made several more remarks about how hungry he must be and how he'd be eating the Wolf's cock soon enough.

The slow burn of anger curled in his stomach and helped distract him from the hungry pangs that were almost painful.

Fuck them.

He and Bella were led up to the stage where the Wolf was talking and joking with some of his men. Jordan was there, which meant Trish was. She was dressed in a very low-cut, dove-gray dress that was loose on the top and had a short, flowy skirt. Her big, blue eyes were fixed on Bella, her expression anxious. She was tucked up under Jordan's arm with no way to approach them, but Alex thought Trish looked like she wanted to reassure Bella, who was obviously having trouble looking at the other woman.

The Wolf looked up and grinned as he saw them approach.

"Ah ... it's my sweet anal virgin," he said, spurring a bout of laughter round the room. Bella's face turned beet red. "Don't worry Pet, we won't be taking that last cherry this evening ... but I don't want people to think I'm cruel. We can help prepare you for when we do."

His broad wink at his audience made sure all eyes were on him, center-stage on the dais.

———

Bella tried to be strong and not make Alex's situation worse when he was obviously feeling weak from lack of food. She stifled her whimper as one of the soldiers pulled her up onto the stage. An apparatus was pulled out from underneath the table there—like a smaller table, but slightly lower and much narrower. One of the soldiers bent her over it before kicking her legs apart and securing her ankles to the base.

One board ran down the front of her body, right between her breasts, allowing her head to hang off the end. There was a support beam, perpendicular to the board that held up her body, with places for her wrists to be secured. She saw Alex watching from the corner of her eye, and he looked grim but, for once, he wasn't protesting.

Maybe he was finally learning how to bend. Or maybe he was too tired and weak.

She avoided looking at Trish, although she could feel the other woman's eyes on her. Too much guilt welled up inside of Bella every time she did.

"Ready for your plug, Pet?"

Bella tensed as much as she was able with her legs apart the way they were. It didn't do anything to help shield her vulnerable asshole.

Smack!

She yelped as a hard hand slapped against her ass, hard enough to feel as though it had left an imprint behind.

"I asked you a question, Pet."

God, she hated him. If only he would just do it, but no ... he had to ask. Had to make her participate, just like he had at lunch. She'd forced herself on Trish because he'd demanded a show.

Smack!

His hand came down on the other side of her ass and made her jerk against the restraints as her cheek burned.

The Wolf chuckled. "It looks like Toy has been rubbing off on Pet." The way he said it made the statement into a lascivious double-entendre. "Do you want to be punished, Pet? Is that what you're asking for?"

"No, Sir." Fear easily outweighed pride. Although her voice was soft, he heard her anyway. A gentle hand stroked down her flank, as if soothing the burn from his slap away, a reward for her response.

"Good girl. Are you ready for your plug now?"

"Yes, Sir."

She hated how easily she'd submitted, how quickly she'd given in, but Bella wanted this over with as quickly as possible. What did it matter what she said, anyway? Deep down, she knew the truth. Everyone else in the room probably did too, even if they didn't care.

The hard tip of rubber pressed wetly against her anus and pushed in. Bella shuddered and squeezed down automatically, trying to keep it out.

SMACK!

Another resounding slap on her ass, this time directly on top of the place he'd first spanked her, and Bella howled. Her muscles spasmed, and the plug slid in deeper.

"Relax, Pet." The Wolf began to work a couple inches of the plug in and out of her asshole. The tight ring of muscle burned as it stretched around the rubber, forced to open a bit wider with every millimeter of length that pushed in. "Hmmm ... Pet might need help relaxing. Who would like to help her?"

There was a sudden flurry of shouting as people volunteered. Laughing, the Wolf pointed at a woman near the front. Bella turned her head, anxious to see the stranger approaching. Dressed in camo pants and a black tank-top, the woman was both muscular and utterly feminine. Her bright red hair was pulled back into a ponytail, and she looked at Bella with undisguised lust.

Then Bella couldn't see her as the woman moved behind her. But she could feel the woman's slender fingers on her thighs, her hot breath wafting against her pussy.

"Nnooooooo," Bella moaned as the woman began to lick at her cunt, her tongue sliding up the very center and wiggling around. Bella's muscles clenched, but that didn't stop the spasm of unwanted pleasure that rippled through her. She turned her head away from the gathered crowd that watched her humiliation as the tip of the plug slid back into her virgin asshole.

She didn't want to enjoy what was happening to her, not any part. It would have made it easier on her, but she didn't get a choice. The woman had obviously volunteered to eat Bella's pussy out of sincere desire. She licked and sucked on Bella's pussy lips with sexual hunger, her tongue wriggling and questing and sliding into Bella's hole. Every time that clever tongue slid down to tease Bella's clit, her hips jerked upward and pushed the plug deeper.

Slowly, her asshole opened up under the steady pressure of the plug, the slick thrusts in and out. It burned. It was uncomfortable. She felt full. And yet she got more and more turned-on. Not everything about the fullness and probing felt bad—in fact, the closer she came to orgasm, the better it felt. Bella gritted her teeth and tried to stave off the pleasure, determined not to cum for their entertainment.

A sharp pinching flash of pain flared through her as the widest part of the plug was forced past her sphincter, and Bella cried out in shock. She panted, her asshole clenching around the large invader, which was bigger than the one the doctor had put in her the day before. The redhead's tongue still lashed at Bella's pussy, and then her lips wrapped around Bella's clit, and she sucked. Hard.

The combination of fullness in her asshole and the steady stimulation of her pussy was too much. Bella moaned in denial as the itch in her pussy throbbed and exploded. Her hips moved up and down as the woman continued to suck and lick at the sensitive pleasure-organ. That soft tongue licked up her juices as Bella shuddered and came and came ...

"Mmmm delicious." The woman's voice reached Bella's ears through the sexual haze she'd lost herself in. It sounded fuzzy and far away. "She's very sweet."

"Isn't she?" The Wolf sounded amused. "Thank you, Sylvia. Brick and Paul come here. You've earned rewards today. Choose which of you gets her mouth and which of you gets her pussy."

"Please nooooo," Bella begged, looking up at the men who approached. They were already hard from watching the entertainment, and their eyes locked onto her body and filled with desire. It was useless to beg, but she tried anyway.

"I like shutting a bitch up—I'll take her mouth," one of them said, laughing. He was huge, a mountain of a man, and the thing she was bent over and attached to put her at the perfect height against his crotch. "Open up, Pet ... and if you bite me, the Wolf will let me have you for the night."

Bella shuddered and looked over at the Wolf, but he'd

already lost interest and was walking toward where Alex knelt on the ground, between two soldiers.

She didn't know if the soldier was right about the Wolf lending her to him for the night, but going by the hard, cruel smile on his face, she didn't want to find out. Obediently, Bella opened her mouth and stifled a sob as he jammed his cock between her lips.

The man took a firm grip on her hair and leveraged her head back so he could more easily fuck her face. His cock was fat and long, and shoved deep into her throat—and Bella had another opportunity to be thankful for the gag-reflex gel Doctor Monroe had given her. Otherwise, she'd probably be choking on her own vomit instead of just struggling to breathe around the massive piece of equipment.

Another thick cock speared her from behind, shoving a couple inches into her tight pussy before it had to retreat and make another assault. Bella screamed as her insides burned; she was so full from the plug in her ass that it made her other tunnel even tighter than usual, and it burned as the man forcibly pushed his cock into her.

"Awww fuck, that feels good—make her do that again," the one in her mouth said gruffly, his head tipping back as he thrust his hips forward. The one behind her drew his hips back, his fingers digging into her sides, and then plunged forward again, this time filling her completely. Bella's gargled scream vibrated along the cock stuck in her throat as tears filled her eyes.

"Fuck, she's so tight." The one behind her rubbed his body against hers. Her sensitive pussy lips sparked and flared, still swollen from her orgasm, and she clenched around him as his body jostled the plug in her ass.

They began thrusting, taking turns, so each jab of

cock in her throat pushed her slightly back onto the one driving into her pussy, and that pushed her back onto the man fucking her face. Bella moaned and shuddered, breathing deeply whenever she could. The huge soldier using her mouth fucked her just as hard and rough as the one in her pussy, his big cock battering her throat. She pulled at her restraints instinctively, trying to get away, but there was nowhere to go.

The one behind her leaned over, his body grinding into hers as he reached underneath Bella and cupped her breasts. More tears gathered in her eyes as her body responded. It wasn't her fault she was still sensitive from her orgasm on the woman's tongue! If she hadn't been, this wouldn't be doing anything for her, but the lingering pleasure built again, despite the burning of Bella's throat and her utter disgust with the situation. The soldier rolled her hard nipples between his fingers, tugging painfully on them and making her pussy tighten around him.

"Aaahhh fuck yeah ... work that ass against me, baby." He moaned and pinched her nipples tighter, making her writhe. She squealed and spasmed as his body rubbed against the base of the plug, making it move inside her.

The beast in her mouth began to move faster, harder, and Bella got less and less air. She began to panic, but there was nothing she could do. She started to feel dizzy and disoriented. As she gasped and struggled to breathe, the strangest sense of euphoria began to well up inside her, on a straight line from her head to her pussy.

No ... No, this couldn't be happening. Not like this.

The oxygen depletion made her body hum and buzz even more; the man hammering into her pussy made her shudder and clench. The edges of her vision started to look black just as the man in front of her gave a shout and shoved his cock all the way, burying her nose in his pubic hair. Her throat spasmed around his cock, milking it, and Bella struggled to swallow the copious amount of cum that flowed straight down into her belly.

Behind her, the other man reared back, his hands on her hips again, and fucked her for all he was worth. Her body tightened, inevitable, even as she internally wailed in protest.

The orgasm was like a shockwave, sending fireworks ricocheting through her body. In the blackness that grew on her vision, Bella saw bright white sparks of ecstasy. Writhing, shuddering, her entire body was consumed by the rapture, caught in a place where pain and pleasure became one, and she was lost in the burning euphoria.

———

The Wolf gripped Alex's hair as they watched his men raping Bella; the front of his pants bulged with his cock. For once, Alex managed to keep his own erection down, even when Bella started to respond to the brutal fucking. He could tell she was coming, but he could also tell from the glassy look in her eyes that wherever her head was, it wasn't here and now. She looked barely cognizant of what went on around her.

Alex was too distracted by the food people were eating to be turned on. The smells and sights of people eating were enough to make him a little crazed. Would he be willing to suck the Wolf's cock already if it weren't for those soldiers tweaking his pride?

As if reading his thoughts, the Wolf looked down and

aggressively pulled Alex's hair back so he was forced to look up and meet the man's gaze.

"Well, Toy? Are you ready to eat yet?"

"Fuck off." Alex repeated his words from before, but even he could hear how they didn't have the same impact. The same determination.

The Wolf chuckled, not at all perturbed. "You'll be sucking my cock soon enough, Toy. I can wait."

His green eyes glittered with anticipation. Alex wanted to jerk his head away, to look somewhere else, to deny the Wolf's words, but the man was right. The Wolf held Alex's gaze for one more long second and then released his head, allowing it to fall forward. Alex panted, feeling strangely violated by that intense gaze.

He looked up and was swamped by shame for feeling that way. Two soldiers were undoing Bella's restraints, and she was hung limply, shuddering all over as she gasped for air. Cum dripped down her inner thighs, and she looked completely wrung out.

The two soldiers who had used her left Bella hanging there, and the expressions of the men freeing her said that they would rather have taken the previous soldiers' places than let her go. Alex burned with anger, all too aware of how weak he was.

Tomorrow, he would give in to the Wolf. Not because he couldn't bear to be hungry, but because he needed his strength if they were ever going to escape. His pride would take the hit, but if that's what he had to do in order to stay fit and healthy enough to be able to help Bella, then that's what he would do.

11

"Did you enjoy your afternoon entertainment?" the Wolf asked Bella as he fed another tidbit into her mouth.

Unlike the previous meal, he had her sitting next to him, in a chair. Alex was on his other side, kneeling on the floor and staring at the ground. It made Bella supremely uncomfortable, although she figured it was supposed to make a clear distinction between the two of them: the one who had earned a meal and the one who hadn't. Not that she'd really had a choice this evening.

But she'd shown herself willing to do what she had to in order to eat, earlier in the day, hadn't she?

She wasn't allowed to feed herself though. The Wolf fed her and seemed to get some kind of pleasure from it. His eyes were practically glowing green as he watched her take the food from his hand. Bella was just grateful for the food and that he hadn't demanded anything further after his two soldiers had finished taking their 'reward' by using her body.

"You mean the news program?" she asked. "It was … informative."

"Was it?" There was something in his voice, as if he were amused by her answer or … or … she didn't know what. "Did you enjoy seeing your boyfriend?"

"He's not my boyfriend," she answered automatically and then opened her mouth like a baby bird as he brought another piece of meat to her lips. She shifted uncomfortably under his gaze, all too aware of the plug in her ass when it rubbed against the seat. In certain positions she could almost forget it was there, but in others it was almost painfully noticeable. "I don't care what he says."

The Wolf laughed as if truly amused by her answer. Bella locked eyes with Alex and hated that she couldn't get him some food. He still stared at the ground, unwilling to look at her or the table. She couldn't blame him. But she hated that she was eating, and he wasn't.

"May I ask a question?" Bella was hesitant, unsure whether the Wolf's high spirits would extend to that. But he did seem to be indulgent of her at the moment, and there was something she was desperate to know.

"Of course, Pet." The Wolf reached out to stroke her hair. He curled a strand around his finger, a strangely intimate gesture that made her shiver. Right now, the Wolf really was treating her like a pampered pet and not like a fellow human being—something she would do well to remember. "You may ask."

But he might not answer. "What about Abby?" she asked, her voice low.

People could hear the conversation on the dais throughout the main room if they felt like it, of course, but everyone was so loud she doubted any of them were paying attention.

"Slave? What about her?"

"What happened to her?" Bella asked anxiously, hoping he would answer and the answer wouldn't be awful. The question had occurred to her as she'd been sitting there, eating, and wondering about the people who had come before her. Perhaps who'd sat in this very seat. "Why didn't you send her home yet?"

The Wolf looked at Bella through hooded eyes, his fingers rubbing across the strand of hair he'd wound up. "I did, Pet. She was released and returned to your people an hour after you saw her."

"Then why weren't they reporting it?" Bella asked, insistent. It was always big news when someone came home from captivity with the Wolf.

The Wolf looked thoughtful and held up a green vegetable to her mouth, and she obediently opened and took it. "That is the question, isn't it, Pet?" he asked silkily.

Then he looked away and reached for his glass of wine, and Bella got the impression the subject was now closed. But what did he mean?

Had he really released Abby when he claimed? Was she already back on the Moon? And if so, why hadn't the reporters known about it?

———

When they got back to their room, Bella told Alex about the conversation with the Wolf and his claim that he'd released Abby the same day they'd seen her. Alex hadn't thought of it before, probably because he'd been focusing on other things, once she'd brought it up, the questions kept whirling around his head, too.

The Wolf didn't have any reason to lie about releasing her. Did he? Neither of them could think of one.

The other question they couldn't answer was why Trish's disappearance hadn't been reported yet.

Maybe when his head wasn't so fuzzy he'd be able to think better. Right now, not eating was taking its toll; not just on his body, but on his mind. He wasn't functioning on his normal level, although Bella was as alert as usual and her brain seemed to be firing on all cylinders.

Both of them shut up the moment the door to their room opened and the Wolf walked in, accompanied by three soldiers. There were no clocks in the room, but since they'd eaten a few hours ago, Alex assumed it was time for bed. He growled, knowing it was useless, as the soldiers approached him.

The Wolf ignored him and went around to lay on the other side of the bed. He pulled Bella up against him as he watched his soldiers secure Alex to the bed frame. She didn't resist and neither did he, although Bella looked unhappy and frightened as the Wolf put her back against his front and played with her breasts while they watched Alex being cuffed down.

Just like the night before, his arms were pulled above his head and his legs stretched out, wrists and ankles attached to the bed frame. Bella whimpered, and he looked over to see the Wolf cupping her chin with one hand, holding her in place, as his mouth moved down her neck. The Wolf's other hand was between her legs, stroking her pussy, but his eyes were on Alex.

Once the soldiers had Alex fully secured, they stepped back and looked at the Wolf. He barely glanced at them as he lifted his head from Bella's neck. "Leave us."

Bella shivered as the soldiers left the room. The Wolf's fingers still stroked her pussy, which became wetter and wetter under his skilled touch. He'd sucked on the skin of her neck hard enough to leave a mark, later. Even though she hated the reaction her body had to him, Bella couldn't stop the pleasure building inside her.

He pushed her onto the bed and cupped her buttock as she crawled forward. "Go on Pet, I want to see you suck on Toy's cock."

'I'm sorry,' Alex mouthed at her. Bella couldn't see behind her, but she assumed that Wolf must be looking at her vulnerable backside if Alex was daring to even mouth the words. She gave him a small, encouraging smile.

She didn't mind having to do things to Alex. She just wished they weren't forced into the situation. Bella felt more attached to him every hour they were in this situation, even when they didn't agree on things. He was her fellow captive, her safe harbor.

She leaned forward and felt the Wolf's hands on her hips, keeping her ass high in the air. Bella dragged her tongue along Alex's cock, and it stiffened under her ministrations. She curled her tongue around the head and teased the fat crown, trying to distract herself from the dip of the bed as the Wolf came up behind her. His legs were on the outside of hers, keeping her legs trapped between his.

She stiffened, anxious as he twisted the plug in her asshole and tugged on it before shoving it back in, deep. Bella whimpered and pulled Alex's quickly hardening dick between her lips to let it expand inside her mouth, where it effectively gagged her. If she didn't, she might beg the Wolf to leave her ass alone, and Bella didn't know whether that would help or hurt her situation.

When the cock pushed against her pussy, she almost sighed with relief. The Wolf would take her anal virginity eventually—he seemed fascinated by the untouched state of her rear channel—but she kept wanting to put it off. The further Bella could put it off, the happier she would be.

The rough thrust forward pushed Alex's cock deeper into her throat, and he moaned. She could see his eyes close to shut out the sight of her and the Wolf, as his body arched upward. This position made it easier for her to breathe than when the two men had taken her before dinner; she had slightly more control over how deeply she took Alex in her mouth. But not entirely—his hips thrust upward, and she pulled off a bit, which shoved her back onto the Wolf's rod.

This kind of sex, with two men, was something she'd never fantasized about, but Bella couldn't help that it made her hot. There was something extremely erotic about being sandwiched between them, and with Alex in front and the Wolf behind her, it was easier to imagine herself in a more ... consenting situation. Especially since, this time, she wasn't tied up.

Bella whimpered as the Wolf's fingers dug in and he fucked her harder, her pussy squeezing down as the head of his cock slid over her g-spot. The whimpering made Alex groan and shudder again, and the vibrations pulsed over his cock as she sucked him deep into her throat. She almost liked being able to fit his entire length between her lips—something she had never been able to achieve before the gel. It hadn't felt like an accomplishment earlier, but now, with Alex, it kind of did.

She was getting into sucking on his cock, wanting to pleasure him, wanting to be able to choose—for once—whose cum she swallowed.

But then the Wolf grabbed onto her hair and pulled her up, and her mouth slid off with a wet, slurping sound. He pulled out of her pussy too, leaving her empty and clenching. Bella shivered at how close she'd been coming to orgasm.

"Let's switch places. I think I'd like to try that sweet mouth, Pet."

———

Alex narrowed his eyes into slits and watched as the Wolf arranged Bella to his satisfaction. She straddled Alex's waist, facing away from him, while his cock pointed upright at her pink, swollen pussy, and the Wolf stood in front of her on the bed. As she slid down on Alex's cock, all wet and hot and welcoming, he gritted his teeth around his moan.

The Wolf stared down at him, watching his expression as Bella took Alex within her heat. It was unnerving how much the man watched him and infuriating it didn't affect the stiffness of his cock, at all. Could he blame the cock ring for that, or was it just Bella's well-rounded ass and sexy back and the plump lips of her pussy that had his balls aching?

The muffled noise Bella made as she sank down meant the Wolf had shoved his cock into her mouth just as she'd lowered herself onto Alex. He did his best not to struggle. As much as he wanted to break through the restraints and beat the smug look off of the older man's face, he needed to conserve energy. His stomach was hollow and empty; it ached in a different and unpleasant way from the warm throbbing in his groin as Bella began to bounce up and down on top of him. The plug made her even tighter than before and it rubbed along the length of his shaft, but even that couldn't distract Alex from the man who stood above her.

It felt like the Wolf was using her mouth as a substitute, taunting Alex with what he would endure tomorrow. The Wolf stared down at him, his hand fisted in Bella's brunette curls, the movement a slow, deep thrusting as he filled her mouth. The sloppy, choking sounds made Alex's soul burn even as his hips arched upwards to spear her pussy.

He couldn't close his eyes and look away—it would be too much like acknowledging defeat. Submission. And yet it was incredibly disturbing to look back into the Wolf's expectant green eyes and see the man's anticipation, not to mention his pleasure as he thrust into Bella's mouth, all while Alex was pleasured by Bella's pussy.

Her hands held onto the Wolf's hips to help her keep balance as she bounced and ground down on top of Alex. He shuddered uncontrollably as her pussy spasmed around him. The tightening of his balls became unbearable, the firm hold of the cock ring taunting him as his need to come crested but went unsatisfied.

Alex jerked beneath Bella and couldn't stop the groans that began working their way up out of his chest. Bella's movements became more frantic, more needy as she neared her own climax, and knowing she was about to come on his cock was as exciting as it was frustrating.

Her muffled, gurgling scream of pleasure filled his

ears as her hips rotated, rubbing her clit against him. Her pussy pulsed, rhythmically, pulling at his cock. And Alex stared up into the green, triumphant eyes of the Wolf as he came.

The Wolf grabbed Bella by the back of her head and shoved deep. Her body trembled as she tried to push away, to no avail. Alex's arms jerked as the Wolf stared right at him, coming down her throat as Alex filled her from the bottom. His lower body was in heaven while his mind and his heart were in hell.

The Wolf sighed happily and relaxed his hold on Bella's head, and she came away gasping for breath. "Good Pet." He patted her head and stroked her hair.

To Alex's horror, she leaned forward, her head pressed against the Wolf's hip as she gasped and sucked in air, accepting the stroking. She might not have been aware of what she was doing.

Fuck.

Tomorrow he would suck the Wolf's cock. He would do whatever he needed to get up his strength. He would spend their outdoor sessions either working out or gathering information on how they could get out of there.

Because he had the sinking feeling that, right now, the Wolf was winning.

12

"Trish," Bella whispered. "Trish ..."

The petite blonde looked over at her with a worried expression. For once, she wasn't glued to Jordan's side, and Bella had decided to take the opportunity.

Alex was still doing laps in the pool, slowly but steadily, despite his stomach growling like mad that morning. Both she and Trish had been given breakfast, but Alex hadn't, and he hadn't been given the chance to earn some. The grim expression on his face told Bella what his answer to the Wolf would be at lunch. She couldn't imagine how Alex was still going, and she didn't know whether it was pride, stupidity, or bravery that drove him.

"What?" Trish whispered back after an anxious glance over at Jordan. He was talking with two of the guards, about fifty feet away from Bella and Trish.

"Are you allowed to talk to us?"

Another worried, little glance over at Jordan. "I don't know. He hasn't told me not to."

Reassured, Bella scooted over closer to the bench

where Trish sat. Since Bella was seated on the side of the pool, with her feet dangling in the water, it wouldn't look like they were conspiring. Which, they wouldn't be. Bella just wanted to ask Trish some questions.

"Bella ... I just wanted to say I'm really sorry." Trish's big blue eyes filled with tears. "About ... you know ..."

"No, don't apologize," Bella whispered furiously and made a cutting motion with her hand. "I'm sorry that I had to ... but it's not either of our faults, okay?"

Trish nodded but appeared unconvinced. Today, she was dressed in a pink top and a short, white skirt she'd been able to put on as soon as she'd finished in the pool. Bella envied her only briefly. She had become almost used to being naked on a constant basis, and she'd rather just be naked than naked and walking around with the butt plug. Which, fortunately, so far, had not been inserted today.

"Have you seen any of the news shows?" Bella whispered.

Trish shook her head, and her cheeks turned a bright pink as she glanced over at Jordan again. "He never turns on the television."

"The Wolf let us watch some yesterday. They were reporting on our disappearance, but they didn't mention you." Bella wished she could have phrased it in a way that didn't make Trish sound unimportant, but blunt honesty was the fastest way to communicate. Trish didn't seem distressed by the revelation. She just shrugged.

"I'm an orphan. I was on Earth on scholarship."

"I don't understand."

Trish sighed. Not in a mean or derisive way, but like she was disappointed that Bella needed it spelled out.

"When was the last time an orphan was taken by the Wolf?"

"Umm ..." Bella cast her mind back. Some people on the Moon who were obsessed with the Wolf knew every name of every person taken and as many facts about the victims' past and current lives as they could collect. "Sorry, I've never been a Wolf follower."

"Five years ago. He was kept for one month."

"Oh!" Bella dimly remembered that, mostly because it was such an odd amount of time. Most people were either kept for a few days or months on end. "He was taken with that other guy, Bryce-something." That had been huge news because Bryce had been kept for much longer. It was the only time something like that had happened. "I don't think I realized he was an orphan."

"Why would you? I only knew because he was from the same orphanage as me," Trish said, a sad kind of little smile on her face. "The news stations aren't as interested in people like me as they are in people like you and Alex."

"But that's wrong!"

"You have families. People they can interview. Important people. Connections. I don't have any of that." The young blonde said it matter-of-factly, not at all put out by her own description. She looked at Bella curiously, as if surprised she was disturbed by the implications. "I'm sure if you and Alex hadn't been taken at the same time, I would have been bigger news."

Bella pushed down her gut reactions. Feeling defensive was stupid. If the news shows weren't talking about Trish, that wasn't her fault, and it didn't seem like Trish was blaming Bella, anyway. She needed to focus, not get upset about the disparity of the situation.

"Have you been around the compound? Seen anything that might help us escape?"

Trish shook her head. "I haven't even been able to figure out which doors lead to the outside. Any time Jordan's going out, he locks me into the room."

"Do you have any computer access or anything?" That would have been incredibly helpful.

Trish was already shaking her head again. "Not really. He leaves me there, and I can access games or books or things to entertain me, but it's not connected to anything. I can't access anything that's not saved to the computer, itself."

There were a million more questions Bella wanted to ask, but out of the corner of her eye, she saw movement. When she looked over, Jordan was turning around. Bella snapped her head back toward the pool. Alex was on the far side, holding onto the edge and watching them. He looked exhausted and curious; how long had he been over there staring but not wanting to interrupt?

As Jordan's footsteps came closer, Bella could only hope that she hadn't gotten Trish into trouble with the big man.

"Time to go back in," he said. Bella peeked up at him while he took Trish's hand and pulled her up from the bench. His expression was stoically blank, so Bella had no idea if he was upset with them or not.

———

Food. All Alex could think about was food. Bella had tried to talk to him about her conversation with Trish, but he couldn't focus on it. His body ached. Working out with the anticipation of food, rather than the reality, had been stupid. But what else was he supposed to do? Sit around and think about his upcoming surrender?

He tried to tell himself it wasn't really a surrender, but that was still what he felt like.

The gnawing emptiness in his stomach and the hazy way his brain was working made eating a priority. He wouldn't be able to go another day. Hell, he didn't know if he'd make it to dinner at this rate. Even after his slow, lazy laps in the pool, his muscles felt so weak that, for one awful moment, he'd thought the soldiers might actually need to help support him.

The only thing saving Alex was that no one denied him water. But that had stopped helping the emptiness yesterday.

As he and Bella came into the main room, Alex looked up at the dais, and his gaze crossed the Wolf's almost immediately. Alex could practically feel the hate burning out of himself. The collar around his neck felt like it was choking him, and, for one savage moment, he wished it actually would. But then Bella would be unprotected and alone with the Wolf and these twisted bastards.

To his surprise, the Wolf kept his face blank as Alex and Bella approached. The came around to the front of the dais and stood at the edge. There were only a few people sitting at the mostly empty tables in the room, but Alex didn't focus on them. He kept reminding himself why he was doing this. And the girl to his left—beautiful Bella with her soft, pink lips and nipples, her nervous trembling and bouncing, brown curls—filled his vision.

Yeah. That's why.

"Sit over here, Pet." The Wolf's lips curled up in an anticipatory smile. He pointed to his left, right at the edge of the dais, and Bella obediently trotted forward.

An incredible smell wafted up from the back of the room, and Alex's mouth watered as his knees nearly buckled. God, he was so hungry. His stomach growled loudly enough that he was pretty sure everyone within ten feet of him had heard it.

"Do you want to eat today, Toy?" the Wolf asked, softly. Almost coaxingly. The way a man might do with an animal he wanted to tame.

Alex had never felt more like growling. He nodded his head: one short nod, barely perceptible. That was all the Wolf needed. That one small gesture. He didn't force another answer from Alex. Instead, he just pointed to the spot right in front of him.

"Come here and kneel, Toy."

There were men who stayed on either side of Alex as he approached the Wolf, and he felt a small spurt of pride that they still considered him worth guarding. Unfortunately, he was too weak right now to be of any threat. He practically fell to his knees in front of the Wolf and cursed himself for his lack of control over his muscles. His knees hit the ground with a thud that seemed to echo throughout the room.

Behind him, a few people called out, but the words in their sentences blurred together. He didn't look up. He looked straight ahead at the bulging front of dark-green pants.

"Undo my pants, Toy."

The Wolf's voice was a low purr in Alex's ears. He gritted his teeth and reached up to undo the heavy buckle on the brown belt and pull it open, and then he undid the snaps holding the Wolf's pants closed. Alex wished it was a zipper so he could try to catch the Wolf's obvious erection in the metal.

The heavy, thick cock sprang out, nearly hitting him in the face. The Wolf hadn't worn any kind of underwear. He was already completely hard, and the masculine musk of his body filled Alex's nose.

Alex jerked as a large hand caressed the top of his head and wound around to grip his hair and pull his head back. He was forced to look up at the Wolf's glowing green eyes, to see the hungry anticipation in them. With his other hand, the Wolf gripped his dick and rubbed it over Alex's lips, smearing pre-cum across them.

"Lick me," he said throatily.

As if in response, as if warning Alex not to follow his instincts, his stomach rumbled again. He wanted to do nothing more than dart forward and bite the bastard.

He saw a hint of movement and glanced over at Bella. She was watching. Worried.

I'm doing this for her.

And he stuck out his tongue and licked. The Wolf hummed his approval. Alex closed his eyes and tried to pretend he was somewhere else. With someone else. Back when he'd been experimenting with friends, young men he actually cared about. Not some twisted, older asshole.

He went by feel so he didn't have to look, and slid his tongue up to the tip and away again. Back down the shaft. The skin was soft; the cock hard as rock underneath.

"Open up."

Alex opened his mouth, his muscles tensing even as he tried to force them to relax. The Wolf's grip on his hair tightened to tip his head back slightly. Then something hard whacked him on the cheek. It didn't hurt, but Alex had just been cock-slapped.

He growled, and his eyes flew open to glare up at the Wolf.

"Good. That's what I wanted to see." The Wolf's lips curved up. He held his dick in his free hand and tapped it against Alex's cheek again. Alex tried to jerk away, but he was held in place by the Wolf's hand on his hair, which tugged painfully. "Bite me and you'll regret it."

He shoved his cock into Alex's mouth.

For a moment, Alex seriously considered biting down on the thick shaft of meat that pressed in, heavy and salty on his tongue. But looking up into the Wolf's eyes, he saw a cold flatness. It wasn't a threat; it was a void, an emptiness. Maybe people were allowed to go free, unharmed, because no one ever went against the Wolf's orders. Maybe no one before had ever fought against him.

But Alex didn't want to get killed. He didn't want to be the first discrepancy in the Wolf's record. And he sure as hell didn't want to put Bella in real danger.

The Wolf stared down at him, waiting, as if he knew Alex weighed the consequences. It took every ounce of willpower he possessed to relax his jaw, and Alex closed his eyes again. Submitted.

Animals attacked when threatened, out of fear or instinct. The difference between animals and humans was that humans could stifle their instincts, they could think and reason. They could wait.

Besides. Perhaps Alex had been going about this the wrong way. The constant guards, the Wolf's vigilance ... It all stoked Alex's pride to know he was considered a threat. But how would they ever get a chance to explore the compound, to find routes to escape, when they were constantly watched? He could bend. Let the Wolf and his men think he was beaten, that he'd be compliant. The entire time, he'd be watching and waiting for the right moment.

He wouldn't risk Bella, or even risk being separated from her if he could help it.

So, he sucked. Hard. And heard the Wolf's groan, felt the man's fingers tightening in his hair. This time, the older man allowed him to keep his eyes closed as his cock began to move in and out of Alex's mouth. It was a rhythmic, almost hypnotic rhythm, and he found it easier and easier to let his mind drift. He focused on breathing whenever he could get air and on sucking and licking the underside of the cock that was fucking his face.

His throat easily accepted the thick length without gagging or choking, and Alex let the Wolf take over and move his head back and forth. Letting go completely was a relief he would have to be wary of. It was easier to bend, to submit, but it was also dangerous. And Alex wasn't going to let his guard down while he was waiting for the Wolf's to fall.

———

The Wolf shoved his slick cock in and out of Alex's mouth, and Bella was shocked at how riveting she found the sight. She knew that eventually he would have to give into the Wolf, but she hadn't been able to picture it. Now she was watching it.

The look the Wolf had given Alex when he'd first pushed between Alex's lips had made all the hairs stand up on the back of her neck as she shivered uncontrollably. As cruel or toying as the Wolf been with them, she'd never seen that look before. Then again, the Wolf hadn't considered her a problem the way he did Alex.

His domination over Alex meant more, and he was enjoying it, fucking Alex's mouth with long, hard strokes, his hands holding the back of Alex's head. There was something intoxicating about seeing a strong, alpha male like Alex forced to his knees before another alpha male. The guards still stood close; no one truly believed Alex had been beaten.

The entire room was silent, watching the scene. No one cheered or called suggestions the way they had with her. They just savored the sight.

The Wolf groaned and thrust harder, faster. The wet slurping sounds increased, and Alex growled low in his throat. Bella's breathing increased as she watched, completely wrapped up in the strangely erotic, horribly fascinating scene in front of her. She shuddered as the Wolf threw back his head and the long line of his body surged forward as he buried himself in Alex's mouth.

Alex's throat worked as he swallowed, and the Wolf's fingers and buttocks flexed as he poured his cum down Alex's throat.

When the Wolf pulled away, Alex's eyes opened again, and he glared up at the Wolf before looking down at the ground. It was oddly submissive and seemed wrong.

"Good Toy." The Wolf patted Alex on the head absentmindedly, as though now that Alex had given in, the Wolf had lost interest. He looked over at one of the guards who still hovered behind Alex—the soldier was grinning from ear to ear—and waved his hand. "Take Toy back to the room and feed him."

Alex's head swung upwards again to look over at her. "Bella ..."

"Ah yes ... Pet will stay with me for the afternoon."

"Bella!" Alex lunged, but the guards caught him.

"Alex, just go!" Bella said loudly enough for him to hear her. The Wolf had returned to ignoring them as he walked back around the table. He didn't look up at Bella's insistence that Alex leave or watch Alex struggle against the guards. Bella glared at Alex; his stubborn reluctance was written clearly across his face. "Go."

Her voice dropped to a whisper, but she couldn't stand to see him tormented further because he thought she would be unsafe unless he was there. What could he do to protect her anyway? She felt better when he was there, but practically, he couldn't help her at all.

The guards dragged Alex away, and Bella's heart sank as she watched him go. When the Wolf spoke again, she shivered and goosebumps covered her body.

"Come here, Pet."

———

The guards joked and laughed as they dragged Alex back to the room.

"Thanks." One of them patted his back as they pushed him into the room. "We won a hundred bucks each after you held out till today!"

"Longest any of these whining Moon Boys has ever gone," the other said, laughing.

That was when Alex recognized them as the same guards who had pricked his pride the evening before by taunting him. Even with his brain fogged by shame and hunger, he realized they had done it on purpose. They'd been part of a bet about when he would eat. What kind of people did that?

And he wasn't the first, either. Others had been

subjected to the same treatment. He supposed he should feel glad he'd lasted longer than any of them.

"You'd probably be whining too if you had to go without food for that long," Alex snapped at them.

They just laughed.

"If you were from Earth, you'd know that most of us have gone that long without eating, and not by choice, like you. Now stop whining and be thankful you get to eat at all," the first one said, smirking at him. He pointed at the table. "They'll bring more solid food in a couple of hours."

A clear broth and some bread waited for him, along with something that looked like fruit juice. The door closed while he looked at the food. His reflexes were all messed up.

He needed to eat. Prepare. Get himself back together because, right now, he needed to be as strong as possible. Not a whiny Moon Boy.

And hope that nothing awful was happening to Bella while he wasn't there.

13

Bella approached the Wolf, who was sitting at his table. He didn't look at her; he just snapped his fingers and pointed at a spot on the floor next to his chair. There was already a cushion sitting there, waiting for her. Bella kept her head down, not wanting to look at anyone, and knelt on top of it.

As if she were an actual Pet, the Wolf reached out and began to stroke her hair while he talked with the man who sat to his left. Bella tried not to let herself feel as though the motions were in any way soothing. Though he treated her almost gently at times, he could be incredibly brutal, as well. Not just in his own actions, but because he could pass her off to anyone at any time.

The thought made her shiver. More than one man and woman who came up to speak with the Wolf gave Bella a lascivious look as he pet her and fed her from his plate. She stayed quiet and tried to fade into the background, where most people seemed to relegate her.

Being silent had its own rewards. She heard several of the men talking about the money they'd either won or lost betting on when Alex would give in and suck the Wolf's cock. Several of them seemed impressed Alex had held out as long as he had; others were more derogatory, though even they were surprised at his continued resistance. The latter were the ones who sneered at her, as if her own meek behavior was nothing less than they expected. The Wolf spoke with Jordan and some of his other soldiers about a warehouse they were watching.

And, most importantly, she learned the main entrance to the compound was on the northeast side. Surely, that knowledge could help her and Alex.

Just after that, the Wolf pulled her by her hair over his lap so her bottom was turned up as if asking for a spanking, and her head, arms, and legs hung down toward the floor. Bella shivered as he stroked her bottom. How much of her body was on display, even from behind his desk? Surely, everyone who came up to speak with him could see what he was doing, but none of them said a word.

"Oh!" she cried out as a slick finger prodded her asshole. She was pretty sure it was the Wolf's. It dipped into her virgin ass, stretching the little hole and making her tense all over.

Never knowing what the Wolf would do was the worst part, and Bella dreaded when he would finally take her anal virginity. But sometimes—like right now—she almost wished he would do it and get it over with and stop tormenting her. The first finger was joined by a second that stretched the small orifice and made her whimper again.

His voice droned on as he talked to someone who stood on the other side of the desk, but Bella had trouble concentrating on his words when she was so worried about what he might do to her body next. Alex wasn't here to lend his support, and she was surprised at how frightening it was to be without him. He couldn't do anything to help her, but just having him there had bolstered her. Now they'd been separated for the first time since she'd been sent to the doctor and he'd been taken to Nurse Roche.

Not that the Wolf seemed interested in letting someone else have her for the moment. His erection began to grow, and the front of his pants bulged against her side as his fingers pumped in and out of her ass. It almost felt good now that the burning discomfort of the initial stretch had passed. When he removed his fingers and pushed a plug into her, Bella couldn't stop herself from squirming and moaning.

The plug wasn't huge, but her sphincter protested as it was forced open for the widest part. Bella panted a bit, her pussy spasming, and she moaned a little as she realized she was getting wet. She moaned loudly as the plug began to vibrate.

The Wolf moved her, bending her over his desk so she faced the rest of the room with her bottom and pussy right next to him. She closed her eyes against the grins on the faces of his soldiers and turned her head away from both them and the Wolf. Unfortunately, with her eyes closed, the pleasurable sensations from the vibrating plug seemed to increase.

Bella clenched her jaw and shuddered as the Wolf stroked her pussy, teased the sensitive folds, and tapped on the base of the plug. His hand moved away and left her standing there, bent over and aching. The plug hummed away inside her and kept her aroused, even when he wasn't touching her.

Over and over, he repeated the sequence, stroking her

pussy until Bella thought she might scream from the need to come, and then removing his hand and continuing to work while she remained in place. Any time she began to move or squirm too much, his hand would come down hard on her ass to leave her gasping and clenching as the pain and pleasure mingled inside her.

It felt like she lay there for hours trying to listen to his conversations but she mostly had to concentrate on keeping her body from going absolutely wild. The desk was hard under her nipples, hard against the front of her groin, and she was ashamed and excited the entire time. The Wolf kept her excited with his infrequent attention to her pussy and the relentless vibrations of the plug in her ass—which made her ashamed every time she started to come down from the arousal. But then he would touch her again, and her body would ramp right back up.

It was a torturous cycle, and Bella had begun to consider pleading with the Wolf to let her come when she saw Dr. Margolius headed up toward the dais, a gleeful smile on his face. She jerked back, which earned her two swift and painful slaps on her bottom. The doctor looked even more pleased. He could probably see the fear on her face; something he obviously enjoyed.

Bella tried to blank her expression but she couldn't stop herself from shivering as he neared.

"Do you have it?"

"Yes, Sir," Dr. Margolius said, his voice respectful. Bella watched him with all the wariness of prey in the presence of a predator.

"Good. Come administer the dose."

The Doctor gave her another gleeful look as he came around the desk. Bella whimpered and she might have bolted, but the Wolf's fingers plunged into her pussy to keep her trapped in place. His fingers were rough as they probed her insides, distracting her.

She couldn't turn to see behind her, but she felt the Doctor's hand on her lower back and then a sharp pinch on her butt-cheek made her squeal. He pulled away, syringe in hand and a satisfied smile on his face.

"All done. It should only take a few minutes to take effect."

"Good. Marcus, Bruno—take Pet back to the room." The Wolf thrust his fingers in her pussy one last time, making her squirm and gasp, and then pulled them out completely. "Dr. Margolius, thank you. You may return to your office."

With a wistful look at Bella, the doctor retreated. She wasn't sorry to see the back of him, but she couldn't enjoy it because she was too upset. What the hell had they just put in her?

———

Alex paced back and forth around the room and counted his steps. Twenty-six along the side with the door and the side opposite, thirty-five along the perpendicular walls. Well, if he didn't count having to walk around the bed. He wasn't sure how many times he'd re-traced the path at this point.

After eating all his broth, which had made his shrunken stomach stand up and take notice, they'd eventually brought him a small meal of rice, flavored with a light, creamy sauce, carrots, and bland chicken. It had tasted like heaven. Anything heavier or more strongly flavored and he probably would have thrown it all up.

Once he'd eaten, he'd napped. And then he'd awoken

with a surfeit of energy and anxiety. Bella still hadn't returned, and his imagination worked overtime as if, now that his mind had turned back on, it was overloaded. He inspected every inch of the walls, including the wall where they knew the screen was, but couldn't find anything to help. He couldn't even figure out how to get to the screen, which was frustrating in the extreme.

When the door finally opened, he spun around, both relieved and anxious.

Bella stumbled in, partially held up on either side by the two soldiers escorting her and let out a little moan.

"What did you do to her?" Alex snapped out, jumping forward. He tensed, torn between trying to grab one of the soldiers by their neck or helping Bella. They let her go, and he reached out and caught her. She clung to him, her smooth skin pressing against his, and he ignored his body's instinctive reaction to the warm, feminine press of her curves.

One of the soldiers snickered. "She's just fine. You'll see."

The men smirked at him and left the room. Bella was trembling. Alex pulled her toward the bed, and his worry mounted as she moaned and whimpered with every step. He thought he heard her murmur his name.

"Bella? Bella, are you okay?" He was almost frantic as he sat her down on the bed. Her head tilted back, and she looked up at him. Her face was flushed, her eyes wild-looking and her pupils dilated. Her lips parted as she looked back up at him. "Bella, talk to me."

She reached up, grabbed him by the neck, and dragged his lips down to hers.

The movement caught him so off guard that she easily pulled him down on top of her. Alex bent over

Bella, her legs spread to accommodate him, and his cock nestled against the soft flesh of her pussy as she sucked his tongue into her mouth. For a moment, he lost himself in that erotic kiss and the feel of her body beneath him as she arched, but then he planted his hands on the bed and pushed himself up as much as he could. With Bella's hands locked around the back of his neck, it wasn't far.

"Bella—what—"

"Fuck me, Alex, pleeeeeeease." Bella moaned as she writhed beneath him and rubbed her wet folds against the length of his cock, which was completely hard now. "Oh god ... I'm sorry. They gave me something. I'm on fire, please, Alex, please, please fuck me."

Alex cursed. He could tell Bella was out of control, unable to stop herself as she writhed underneath him. His body had already responded—his cock was so hard it ached, and the underside of it was covered in her juices. Whatever they had given her was making her pussy cream like mad.

"It hurts, Alex please, I need you inside me ... please ... oh god, just fuck me pleeease, it hurts, it huuuuuuuuuuurts."

She surged up underneath him, her pussy rubbing along the length of his cock, and that was enough to spur her orgasm. Bella cried out as she rocked against his body. Her erotic, sensual movements created all sorts of havoc for Alex as she came against him, moaning with pleasure. His muscles strained as he forced himself to hold still, to not draw his hips back and plunge into her wet haven.

Whatever they'd given her had made her act like this. If Alex fucked her, it would be rape as surely as it had been when she'd been forced to 'choose' him on their first day here. She wasn't in her right mind.

"Ohh … fuck …" Bella breathed out, shuddering beneath him. Her body went limp, and Alex looked down at her, searching her face.

"Bella? Are you okay?"

She blinked, the wild look in her eyes clearing a little. "Oh my god, Alex, I'm so sorry."

"What did they give you?"

"I don't know." She whimpered a little and looked frightened. "The doctor had something in a needle, and, once he'd given it to me, the Wolf sent me back here. I started feeling all hot and tingly, and then it was like this awful itch that I couldn't stop, and by the time we got back here it hurt. It was starting to hurt so bad, and then I came and …" Her breathing had picked up as she'd talked until she was almost panting, and now her eyes widened and she looked up at him, horrified. "Oh no … I think it's starting again. I can feel it."

"Shit."

She began to tremble and shiver beneath him as her pupils began to dilate again.

"Bella, you have to fight it. You have to *fight* it."

"Oh my god, shut UP." Her nails dug into his arms as she arched beneath him, rubbing her pussy over his already wet cock. "You have no idea what this is like … no idea …" Panting, Bella writhed and shuddered. "Alex please … you have to fuck me. It hurts. It actually *hurts*. I need you inside me."

"You don't know that will help." Alex shook his head, barely managing to keep control over himself. His balls were tight and hot, the ring around his cock made his pulse pound through his body, and his entire lower body screamed to just do what she said.

"I do, I do," she insisted, rubbing her breasts against his chest as she tried to lift her upper body and her lips aimed for his. "Alex, please ... why are you torturing me?" Her voice was plaintive as her hips rotated and rubbed her pussy lips against him, Alex was torn.

She shuddered again, rocking her lower body against him, begging him to fuck her as though it were a mantra she couldn't stop saying. Alex shook his head, but the pain began to grow on her face, and the anguish in her voice rose. His resolve weakened. Alex pressed her wrists firmly into the bed on either side of her face and shook his head again.

Bella wrapped her legs around his hips and managed to lift her body in such a way that his cock twisted painfully. He jerked back, giving her just enough room to line the head of his cock up with her pussy. They both gasped as he entered her, the wet heat of her pussy engulfing him. Alex groaned, and his body surged forward to fill her before he could stop to think or resist.

"Yes, yes, yes," Bella chanted, rolling her hips as her pussy clamped down on him and squeezed.

Alex groaned. Her pussy felt like a hot vise massaging the length of his cock, trying to suck him further into her body. She was so wet her juices smeared across his entire groin. The plug in her ass made her incredibly tight, and the wide bulge of it rubbed against his cock. When he tried to pull out, her legs tightened around him and drew him back in with a reluctant thrust.

"Dammit, Bella," he grated, trying to pull himself out again.

"Alex, please .... fuck ... I need this. Just fuck me." Tears leaked out of her eyes, but there was relief in her voice. Relief, just from having his cock in her.

With another groan, Alex gave up the fight and gave into what his body demanded.

———

Bella cried out as Alex began to thrust hard and fast into her hot pussy. It was as if she was burning up from her cunt, outwards. The stretch of her tunnel around his cock felt wonderful and eased some of the needy pain that had built up inside her. She was still burning up but in a different way that didn't cause her pain. His mouth came down hard on hers, demanding, and she kissed him back with every ounce of her need.

It was rough, wild. He let go of her wrists to grab onto her legs and spread them wider so he could pound into her, hard. Bella moaned uncontrollably into his mouth and reached up to wrap her arms around his neck to leverage her hips up to meet his rough thrusts.

She felt like she was splintering apart. Her nipples were swollen, throbbing, and felt like tiny explosives on her chest that went off every time his chest rubbed against hers. The plug in her ass made her feel ridiculously full, and the inner walls of her pussy were more sensitive than ever.

Bella keened and shuddered beneath him as her orgasm exploded, so much better now that he was inside her and she wasn't just rubbing against him. Alex groaned, and his hips continued to piston as he fucked her through the waves of pleasure. She clawed at his shoulders and felt utterly, wonderfully fulfilled as he moved inside her.

It did more than scratch an itch: it was satisfied an aching need. The need had been artificially created, but that thought seemed distant and unimportant. All that was important right now was Alex's hard body, his demanding kiss, and the way his cock massaged the walls of her pussy as he fucked her hard into the bed.

Bella screamed as pleasure ripped through her again. She arched and thrashed, and her thighs tightened around Alex's body, trying to get him even deeper into her. It felt amazing. He felt amazing. She immersed herself in the pleasure and the heat and the need.

———

Bella's body throbbed around him again, and, this time, Alex went off like a rocket. The cock ring had made it harder for him to come, or he probably would have gone off the second he'd pushed into Bella's pussy. When he did finally come, it was incredibly intense. He could feel the jets of liquid streaming out of him, taking his energy, all his pent-up anxiety and tension, along with it.

He groaned and lay himself out over her body, his knees too weak to hold him in the standing position anymore. She shuddered and clenched beneath him, milking his cock, her fingers massaging little circles on the back of his shoulders.

"Fuck," he said hoarsely. Her crazed passion had been exciting ... but ...

Her hips rolled again, and she shivered; fine tremors went through her body.

"Again," she whispered, her voice husky.

"I can't."

Alex rolled away and crawled fully onto the bed. His

cock was wet with their combined juices, and he needed a few minutes to catch his breath. Bella followed him, her eyes practically glowing as she knelt beside his hips and lowered her mouth to lick at his groin. Her hand was already between her legs, stroking her juicy pussy.

"Fuck!"

The rasp of her tongue against his sensitive cock was painfully pleasurable. Bella moaned as she rubbed herself, her hand working between her legs, searching for more pleasure. Alex grabbed a chunk of her hair and pulled her off his dick. She looked at him with glazed, needy eyes, her lips shiny with their juices.

"Bella, you have to stop." He phrased it as an order, but he could hear the pleading in his voice.

"I'm sorry. I'm sorry." She gasped, but her hand was still moving. "I can't, Alex … it huuuurts."

The anguish in her voice broke his heart because he wouldn't be able to resist. Not now that he'd heard the relief sex had given her; not knowing he could erase the pained note. Alex groaned and released her hair, and Bella bent over him and cleaned his groin of cum and cream while she played with herself.

She sucked his cleaned cock eagerly into her mouth, her tongue laving over its surface as she became more visibly excited. Alex groaned and held his hands gently on her head, stroking her hair and trying not to enjoy himself too much—a nearly impossible task.

There was no one here watching them. No one judging them. It was just him and Bella.

Him, Bella, a cock ring, an electric collar, and drugs running through her system. It was almost too easy to forget. As she shifted, he could see the butt plug in her virgin asshole, another reminder that he was a jerk if he forgot what was really going on here.

But her mouth was eager and hot and sweet, and she sucked him deeply, as if she couldn't get enough of his cock between her lips. Every bob of her head sent him pressing into her throat, and her muscles squeezed the tip of his dick as her tongue danced along the underside. It was the best fucking blowjob of his life, and it made him feel like shit.

Her soft hair curled around his fingers as his hips thrust upward, going deeper, and she sucked hard again. Then she pulled away and began to climb on top of him. Her pussy lips were dark pink, her swollen clit peeking out from between the folds, and she was wet and hot as she sank down onto his cock.

Alex gripped her hips and gritted his teeth, determined to give her what she needed while he still tried his best not to enjoy it. Bella sat straight up, taking him deeply and completely into her body, so wet with their combined juices and the saliva on his cock it only took one thrust to bury him inside her. They both moaned as her muscles gripped him, and the look of relief on her face did a lot to mediate the feelings of guilt that crept inside him.

Bella cupped her breasts and squeezed them hard, rolling her nipples between her fingers as she began to bounce on his cock. She looked like a sex goddess using him for her pleasure—which was exactly what was happening, except it wasn't her choice. But he chose to give freely because he couldn't bear the alternative.

Since he'd already come once, with the help of the cock ring he managed to keep from coming again as she rode him through orgasm after orgasm after orgasm ....

———

The sound of the door opening and men laughing woke Bella. She'd been curled up on the bed next to Alex; her entire body felt like it had been pushed through a wringer. Just moving her legs made her whimper; her pussy was swollen and sticky and beyond sore.

Alex stirred next to her, one heavy arm reaching around her body and pulling her closer to him as he looked up to see who was coming into the room. Bella stifled a moan as her muscles protested even that small movement.

She remembered everything that had happened, but it was like remembering a movie. Like her memories had happened to someone else, with only the physical state of her body proving it had been her. She'd ridden Alex to orgasm after orgasm until he'd finally flipped her onto her back and fucked her with long slow strokes that had her constantly coming … and then she couldn't remember. Maybe she'd just passed out, finally.

"Come on lovebirds, wake up," one of the soldiers said.

They were taken to a bathing room where one of the soldiers bent Bella over and removed the plug before fingering her sore pussy, his fingers coated with the healing cream that had helped her so much before. She couldn't help but moan with relief as her abused lips and insides were coated, soothing the flaming ache. Alex got the same treatment on his cock, which also looked like it had been abused. By her.

Afterward, they were given a shower and allowed to do their business before being taken to the main room. Bella still had to take small, mincing steps, despite the effects of the cream, and did her best to keep her thighs from brushing the lips of her pussy. Alex kept his arm wrapped around her waist, allowing her to lean on him, which she was eternally grateful for even though she couldn't look him in the face. Remembering the way she'd acted—despite being drugged—made her feel incredibly ashamed, as though she should have had more control.

The main room was filled with people, most of them already eating their dinner. Bella's stomach growled, and she felt her heart sink at the idea of having to earn her food now. She was starving and sore and not feeling entirely sane. Punching someone right now would feel really, really good, even if it did get her a punishment.

As soon as she had the thought, Bella was torn because she really couldn't take any kind of punishment in her current condition.

The Wolf looked up from his meal to see them approaching and he smiled, warmly, like a host greeting his guests. It was strangely unnerving.

"Ah ... good. You're here. Now we can begin the show."

Dread was like a lead ball in her stomach and the back of her throat, but, to her surprise, the soldiers sat her and Alex at the front of the dais and handed them each a plate of food. Uneasiness skittered across her senses. More of the Wolf's unpredictable behavior. She'd already learned today she couldn't anticipate what he might do.

A huge screen on the other side of the room lit up, and Bella gasped as she recognized the bedroom with Alex in it, just as she entered on the arms of the soldiers. She moaned low in her throat, the food in her mouth suddenly dry and tasteless.

They'd been recorded. Every movement. Every begging word.

Heads turned between her and Alex on the dais, and her and Alex on the screen, wanting to see their reactions. Bella didn't have one. Everything felt numb as she watched Alex fuck her while she writhed beneath him. They'd been watched … and something inside her hurt as she saw what they'd done.

Something that could have been beautiful, that should have been private, was splayed across the screens for all these voyeurs. She was attracted to Alex, she was coming to depend on him. There was a connection between them and it had been made into something ugly. Something to be watched. Something ruined.

It wasn't enough for the Wolf to just fuck them—he had to fuck with their heads, too. So, Bella did the only thing she could do.

She shut everything out.

———

Alex ignored the sights and sounds of the tape, even as anger boiled in his chest, to wrap his arm around Bella and turn her so she wasn't facing the screen.

"Come on, Bella, you have to eat," he said gently. She hadn't taken a bite since the movie had started playing.

And he was calling himself six kinds of dumbass for not realizing—of course—the bedroom was bugged for both visual and audio. It wasn't the kind of thing he'd ever had to think about in his life, though he'd seen things like it in movies. They were so isolated, so protected up on the Moon it hadn't occurred to him to think they might be watched. The Wolf probably knew everything he and Bella had ever said to each other when they thought they were alone and safe. This was his way of telling them that.

As Alex fed her, he looked around the room for any hint of sympathy. Empathy. Anything he might be able to use to find an ally. He saw nothing but amusement and enjoyment at their expense.

The one bit of relief they got for the evening was that after they ate, they were dismissed. Their afternoon was still playing on the screen, with Bella on top, riding him And looking just as gorgeous as he remembered. His cock twitched a little, despite being overworked already.

The Wolf didn't come to them that night, but it wasn't a relief to Alex. What was the man was planning while he gave them time to recover?

14

Everything was back to normal in the morning, including Alex's cock. Whatever was in the cream the soldier had rubbed onto him had worked miracles. He noticed Bella was moving easier too, as if she were barely sore anymore.

They were given their breakfast and then taken to exercise. Now that he was eating again, he was much more energized. Bella told him everything she'd talked with Trish about the day before. Now he just had to figure out which was the northeast side of the compound and where the entrance there was located. And if there were other ways to get in and out of the compound—there had to be.

Now that his brain felt like it was working again, he'd woken up with a flurry of new thoughts. Most of them were based on movies he'd seen, unfortunately, but he had to stop thinking like he usually did. He had to stop making assumptions about the place they were living. Now, though they were outside, he didn't trust that there weren't listening devices planted all around. He'd been assuming the Wolf relied on the electric collar around Alex's neck and the trackers that had been planted in his and Bella's arms to catch them if they escaped. It hadn't occurred to him they'd be monitored beyond that.

Now he tried to be smarter about their situation, but he didn't have much to go off, except fiction. The petty wars and conflicts of the Earth didn't touch the Moon; they were almost completely separate entities. Even when the Moon families did intervene in Earth affairs in a military way, it was always with the use of mercenaries, not their own children.

For the first time, Alex wondered if perhaps that was a mistake ... because how could he, or any of the victims taken by the Wolf, ever be prepared?

Bella's swim didn't last as long as his; she still seemed tired. Alex pushed himself to the limit, now that he was getting steady food again. Would the Wolf make them start earning their meals again or, now that Alex had done what the Wolf wanted, would the man move on from that particular torment?

Alex's muscles burned by the end of his workout, but his energy was up. He felt good. Maybe even a little bit hopeful.

———

Bella watched Alex's powerful body plow through the water and couldn't help but wonder what her life might have been like if she and Alex had met before they'd met Ken and Lisa. She was incredibly attached to Alex, though their connection might only exist because of their situation. But she felt safe when she was snuggled in his arms.

It had hurt yesterday, to see their ... their interlude in

the room broadcasted and used. To know it hadn't been either of their choices, even though they'd been alone. It had made her realize her feelings for him might be a bit more than just those of friends caught in a situation. Maybe it was because she'd become used to relying on Alex, but she also felt an incredible amount of resentment toward the Wolf for taking away something she hadn't realized she wanted—sex with Alex. But not just sex.

Bella pushed down those emotions and sighed. It was pointless wondering what would have happened between her and Alex if they hadn't been captured after they'd caught Ken and Lisa cheating on them. If she was honest with herself, it was doubtful they would have seen each other again. Seeing each other would have reminded them of their significant others' infidelity.

Feeling like something had been stolen from them made no sense.

Shifting on her bottom made her wince. The soldiers had plugged her before letting her into the pool; they'd made her bend over and spread her cheeks. She'd been fortunate Alex had already been in the pool swimming laps, so he hadn't seen her shameful position as she'd held her butt cheeks open for the soldiers while they'd talked about her pretty, virgin asshole and pushed the plug in and out of it. While she had gotten more used to having something in her ass, and it didn't really hurt anymore, she still didn't like it.

And having it inside her made Bella increasingly nervous. She'd been so sure yesterday the Wolf would take her anal virginity when Alex had been taken away. Now she worried he'd just been waiting for when Alex could be an alert and energetic audience.

After Alex got out of the pool, he came and sat next to

Bella to dry off in the sun. She tried not to look at his body or think about how attractive he was with the droplets of water rolling down his skin. It always seemed wrong to check him out, considering their situation.

Even more wrong when she sometimes thought he was looking at her and she'd feel a thread of pleasure at his attention.

"Hey," she mumbled, peeking at him from underneath her eyelashes. She still wasn't sure how he felt about her behavior the afternoon before, drugged or not. He acted like everything was normal between them—well, as normal as it could be—but maybe it was just that: acting.

"Hey." His eyes were fixed on some of the soldiers who had gathered together and were talking in a circle, not paying any attention to her and Alex. Jordan wasn't anywhere near them; he was walking around the pathways with Trish, and it looked like they were talking. "What do you think they're talking about?"

Bella looked again to make sure he was referring to the soldiers. "Us maybe?"

"Maybe, but they haven't looked over here once." Alex said softly, as if he were talking to himself more than her. "They're distracted."

Was he really thinking about trying to escape right now? Had he somehow already figured out where the main entrance to the compound was? She hoped not—it seemed like the perfect way to get caught. Plus, they still had the trackers in them, and he still had the collar on.

He glanced over at her and must have seen something of her thoughts on her face. "Don't worry, I'm not going to try anything right now. I'm just wondering why they're talking rather than paying attention to us, for once."

"Maybe they're just finally used to seeing us naked." She hadn't meant it as a joke, but a grin flashed across Alex's face, and she found herself smiling back. It felt odd to smile. But something in her chest loosened, as if her heart were just a little bit lighter.

"Maybe," he said as his smile faded. The brief moment was gone as quickly as it had come.

———

When they were led back into the Wolf's lair, as Alex darkly thought of it, he didn't know what to expect. It was lunch time, but would they be required to earn their meal? They hadn't yesterday, and look how that had turned out. Bella still seemed uncomfortable around him, which Alex understood, but it still grated on him.

They were both still adapting to being completely out of control of their lives. He had to admit, she was already working better within the framework of their new reality than he was. Submitting to someone else was not natural for Alex, and he had to fight his instincts, had to stop and second-guess his reactions. If he could imitate Bella, could lull them all into thinking he was beaten, that he had accepted what was happening to them …

Perhaps.

Besides, he'd come to realize the Wolf didn't get off on just having him and Bella as prisoners. He got off on Alex's resistance to everything more than he did on toying with them physically. Maybe if Alex acted beaten, the Wolf would get bored with them, as well as careless.

It was worth a shot, anyway. If they could just have

the opportunity to explore more of the compound, even with the cameras watching, that would be something. He needed to find out how and where to get his collar and the trackers in their shoulders removed, and how to get out of the compound. From watching the guards in the outdoor area, he knew their normal routines, but as today had proved, they didn't always follow that.

That meant something must be going on. Probably not with him and Bella, since none of the guards had paid attention to the prisoners—which was also important. Something that would distract the entire compound and allow Alex and Bella a tad more freedom.

Or maybe they would just be locked into their room, but perhaps he could use that to his advantage. If people weren't watching as closely, maybe he and Bella could try to take his collar off.

The Wolf ignored them all through lunch while he had a series of intense, low-voiced discussions with his people. Jordan was there without Trish, which meant something was happening. That, or something had happened to her, but since Alex had just seen her a few hours ago, he tried not to be unduly worried.

Once he and Bella were done eating, they were left sitting there, only nominally guarded and waiting. Bella was somewhat curled up, hiding her body from the people seated at the tables, more than one of whom looked at her and Alex. He ignored their attention and didn't bother to hide any of himself. It gave them something to look at so maybe no one would care that Bella was mostly hidden from their view.

He and Bella didn't talk, although they exchanged several looks. Alex was too busy straining to hear the conversations between the Wolf and his soldiers. He couldn't hear much.

"She's requested that ..."

"... and set the usual guards ..."

"... what does she offer for ..."

Snippets of conversation tantalized but didn't give him a clear idea of what was going on. Something was being planned—something involving a woman—but since they all referred to her as 'she,' rather than by name, he wasn't sure who the woman in question was. Or what was being planned.

He glanced at Bella, who also had her head tilted as though she was listening. Bella did a lot of listening, he'd noticed. More than he did, sometimes. Quiet, unobtrusive, and not nearly as rebellious as Alex, he bet some of the Wolf's people even forgot she was there when she wasn't providing them with entertainment. Somehow, he didn't think the same kind of tactic would work for him.

A sudden lull made him look up, directly into the Wolf's green eyes, which were now focused on him. Beside him, Alex felt Bella shiver. His own reaction was to tense, his muscles ready to go. Even though he'd pushed himself during this morning's workout, and he was tired, adrenaline sent energy surging through him. Besides, he'd gotten to rest for a little bit while they'd been sitting on the dais.

"Ah, Pet and Toy ... Don't worry, I didn't forget about you. In fact, I have plenty of time for you now." The anticipatory gleam in his eye made Alex clench his fists. Whatever the Wolf had planned, he already knew he wouldn't like it. The Wolf snapped his fingers, and Alex turned his head around as he heard the whir of machinery.

People were moving back as the floor opened and the

erotic torture chamber came up through the opening. The platform ground into place, ready and awaiting use with its multitude of apparatuses.

The soldiers moved. Alex had his back to the Wolf and he'd missed the hand signal; he had to force himself not to lash out as they pulled him away from Bella. To his surprise, she tried to hit one of them, but the woman just laughed and pinched Bella's nipple, making her shriek. He wasn't sure what had made Bella try to do that; it was as if they'd reversed roles. He hadn't protested or even moved when the soldiers pressed down on his shoulders, whereas Bella was fighting for the first time.

"Ah, Pet's in a temper today," the Wolf said, sounding amused. "We'll have to see what we can do to help her … feel better." Those in the room laughed, as the last two words were laden with all sorts of sexual intensity. There was no doubt what the Wolf meant by making her 'feel better.'

The soldiers took Bella to a padded bench that was on a slight incline and bent her over it so her bottom was up in the air. Although there were armrests, her wrists were cuffed to the base of the bench, limiting her movement even more than the armrests would have. At least there, she'd have been able to bend and flex her elbows to get some give.

Alex's cock twitched at the sight of the plug winking between her cheeks, where it was buried in her asshole, and the splayed lips of her pink pussy as her legs were pulled apart and also cuffed to the bench. Bella squirmed, but she'd already stopped fighting; now it looked like her movements were involuntary reactions to being restrained in front of so many people. She had to be nervous. He hated that seeing her like this still made him a little hard, which—with the tight cock ring—started a reaction that would inevitably lead to a full-fledged hard-on, whether he liked it or not.

"Our sweet little anal virgin," the Wolf said from behind Alex, his words rolling out as if he were tasting each of them as they left his tongue. Savoring them. "But not for much longer. Put Toy in place."

Now Alex was brought to his feet, and he dug in his heels and tried to swing his head around to look at the Wolf to see what he meant. But the soldiers were already dragging him toward Bella, and he couldn't turn his head around far enough to see the Wolf's expression. What he could see was the woman Bella had tried to hit pulling the butt plug from Bella's anus. The little hole gaped slightly, and Bella's body squirmed even more now.

Cheers rang around, and Alex recognized the sounds of bets being settled as the soldiers put his feet outside Bella's and cuffed his ankles to hers. One of the men stood behind him, holding his wrists and keeping him off balance.

"What the fuck?" he growled and tried to pull away as one of the men cupped his dick—which was half-hard and unable to go down from his looking at Bella's body—and began to stroke it. Alex's stomach sank, but he had been too slow. His ankles were already attached to Bella's, and he couldn't get away. Under the man's squeezing strokes that spread lube over his shaft, his dick came to life, blood rushing in, tightening the ring around the base of his cock and balls even more.

Fingers stroked down his back, and he arched away, trying to jerk his wrists out of the soldier's grip. The Wolf's hot breath wafted against his ear. "Have you figured it out yet, Toy? You're going to get the chance to save our sweet Pet's ass. All you have to do is not fuck her and no one will."

"Like I'm supposed to trust your word," Alex said through gritted teeth.

The Wolf stroked Alex's face with one finger, and Alex stood there, refusing to move or jerk away now. It was like a game of chicken, to see who would flinch first. The older man's glittering, green eyes looked almost sorrowful. "Have I lied to you yet, Toy?"

"You said you let that other girl go days ago, but she hadn't been returned home when we watched the news."

"I didn't lie. Perhaps you do not believe," the Wolf said with a shrug, as if Alex's belief didn't matter one way or another. "But I did not lie. And I do not lie now. Although, it doesn't matter whether or not you believe, I think you will try anyway. To protect Pet. Won't you, Toy?" He ran his finger over Alex's lips and Alex had to steel himself against jerking away.

Of course he'd do what he could to protect Bella.

The soldier gripping Alex's cock lowered it and pressed it against her virgin anus, and Alex groaned as the man behind him pushed forward. Bella let out a gasping shriek as the tight ring of her anus was forced open to accommodate the head of his cock.

"Stop it!" he shouted, trying to pull back, but they were already taking his wrists and forcing him to bend over her. Alex arched his back and his hips and tried not to think about how good the tight clasp of her hot, back entrance felt around the head of his cock. Only the tip of his dick was lodged inside her body as the soldiers cuffed his wrists to the armrests.

The position put an incredible amount of strain on his arms, his hips, and his legs as he hovered over her, keeping as far away from her as possible. The position didn't allow him to pull out of her completely, but he could keep from allowing more of his lubricated cock to slide into her tight hole.

For now.

"All you have to do is not fuck her sweet little ass," the Wolf said, as wet fingers began to rim and play with Alex's asshole. He gritted his teeth and shuddered with the effort of staying in the uncomfortable position, and also against the surge of pleasure as he was stimulated from both ends. It was just like their first day, except this time Bella hadn't been given the facsimile of a choice, and this time Alex had a thin chance of protecting her from further violation.

"Please no, please no, please no," she chanted softly; so softly it was a whisper tickling his ear. He groaned as she clenched around him, like she was trying to force him out. Unfortunately, it only made him want to thrust in, to fill her completely because it felt so damn good. The heat of her ass scalded the head of his cock, and the need to bury himself inside her was killing him.

"Bella, stop," he begged, as one of the Wolf's fingers slid into his ass, breaching the tight hole. Unlike Bella, he hadn't been prepared with a plug, and the intrusion burned a bit. "You have to stop clenching."

Another finger slid into his ass, spearing him, and Alex groaned when Bella's ass spasmed at the same time. His hips jerked involuntarily, pushing him a little deeper inside her, and she squealed.

"Sorry, sorry," he groaned, pulling his hips back, which had the double effect of forcing the Wolf's fingers further into his ass.

"Mmm, so eager, Toy, I like that," the Wolf said, chuckling.

"Fuck you."

"That's what I plan to do," taunted the Wolf, his fingers twisting inside Alex, opening his ass up further. Alex snarled, but he couldn't pull away without pushing deeper into Bella's body. She'd finally relaxed, adjusted enough that she'd stopped squeezing his cock.

The Wolf withdrew his fingers, and Alex braced himself over Bella, waiting for the rough thrust he knew was coming.

Instead, the Wolf pressed his cock against Alex's anus and very, very slowly began to push in. Alex groaned, the combination of the slow penetration and his burning muscles as he tried not to let what was happening to him affect Bella was incredibly difficult to withstand. His legs and arms wanted to give in, and his muscles begged for relief as his ass was opened up.

The thick cock burned as it slid in, going slow and deep. The inward slide was relentless, pushing forward without once drawing back to gain an easier entry, and Alex panted and tried to relax the tight ring of muscle while he kept himself braced. It hurt. It felt good. And his cock twitched inside Bella's ass, wanting more than ever to fully embed itself in her heat.

———

She was a selfish bitch. And she knew it.

Alex's body hovered over her, protecting her, at a cost to himself. His legs made a tense line against hers, his wrists trembled on either side of her, his cock twitched inside her, and he groaned. From their words,

Bella knew the Wolf was fucking Alex; raping his ass again.

And Alex held himself in position for it, straining to resist doing the same to her. Because he didn't want to hurt her.

She hated herself for hoping he could withstand the Wolf's assault. After all, if Alex was being raped, hurt, and she wasn't—because of his efforts—that was shameful. Selfish.

Wrong.

But if he didn't … then she'd be protected. Strangely, she believed the Wolf when he said he would allow her to remain an anal virgin, with a cock never having penetrated her ass deeper than Alex's currently was.

It hurt in the strangest way, making her hole throb. Nothing like the butt plug, because his cock twitched and moved inside her, and she could feel it pulsing. She had no idea how much of him was in her, but it felt huge.

Bella gasped as it slid deeper before Alex cursed and pulled away again. He was tiring. The Wolf's thrusts into his body were slow, deep, and purposeful. It was a waiting game. Perhaps he could have forced Alex into her with fast, rough strokes, but this long, slow fucking would slowly wear Alex down, a little bit at a time.

And with every inch, he would curse himself.

Bella shuddered and closed her eyes. She could still feel everyone watching them, but at least she wouldn't see it.

"Alex, just do it." Her voice was little more than a whisper.

"No."

"Alex, please, just do it." Maybe he would think her a coward, but she couldn't just lie here and let him torment himself, let him fill himself with guilt as he was pressed into her. It was inevitable.

So, she squeezed his cock. His body buckled slightly and pushed his cock deeper, and Bella gasped as her anus spasmed. It hurt with a burning itch, an unbearable stretch that made tears spring to her eyes.

"Dammit, Bella ..." Alex's voice rasped, and he struggled to push himself back up. But his muscles were tired. Sore.

Her voice caught in her throat as she underwent her own struggle, trying to breathe through the waves of discomfort and burning his cock caused in her virgin anus. She wanted to tell him it was okay, she wanted to tell him to keep going, but she couldn't.

Then he surged deeper. She could feel the push of the Wolf's thrusts, which got harder, and Alex was in a terrible spot. Every tremor of his body went through her. The heat of him came closer, and he wasn't anywhere near being all the way inside her yet. Bella whimpered and tried her best to be quiet and not increase Alex's ordeal.

His muscles gave out almost completely, and he managed to keep from crushing her, but the entirety of his cock pushed into her asshole.

Bella shrieked as the flaming pain licked her insides, her tight hole clenching against him and trying to reject the thick intrusion so deep inside her.

"Sorry, sorry," Alex's voice whispered in her ear, thick with guilt.

"It's okay," she gasped out, lying through her teeth.

His hips pulled out slightly and then shoved back in, and Bella shuddered.

"Pet's ass just got its first cock!" the Wolf shouted above the cheers that exploded around them.

Tears leaked through her lashes—shame, humiliation, fear, and pain. It hurt as Alex's cock dragged out of her, and the Wolf's fingers wrapped around Alex's hips and pulled him away before pushing forward again. The thrust made her writhe, made her groan and shudder as her body tried vainly to adjust to the thick cock that had deflowered her last, virgin hole.

The movement was even worse than the overly full feeling that burned as his cock receded, the strange drag of his flesh against her sensitive inner walls that exacerbated her discomfort. It almost felt better when Alex shoved back in again and the back of the Wolf's fingers dug into her buttocks with Alex's thick cock buried deep inside her. The Wolf was fucking them both again, using both of them at the same time.

Bella groaned and took it because there was nothing else she could do. Alex struggled above her and tried to fight the Wolf's forceful thrusts; tried to resist the push and pull of his hands, which made for inconsistent thrusts into her own backside.

"Stop fighting, Alex, just stop!" she cried out, frustrated. Didn't he realize struggling and fighting only made the entire event take longer?

"Listen to Pet, Toy. You might be the brawn, but she's definitely the brains," the Wolf said, laughing. "The more you fight, the worse it will be. Or maybe you're too thick to have learned that lesson yet."

She hated the way the Wolf taunted Alex but couldn't help feeling a surge of relief as Alex stopped his useless resistance. The rhythm of thrusts became smoother, less painfully unpredictable. Her body relaxed as much as it could under the circumstances.

It already hurt less, although her level of guilt was higher now. There was never any benefit for free here; it was always a tradeoff.

The burning began to lessen, to morph into something else. Bella found the thrusts easier and easier to take; the steady rhythm stroking inside her became almost hypnotic.

It was starting to feel good.

That elusive 'different' good she'd heard about but never been interested in. It didn't help that these smoother, steadier thrusts pressed the front of her mound against the padded leather, something she could appreciate more now that she wasn't writhing in pain.

Her pussy began to feel hot and a little needy, and her ass clenched as her body demanded a response. Bella stifled a moan—was she beginning to enjoy this?

The first lift of Bella's bottom up against his thrust was so subtle Alex thought he might have imagined it. Then came another. And another.

It felt incredible: the tight heat of her ass pushing against him, pulling at his cock, while the Wolf's deep thrusts stroked his own heated interior, rubbing over his prostate again and again. Alex writhed between the two of them, caught by pleasure on all sides, as much as he hated it. As if sensing something had changed, the Wolf began to fuck him harder, spearing Alex's anus with his cock and making Alex, in turn, fuck Bella harder.

Soft gasps beneath him indicated she'd begun to

enjoy it; she wasn't in pain anymore, which soothed some of his guilt. His muscles were incredibly sore now, although he still kept the Wolf from putting their combined weight onto her. Alex hated how much he enjoyed the silky heat of her ass, the way her muscles spasmed around his cock, and the soft cushion of her bottom against his groin ... but he couldn't help it.

"Fuck ..."

The relentless press against his prostate was taking its toll, even with him fighting his orgasm and the tight cock-ring helping to postpone it. The Wolf was nearing his end, and Alex's balls tightened in response: an erotic reflex he couldn't control. Bella bucked beneath him, wriggling in a way that made him think she was rubbing her front against the bench, getting closer to her own climax.

Let go, said a little voice in his head. *You wanted the Wolf to think he was getting the better of you anyway, just let go ...*

But that voice also worried him. The path of least resistance was dangerous. But at the same time, it was right.

Alex surrendered, the same way Bella had, but only for this moment. Only for right now while his cock plundered her virgin ass, while he was fucked from behind at the same time. He let the sensations overtake him, let them cloud out logic and reason and overpower his emotions.

The Wolf pounded harder into him, gripping Alex's hips and forcefully shoving him into Bella's tight ass. Every time he drew out, the Wolf's hips surged forward and filled him, and he filled Bella in turn, fucking her harder and harder. Her gasps were louder now that he wasn't holding back, and yet just as filled with a painful kind of pleasure. He'd heard her come often enough to know she was getting close.

When she did, her ass clamped down on him like a vise, sucking his cock in. Alex groaned and arched his back as her asshole squeezed him almost painfully, and he was unable to move in or out. The impossibly strong grip of her sphincter held him in place while the Wolf pummeled his own vulnerable asshole, the head of his dick sliding over Alex's prostate with each thrust.

Cum pushed against the cock ring and then exploded through it, forcing its way past the tight constriction, past the spasming rim of Bella's asshole and deep into her rectum. As he cried out, his body writhing with pleasure, he could feel the Wolf's liquid explosion deep inside him, brought on by his own shuddering clenches. Heat filled him and ecstasy ripped through him, swinging him up and sending him crashing back down along with reality as wild applause filled his ears.

Alex hunched over Bella and took a shuddering breath. She mewled beneath him, and he realized he was crushing her. With the last of his strength, he pushed himself up so she could breath. Her asshole massaged his shrinking cock, and his did the same to the Wolf's.

When the Wolf pulled out, a slimy track of cum slid out as well and began trickling down the back of Alex's thigh.

"Are you okay?" he whispered in Bella's ear, worried. She nodded, but he couldn't see her face.

"Alright people, we only have another day and a half. Back to work," the Wolf said loudly.

Soldiers pulled Alex off Bella, and he had a momentary glimpse of her reddened asshole gaping at him between her pink cheeks before he was led away. He was surprisingly wobbly on his own legs and allowed the soldiers to support him as they steered him out of the room while he vainly listened for more clues as to what exactly was going down in a day and a half.

After being cleaned in the showers, Bella and Alex were returned to their room. He was absurdly grateful when she crawled into his arms and rested her head on his shoulder as they cuddled in the bed.

"I'm sorry," he whispered to the top of her head, stroking her hair.

"Don't be stupid," she whispered back, sounding sleepy. "I don't blame you."

Well, that was something, although it didn't completely assuage his feelings of guilt. He kept feeling like he *should* have been able to do something.

———

Bella murmured more reassurances to Alex; she could tell from the tension in his body that he still blamed himself —the big idiot. Although she understood, there wasn't anything he could have done. He took way too much of the responsibility for what was happening to them onto his broad shoulders. Eventually, he would crack under the strain if he overloaded himself.

She snuggled up to him, trying to ignore the soreness in her ass, and stroked his chest; curled her fingers through the wiry hairs.

"It's okay," she repeated. "Besides, I'd rather it be you than him." It was the closest she'd come to telling Alex she was starting to have feelings for him that were more than friendly. What Bella meant was she was kind of glad it had been him if it had to be somebody. If it had been anyone else, even Ken, she would have suspected they'd been secretly overjoyed to be the one to pop her cherry.

Alex obviously respected that it hadn't been something she'd wanted, and he'd done his best for her.

Sure, it had hurt, but it had also felt better in the end than she could have ever imagined. She still wasn't sure what had happened—it had kind of felt like an orgasm, but different, too.

Slowly, the tension leaked out of Alex's big body, and then soft snores told her he'd fallen asleep—probably exhausted. He'd definitely expended more energy than she had. All she'd done was lie there.

Bella wanted to get through this, more or less intact, and the best chance for that was to try to fly under the radar—not something Alex excelled at. Would the Wolf have been less interested in them if Alex wasn't the way he was? He couldn't help it, but the Wolf seemed to enjoy the process of breaking Alex more than he was interested in Bella.

Which, if she was only in this for herself, would have been a major advantage. But she and Alex were a team, and right now she didn't know if they were winning or losing the long war.

15

That night, Bella and Alex were served dinner in their room, during which time they talked about what might be going on that had the Wolf and his men so busy. Not that either of them were upset about being ignored—although being cooped up in the room meant they couldn't learn anything more—but it was unusual.

"I feel like we were entertainment this afternoon; a distraction. Like watching tv during a break," Bella said, a bit miserably. After all, who liked to think of their pain and humiliation in such terms? It still wasn't comfortable to sit. If she'd thought the butt plugs were bad, the aftermath of anal sex had left her a lot more tender in that entire area. Still, she didn't say anything about it because she could tell that Alex was still feeling guilty, even though it wasn't like he could have done anything.

"Yeah … I don't know exactly what is going on, but I feel like maybe someone important is coming here. For a visit or negotiations or … something," Alex said. He wasn't able to look her in the eye, which made her bite her lip in frustration. But bringing it up would only make him more awkward around her. Probably better just to act normal.

"I wonder who."

The news stations they watched had always focused on the Wolf because he was so interesting and big and splashy. Although everyone knew there were others who ruled over large swaths of the population of Earth, for the most part, the Moon families didn't pay attention to what didn't affect their day-to-day lives. Bella was starting to realize how isolated, how ignorant that made them. From the disgruntled look on Alex's face, he felt the same way.

Neither of them had any real theories, which made their conversation go around in circles a bit, but what else were they supposed to talk about? Eventually, Bella got into bed and watched Alex pace around the room. He ran his fingers over any seams in the wall he could find, especially around the area where they knew the television was.

"He could let us watch something again," Alex muttered under his breath, obviously referring to the Wolf.

After he'd made several circuits of the room, Alex sighed and stood there, staring at the wall. Bella couldn't help but admire the muscles in his back and the firm cheeks of his butt. She wondered if he was as sore back there as she was—it wasn't exactly something she could ask.

Bella was exhausted but she couldn't fall asleep, and she'd finally figured out why. "Come to bed, Alex," she said softly, a hint of pleading in her voice.

Alex sighed again and turned around, frustration evident on his face. Bella's heart twinged; she wished she had a better suggestion for him, but what were they supposed to do other than get their rest? They often needed more than they got. And she couldn't sleep until Alex was there, holding her and protecting her from the terrors of the night.

If they needed any confirmation someone was watching—after having seen video evidence of their own interlude together—as soon as Alex had himself comfortably settled in bed with his arms wrapped around her, the lights went out. In the darkness, Bella snuggled closer to him and buried her nose in his chest hair to breathe in his masculine scent. His cock hardened against her belly, but typical Alex didn't make a move to do anything about it.

Part of her wanted to tell him it was okay; she would be happy to be with him like that ... but she couldn't find the words. Besides, she was so tired and finally felt safe and warm in his arms. Darkness dragged her under.

———

Alex woke the next morning uncomfortably hard. Having Bella snugged up against him all night had been torturous, but she'd slept a lot better for it, and he wouldn't deny her any comfort he could give. He cursed both his dick and the cock ring around the base of it that made it impossible for him to go down.

Next to him, Bella stirred sleepily, her hand trailing along his stomach, and he gritted his teeth as he caught her wrist and pulled it away.

"Wha ...?" she asked sleepily, blinking her soft brown eyes up at him. A glow appeared in their depths as she registered his presence; a glow he didn't deserve but that soothed something inside him.

"Morning." He gave her hand a squeeze. "I guess we're not getting our usual wake-up call."

"I guess not." She glanced at the door then hesitated and looked around. "Do you know if he …"

"I don't think so," Alex said. At least, he hoped he wouldn't have slept through the Wolf coming in and out of the room. Just the idea was disturbing.

Bella shifted, her body brushing across Alex's cock, and every muscle in his body tensed. Bella gasped and looked down at his cock, which was big and red and angry looking.

"Oh my god, Alex. That looks painful."

"Don't worry about it," he said shortly, trying to drag the covers back up over his hips.

"Don't be stupid, I can help."

"Bella, no, don't—" He groaned as she reached underneath the sheet and wrapped her fingers around his cock.

"I don't mind," she murmured, pressing her soft curves against him from the side. "As long as you don't mind … and we keep the sheets up so they can't see."

"Fuck … no, I don't mind, but you shouldn't … I don't …" Alex floundered for words as her hand began to slide up and down his cock. Fuck, that felt amazing. Heavenly. Like he would mind having Bella jerk him off? Was she insane? He was humbled she wanted to touch him at all after yesterday, much less provide him with sexual relief. It was something he could take care of himself, and part of him felt he should, but something in her tone said this was something she truly wanted to do.

"It's okay, just kiss me," she whispered. There was a vulnerability to her request that made him pause. He turned on his side to face her and tipped her head up to see the uncertainty in her eyes.

Her offer absolutely astounded him, though she probably didn't realize how much her emotions were showing. Hope, worry, and real desire all flickered in her dark eyes, along with a connection he'd never seen before. Something had been growing between them, but they hadn't had time to notice because of all the crazy shit going on around them.

But for this moment, they co-existed in a little bubble, just the two of them. They were aware of the cameras, but the sheets would keep anyone from seeing too much. And he didn't care if they saw what he was about to do.

Alex lowered his lips to hers and kissed her. Gently but firmly, he moved his arms carefully around to cup the back of her head and wrap his other arm around her hips to pull her flush against him. Bella moaned a little and wriggled, rocking her hips as he massaged her lower back, tilting her head to open more fully to him. Her fingers tightened around his cock, and he moaned, deepening the kiss as her lips parted for him.

It was a ray of sunshine through the darkness, a slice of something pure amid depravity and trash, a tiny spark of hope to set against the relentless degradation. His hips rocked harder and faster to thrust his cock through her fingers as his pre-cum wet the hole she'd made with her hand. Bella gave herself up to his kiss and allowed him to take her mouth fully, giving him a measure of control he'd been without ever since they'd been taken.

Alex groaned and thrust harder, and the head of his cock stabbed into her soft belly, but instead of moving away, she wriggled closer. He reached down between them and slid his fingers into her pussy and was shocked at how wet and hot she was between the swollen lips. The feel of her arousal coating his fingers blew away the last vestiges of uncertainty, and he groaned as he pressed his fingers deeper.

———

The feel of Alex's fingers parting her folds, pushing into her body, was more intimate and erotic than Bella could have imagined. It didn't matter that they'd already had sex—multiple times—none of that compared to this stolen moment of pure pleasure. No drugs, no audience, no agendas ... Bella squeezed his cock harder and tried to ignore the ring at the base of his shaft as she stroked him, the only reminder of their captivity.

Well, that and the collar around his throat her other hand encountered as she slid it up over his shoulder and neck and into his hair. Alex devoured her with his mouth, their bodies rocking together with heat and need. Bella whimpered and ground herself down on his hand, her swollen clit throbbing as his fingers dipped inside her, probing her wet hole. It felt incredible. He knew exactly how to stroke her, how to touch her, to make her writhe with wanton need. To make her forget everything else and melt into the sensations he created inside her.

His cock throbbed in her hand, and sticky fluid sprayed her stomach, the hot liquid seeming to sear her soft skin. Bella moaned, a bit disappointed. In the past, with Ken, he'd always lost interest in continuing things once he'd achieved his own orgasm. And she'd been so very close to her own.

She should have realized things with Alex would be different.

Instead of pulling away, his kiss deepened further and his fingers pushed completely inside her, stretching her open. Bella gasped with shock as he maneuvered her onto her back, using his body weight to position her the way he wanted—with her legs spread, her pussy open for him. The covers were still over them, so no one could see, but she still felt every movement, every thrust of his fingers; the way his palm cupped her and pressed into her. She groaned and moved her hips up and down in time with his movements, clutching him as his tongue explored her mouth, muffling the anxious sounds that came from her throat.

The pleasure came, fast and hot, buoyed by her excitement and the warmth that spread through her when she realized he had no interest in stopping. The slowly cooling cum on her belly only turned her on more—as if he'd marked her—and reminded her she'd pleasured him, as well. Her pussy tightened down around his fingers, and her hips moved spasmodically as she cried out into his mouth and shuddered with the exquisite ecstasy. He continued to stroke her through her orgasm until she was replete with pleasure, floating on a wave of it.

Only then did he begin to draw away, his kisses coming slower, softer, until he feathered them over her cheeks, lips, and eyelids. Bella made a sound low in her throat as he pulled her in and wiped her belly off with the sheet before moving them to the other side of the bed, away from the soiled sheets. Eventually, this idyll would break, but she was still glad they'd done it. That she'd reached out and touched him.

Something between them, something indefinable, had changed.

When the soldiers finally came to get them and take them to the bathroom and then outside, Bella was much less anxious than usual. She still clung to Alex's side, and he was more demonstrably protective than ever with his arm secured around her and shooting glares at the soldiers who looked at her, but something within her was calmer. It was like they'd reclaimed what the Wolf had taken from them when he'd drugged her and sent her back to Alex.

Unfortunately, Alex's new increased protectiveness meant he ended up trying to fight the soldiers when they bent her over the bench in the group shower.

"Calm down, Toy," one of the women said, laughing as Alex dropped to his knees, his hands going to his collar. Bella shot him a look, her expression pleading with him to listen to the soldier. "Unless you don't want her to have something to help that poor little asshole you abused yesterday." She smirked at him and Alex growled. The man behind him pressed down on Alex's shoulders in warning.

Bella gripped the hard wood of the bench and tried not to whimper as two cream-coated fingers shoved roughly into her asshole. The tiny hole burned and protested, and squeezed tightly to try to force the rude digits out, but they persevered, spreading the cream deep inside her. It would eventually help, but right now the thick fingers and the force being used was more than a little painful. But she didn't want Alex to realize that; not with the way he was reacting.

So, she kept her head down and bit her lip as the fingers sawed in and out of the tight space, violating her.

The sensitive nerve endings had awoken with a vengeance, already sore from being deflowered the day before and now having to tolerate more abuse.

"Hurry up, Vaughn—plug her so that we can take them out to exercise," one of the other men said, sounding bored.

To Bella's relief, the fingers were removed, and a plug was pushed in. It was bigger than the ones she'd had before, but it was coated in the same healing cream that had been used to such good effect on both her and Alex since the beginning of their stay, which made it slide easily enough into her rectum. She still winced though and then sighed with relief as it settled inside her. At least it stayed in place instead of pushing or shoving the way the soldier's fingers had.

She and Alex were led outside, where the day was already bright and sunny. Jordan was there in the pool with Trish, watching her swim laps. Sometimes he confused Bella: although he didn't care whether Trish was humiliated or exposed to others, he seemed to care for her in his own way. Certainly more than the Wolf did for Bella or Alex. It was strange. Even more strange was that Trish seemed less frightened of him every time Bella saw her. Definitely the opposite of how she felt about the Wolf.

Then again, as far as she could tell, Jordan kept Trish protected from the other soldiers with his possessiveness, and he seemed to keep to a routine. It wasn't the psycho-logical battering the Wolf favored.

Alex took to the water with fervor, pounding out his frustrations in physical activity. Bella followed more slowly and sighed with relief as the cool water enveloped her body. Swimming with the plug wasn't comfortable, but her sore insides already felt better thanks to the cream. Right now, she'd take whatever upside she could get.

———

When they reached the Wolf's dais, the man was as busy as he had been yesterday. Alex sat close to Bella while they ate their lunch. He'd worked out hard but not exhausted himself the way he had the day before. They were both quiet, listening to the conversations going on around them, all of which seemed to involve the security of the compound and making 'space' for someone. Alex was more and more sure someone important was coming to visit, he just didn't know who.

And no one said a name, just 'she.'

Going by the serious faces of the Wolf's soldiers, Alex could only guess 'she' was both dangerous and necessary. A trade was in the works. He heard mutterings about various goods, especially weaponry. He didn't know what Bella thought about the various snippets they were able to hear and he didn't want to draw attention to them by trying to talk to her.

Alex knew he shouldn't allow what had happened between them this morning to change the way he treated her—like the Wolf didn't already know Bella was Alex's weak spot. But he couldn't help that he felt closer to and more possessive of her—which, in their current situation, was not only frustrating, it was also possibly dangerous if he didn't get a handle on himself.

Once they finished eating and the remains of their lunch had been removed, the Wolf shooed his minions back.

"Bring Pet and Toy here, to me," he said.

As Alex stood, the Wolf finished signing something off and handed it to Jordan, who immediately trotted away with it.

Then the Wolf's attention focused on his prisoners, and he smiled. Not a cruel smile, but one filled with anticipation, and Alex tensed in response. He and Bella were moved around to the back of the Wolf's desk, where he sat. The man reached out and pulled Bella onto his lap so she sat on one of his thighs.

Submissive as always, Bella sat there, obediently moving her limbs until the Wolf had twisted her around and faced out over the room. It made Alex grit his teeth to see how nonresistant she was, but he couldn't blame her, either. Fighting the Wolf had unpleasant consequences, and she had no chance of overpowering the man. Women on the Moon were not encouraged to develop fighting skills or muscles, unlike the female soldiers they'd been interacting with here on Earth. Bella wasn't a match for any of them, much less a man like the Wolf.

"There we go, good Pet." One of the Wolf's hands casually cupped her breast as he settled her back against him. Alex tried not to look because just seeing her splayed out on the Wolf's lap made all sorts of violent feelings rise up. She straddled the man's thigh, facing outward, her body leaning back against his for support, with both her hands tucked behind her back so her breasts were thrust out as if asking for attention. If the desk hadn't been in front of her and the Wolf, the entire room would have been able to see the splayed pink interior of her pussy.

"There's a news report scheduled that I thought you two might like to see."

The screen across the room flickered to life as the Wolf pushed a button on his desk with his free hand; the other still caressed Bella's breast. Her little pink nipple hardened as long fingers pinched the tiny bud, and Alex had to force himself to tear his eyes away and focus on the screen. It took a minute for the sound to catch up and for him to register what they were seeing.

"Abby's Return!" was the banner across the bottom of the screen, and a heavily made-up news reporter spoke and gestured excitedly as the red-headed Abby came out of the hospital, flanked by her family. The news reporter said Abby had been admitted the night before.

Microphones were shoved at the poor girl, but her family had hired bodyguards for the occasion. They surged forward and pushed the reporters back, repeating the words 'no comment' over and over again, much to the reporters' disappointment. The excitement over a returning prisoner of the Wolf was always high since it rarely happened more than once or twice a year. Abby wasn't willing to talk to the media—like most of the captives the Wolf had held for any length of time—so none of the reporters seemed surprised. In the few glimpses they showed of her, she looked dazed—almost confused.

The view switched back to a reporter who said the government had released a press statement that Abby had confirmed Alex and Bella's capture by the Wolf, as well as that of another young woman, name unknown at this time.

Alex could only shake his head that it had taken them all so long to realize that Trish was missing, even if she was an orphan. Someone should have noticed and come forward before this. Or maybe they had, and it had gotten buried under the interest in Alex and Bella; after all, their families were fairly important. Ken's family was even more so and they were kicking up a fuss.

The broadcast scrolled through more footage of Ken and Lisa. The complete lack of comments from Alex's and Bella's families was glossed over by their ex-significant-others' tearful pleas.

It was a three-ring media circus.

"See?" the Wolf said amiably, bringing Alex's attention back to him. He now cupped both of Bella's breasts, playing with them absentmindedly. Both her nipples were tight and prominent on the soft mounds; he twisted them between his fingers, and Alex had to watch as Bella squirmed a bit. His fists clenched at his sides as he forced his emotions down. "Slave is just fine. Because she was a good girl, and good boys and girls always get to go home to their mommies and daddies. Now Pet, under the desk and show me what a good girl you are."

He pushed gently, and Bella slid forward, tucking herself under the expansive foot-room provided by the desk's frame. The Wolf reached down and undid the front of his pants and brought his hard cock out before sliding his chair forward and trapping Bella there. The Wolf moaned, one hand under the desk, and turned to smirk at Alex.

Two soldiers on either side held him tightly in place.

Alex looked away.

———

The space under the desk had just enough room for Bella and the Wolf's lower body, and barely enough head space for Bella to position his cock where she could slide it into her mouth. The hot, thick meat was heavy on her tongue as she obediently sucked it between her lips, and his answering moan came slightly muffled by all the wood.

She moved by instinct because she was so shocked by what she'd seen on his desk. Her mind raced through the possibilities, horrified by pretty much all of them, so taking his cock into her mouth and sucking seemed easier than facing what she'd seen. Fingers tightened in her hair as her mouth slid down to the base and easily took him into her throat. The gel Dr. Margolis had administered was still in full effect; her gag reflex didn't even twinge.

When she would have moved faster, his grip on her hair kept her bobbing her head at a slow, even pace. Bella wanted to get this over with, to go be with Alex and talk over what she'd seen, but the Wolf wanted to extend his pleasure and her torture. She was forced to move her head up and down slowly, sucking all the way, as her tongue danced along the bottom of his cock. It was all she could do to hurry his orgasm since he wouldn't let her move her head faster.

The muffled sounds of conversation above her let her know he'd returned to work. He didn't focus on Bella as she serviced him with her mouth. She shifted, trying to get more comfortable, and rested her arms on his thighs as she sucked him deep and took him all the way to the root before pressing her nose against his pubic hair and sliding off again. The musky scent of his body filled her nose whenever she pulled away and gulped in air. The bitter taste of his pre-cum filled her mouth as his cock began to leak, but still he wouldn't let her go faster.

Her jaw began to ache from the effort of holding it open so wide, from the hard sucking she was doing. And still, he controlled her pace. Her thoughts begin to slow, her focus entirely on trying to alleviate the tension in her jaw as her mouth slid up and down his cock, the rhythm becoming hypnotic. She moaned, vibrating his length with her vocal cords as the head of his dick pressed into her throat, and his muscles tightened as she did.

The thick rod began to grow thicker, longer, and he allowed her to pick up the pace a little bit. Despite the soreness of her jaw muscles, Bella renewed her efforts and worked his cock hard, desperate to suck him off and gain some relief for herself. The fingers massaging her hair pulled her hard against him, and he groaned as his cock expanded in her throat.

Pulse after pulse of hot liquid poured down into her belly, cutting off her air supply, and she tried not to panic as her throat muscles worked to massage the stiff length of his cock while she swallowed his cum. His hand held her firmly in place, even as he began to soften, and she began to suck in great gulps of air through her nose and around his dick. Bella gasped for breath, her sore jaw throbbing as she laid her head against his thigh, the slick worm of his cock still resting between her lips.

Fingers stroked her hair soothingly. If she couldn't hear the steady murmur of business going on above her head, she might have been able to pretend the person attached to those fingers cared.

The Wolf moved back, and Bella crawled out, looking away from Alex. She didn't want him to see her flushed face or swollen lips.

"Good Pet." The Wolf caressed her breast as she stood and leaned back in his chair to look at her. He tweaked her nipple, causing an answering surge in her pussy. It was involuntary; her nipples had always been sensitive, and he'd been playing with them so much before putting her beneath the desk that her body still craved it. His cool, green gaze moved to the soldiers behind her. "Take them back to their room." Those cat-like eyes flicked back over her and Alex. "Rest up this evening. We have a very important visitor coming tomorrow."

Back in the room, Alex wrapped Bella up in a hug as soon as they were alone. She clung to him in need of the physical reassurance he was happy to give. Not being able to watch what the Wolf had been doing to her had made that interlude both easier and harder.

"It's okay," he murmured into her hair and stroked down the soft skin of her back as he cuddled her close. "It's okay."

She stirred in his arms and pulled back to tilt her head and look up at him. Her dark eyes were wide with a kind of shock. "No, Alex it's not. Did you see what he had on his desk?"

Alex shook his head. He'd been too far back to be able to make out anything on the Wolf's desk clearly. Bella, sitting on the Wolf's lap, would have had a much better view, although he hadn't expected her to look.

"One of the papers—it had the government's seal on it," she whispered as she went up on her tiptoes, her voice so low he could barely hear it.

A chill went through him. "Let's get to the bed," he said softly.

They wrapped themselves under the sheets, creating a little fort of fabric. It wasn't soundproof, but it was the best they could do under the circumstances.

Maybe it was a fake.

Maybe it had been stolen.

Maybe someone in power on the Moon was working with the Wolf.

The first option was the most palatable, but if the Wolf could fabricate official documents, it was still frightening. The idea that he might have the means to steal a sealed document was even more so; especially since neither of them had any idea what it might contain and what he might be able to gain from it.

Deep down, they both believed it was the latter: he had come by it genuinely. It would make sense, wouldn't it? The mercenaries hired by the Moon never came close to catching the Wolf. Those on the Moon had always assumed that was because almost all the mercenaries came from Earth. But what if they were wrong? What if it was because the Wolf was always one step ahead, thanks to his allies in power?

There were other questions, too, though. Was the Wolf telling the truth about when he'd released Abby? If he was, why hadn't she gotten out of the hospital until today? The news reports had always indicated the Wolf's captives were returned to their families immediately ... but what if they weren't? What if the reason they never spoke about their ordeal was because someone on the Moon was keeping them quiet?

Bella was the one coming up with the questions, even as Alex tried to convince her it didn't matter— wouldn't matter—until after they escaped, anyway. He had to stay focused; *they* had to stay focused on the immediate goal at hand. It wasn't like they could do anything until they got out of there, anyway. But Bella wouldn't let it go.

"Even if we manage to escape," she whispered, "if

there's someone working on the Moon with him, who says we'll even make it home?"

"They can't all be working with him," Alex insisted. "The news would leak out. Someone in the media would have figured it out. The Wolf isn't all-powerful."

They lay on their sides, facing each other, hands clasped between them, and so close all he would have to do was lean forward an inch to kiss her. She bit down on her lower lip and worried it between her teeth.

"No one's stopped him before. It doesn't have to be everyone, just a couple of key people. Or maybe even a small group."

They debated in whispers, back and forth, until their dinner arrived, and they came out from under the covers to eat. From the little glances Bella gave him, Alex could tell she wasn't happy with his determination to remain focused on escape rather than on the new information she'd discovered.

16

They had another night completely to themselves, which was more nerve-wracking than it was reassuring. Bella wasn't able to fall asleep for long after the lights went out. Thoughts kept whirling around her head about the document with the Moon-government's seal on it that had been on the Wolf's desk, about what it meant, about how to convince Alex this was important. Then, again, maybe it was better he continued to focus on escaping because that was something she'd never put much stock in … now that she had her own wrinkle to focus on. Maybe it was better if they both concentrated on something different; if each of their focuses were divided, it might just be distracting.

Still, she felt the seal was more important than Alex apparently did.

Even if they managed to escape the compound, what would be their next move? Maybe escape would put them in more danger than ever. Not only did the Wolf have allies on the Moon who might return her and Alex to him, but, as far as she knew, no one had ever escaped the Wolf.

If they were recaptured, what would he do to them? Alex was still ignoring the problem of the trackers in their shoulders. He focused on one step at a time, looking for a way out of the compound before he tackled the next problem.

Maybe that was why he was so focused while she had trouble: he took on one thing at a time, where she looked at the whole big picture and froze instead of acting. The idea of escape, as a whole, seemed insurmountable. Cooperating, getting through their days and eventually being released like everyone else, was easier.

And maybe that was part of the Wolf's power, too.

If Bella was scared for her life or worried he meant to keep them forever, maybe she'd have more of Alex's fighting spirit. But the truth was, for the most part, she felt fairly secure within the mythology that had sprung up around the Wolf. There were moments when she wondered if they were in more danger than they realized, but she hugged to the knowledge that his captives were always released and returned to their families.

She could live through this. Bend. Accommodate. Survive. That had been her plan from the start. But if the Wolf had his claws in the Moon's government, even if it was just through trickery or theft, then their problems would be so much bigger than escaping.

The soldiers came at their usual time, unlike the day before. Food and bathroom first, but then Alex and Bella were escorted to the Wolf's hall rather than outside to exercise. That the Wolf had a "guest" coming was not at all reassuring.

Alex wrapped his arm around Bella and glanced down at her face. Her body was tense, but from the way she wrinkled her forehead and nibbled on her lower lip, he didn't think the tension was entirely from fear or anxiety. She was thinking about something. Of course, he couldn't ask what, but he knew she'd become obsessed with the Moon seal she'd seen. If the Wolf's guest really was from the Moon, Alex didn't know what he would do.

He eyed the gun in its holster on the soldier closest to him. It was strapped in, and he didn't know enough to know whether it was fully charged. He'd shot similar weapons for fun on the Moon, but they had always been kept at half or low charges, meant to stun, not kill. Stunning someone wouldn't do much for him or Bella. If he could even get the gun unstrapped from its holster before being shot, himself.

They were led into the room where the Wolf stood on the dais. His desk had been removed, and there was a small table with two chairs on either side, facing it. A thick, red carpet had been laid down on the dais, and draperies erected behind it to give an overall impression of wealth and decadence. He and Bella were placed on either side of the Wolf; Bella kneeling gracefully, Alex much less so. He stirred at the Wolf's side and glanced up to see the man raise an eyebrow and give Alex's collar a meaningful look … followed by a sidelong glance at Bella.

Alex got the message.

Behave or I'll use the collar, and if that's not enough to deter you, Bella will serve as your whipping boy.

Bella focused on the door at the end of the room; at least she hadn't seen the exchange. She wasn't interested in the Wolf right now; Bella was interested in the visitor, because she was afraid she might recognize the person who came through the door.

When the doors opened and an unfamiliar woman walked through, followed by an entourage of soldiers, a wave of relief washed over Alex, and that same sense of relief came from Bella. It was too awful to think that someone on the Moon had betrayed their own; that someone up there might know what was happening to them and still sat by and did nothing. Confirmation of that ... well, it wouldn't have broken him, but Alex would be lying to himself to say that he'd have been unaffected.

The woman walking toward them had a hard edge to her no one from the Moon families would have. Her dark, red hair was cut short, where Moon females always wore theirs long, and it framed a face that was both strong and feminine. There was something about the way she walked that marked her as a fighter, and not just because of the guns and knives strapped to her body. Her eyes constantly flitted around the room as she walked toward the Wolf, and though she strutted with supreme confidence, Alex got the impression she also took the measure of the Wolf's men, as well as all the exits in the room.

It was like seeing something out of an action movie. He'd never seen people who behaved like this in real life. It was disturbing to realize scenes like this actually happened.

The people ranged behind the woman wore similar clothing to the Wolf's men, but there was something slightly different about them. It took Alex a few moments of watching to notice that, while they mostly wore the same colors, the woman's soldiers all had black bands around all their hems—neckline, armholes, etc. It wasn't especially distinctive, but it was a unifying factor that made them look like an opposing army.

When she came to a halt, about twenty feet away from the dais, the rest of her soldiers stopped as well, all of them still looking around the room. A few of them greeted their friends among the Wolf's men with grins and waves, but they were still watchful. The woman had visited the compound before, done business with the Wolf before, but their relations weren't entirely without tension. Was that usual on Earth or was she someone who could turn out to be an ally?

Her eyes swept coldly over both his and Bella's naked bodies, blatantly assessing in the same detached way the Wolf often had about him, and Alex dismissed the notion that she might be helpful. Better the devil they knew than the devil they didn't, and he wouldn't fool himself into thinking she was anything but another demon.

Next to her was a mountain of a man with dark, brown skin that practically gleamed on his bald head. Such a starkly different skin tone was unusual: while history books had told them the skin colors of Earth's population had at one point varied greatly, most skin tones now were in a range between light tan and dark tan. Very light or dark skin was uncommon. The man dismissed Alex almost immediately, and his eyes settled on Bella, who looked back at him with undisguised anxiousness.

"Cora," the Wolf said, nodding his head slightly by way of greeting. "Welcome back. I trust you didn't have any trouble getting here?"

"Scott. Nothing a few hundred credits couldn't take care of," the woman said with a grin. As if that were some kind of signal, the tension in the room relaxed, and the various parties began to greet each other, the soldiers seamlessly integrating into a mingled mass of greetings and chatter. Cora ignored them all and stepped forward with the large dark-skinned man to close the distance between her and the Wolf, who already moved back to sit down.

The revelation that the Wolf had a first name, and such an innocuous-sounding one, was strangely stunning. Alex felt like he'd taken a blow to the chest. But why? It took him a few minutes, as the Wolf and Cora settled into their seats, to figure out what was so shocking about it.

The media and the Moon government had always cloaked the Wolf in mystery. No name. No sure idea where he'd come from or how he'd achieved his power. He was the most well-known figure from the Earth, and yet few facts about him were ever revealed.

But the casual way he and Cora had exchanged their greetings marked them as equals. The Wolf hadn't cared that she'd called him 'Scott,' yet every one of his men, including Jordan, always referred to him as 'the Wolf.'

Who was she, and why hadn't Bella and Alex ever heard of her? More than that, there were plenty of people on Earth who knew the Wolf's name: no one else in the room had so much as twitched. Yet the Moon remained in ignorance.

There has been a wealth of information in that one exchange, and Alex was certain he hadn't realized all the implications yet. But he did know one thing: he wouldn't think of the Wolf as 'Scott.' It was too normal, too humanizing. The man was 'the Wolf' and he was the enemy.

He had a real name. Bella gave the Wolf a sidelong glance. Not that she could easily think of him as someone as innocuous as 'Scott,' but it was still strange to think he had a real name. A mother and father somewhere, too. She'd pictured him as having sprung, fully formed, as a powerhouse on Earth.

But he was Scott, and this woman was Cora.

Bella looked over at the other woman, only to find she was being studied, in turn. A blush rose in her cheeks as Cora looked her over. She was everything Bella wasn't: hard, strong, powerful. Intelligence shone in her eyes, and the ready violence of a soldier was written in every line of her body. For a moment, Bella felt nothing but envy.

This was a woman who was sure of herself, who was respected. Cora's significant other would never cheat on her. He would never dare. And she'd never allow herself to be used as a sex toy. Or, if she did, she would be more like Alex. Not like Bella.

But that wasn't who she was. Bella was Bella and she couldn't change that with a snap of her fingers. And right now, Bella could only think over everything they'd just witnessed.

If the Wolf had allies—or even just one ally—on the Moon then maybe that's why they'd never heard his name before. Maybe that's why they knew so little about him. Maybe that's why the media focused so much on him. Everyone knew there were other crime lords on Earth, of course, and that the planet was basically ruled by them, but the Wolf was the only one who ever seemed to make the news.

"Have you seen John lately?" the Wolf asked Cora as soldiers came up to offer them refreshments. "There's a shipment scheduled to go up soon that might interest him."

The big, black man standing behind Cora's chair shook his head in refusal before his gaze settled back on Bella. She looked away and peeked at Cora instead, who was no longer looking at her. Truthfully, either of them looking at Bella made her feel unsettled; they looked like they were measuring her and trying to decide if she was a treat that might be offered up along with the food and drink.

"So I've heard." Cora grinned as she took a sip from the glass she'd chosen. "He's visiting me next week. I'll direct him on to you afterward."

"Please do."

Well, that was one question answered. It would be hard for the Moon to intercept messages between the various Earth factions if all real information was done face to face. No electronic traces, no opportunity to hack into a line—they'd have to have a spy in place.

Maybe she could be that spy.

Unfortunately, it quickly became obvious the Wolf and Cora wouldn't be doing any real business right now. This was a kind of opening ceremony; a chance to reacquaint themselves.

Bella learned the huge black man was named Trace and he was Cora's right-hand man. Whatever was going down between the Wolf and Cora, it had to do with weapons. And Cora was the one with access to them—another fact that fascinated. What did the Wolf have that Cora wanted? Something was being traded, but they never specified exactly what. All Bella could gather was that it was cartons of something mysterious.

Then the conversation took a much more disturbing turn.

"So what happened to Slave?" Cora asked—although from the lack of true query in her voice, it was obvious she knew the answer. The question was just a segue into a conversation about Bella and Alex. Bella peeked up to find Cora was looking over Alex, while Trace's focus was still on Bella.

A shiver went down her spine as the Wolf's hand landed on top of her head to stroke her hair. Her fists clenched.

"It was time for her to go home," he said conversationally. "This is Pet and Toy." His hand gripped Bella's hair to force her to look up as he said his nickname for her. She couldn't see what Alex's reaction was, but he must have done something. "Toy's still learning how to be good."

Cora's hazel eyes seemed to glow as she looked Alex's kneeling form up and down. "So I see. Do you think you might be willing to share?"

Bella's muscles tensed. The expectation on Cora's and her man's faces said they already knew the answer. The hot, hungry look in the huge man's eyes as they traveled over Bella's body made her want to cower against the Wolf and beg him to say no. Not that it would make any difference, but there was something even more frightening about Trace and Cora than there was about the Wolf. Maybe because Bella had at least heard of the Wolf before, and now she had a small idea of what to expect from him, whereas these two were complete unknowns.

"What's your pleasure?" the Wolf asked easily.

Cora's eyes were still on Alex. "I think I'd like to play with your Toy."

Not unexpectedly, there was movement on the other side of the Wolf, though Bella couldn't see what. Cora just smiled, the way a viper might before it struck.

Behind Cora, Trace frowned and leaned down to whisper in her ear. The woman's eyes flitted over to Bella. Cora looked back to Trace and shook her head. "Next time, perhaps, darling." She stood and smiled at Alex, her face alight with anticipation.

"Just remember Cora, if you break your toys, you don't get new ones to play with," the Wolf said.

Her small, pink tongue flicked out against her lower lip in anticipation as her eyes returned to Alex. "Understood."

Fear for Alex, jealousy, and possessiveness all washed through Bella in a tumble of conflicting emotions, even as her anxiety for herself leapt higher when the Wolf stood, his fingers tangling in her hair. Soldiers already pulled Alex away toward the center of the room as those standing and sitting there cleared a place.

An all-too-familiar grinding noise made Bella whimper. The platform rose in the center of the room, and the soldiers pulled Alex toward it. Bella turned her head, and her scalp pulled where the Wolf's fingers were, but she had to watch. He wasn't exactly fighting, but Alex was definitely resisting being pulled down there.

Beside her, the Wolf's chair shifted, and he sat down again, this time facing the platform that had risen in the middle of the floor. She didn't fight as he pulled her onto his lap and cupped one of her breasts while his other hand stroked her thigh. They both watched as Cora directed the soldiers who held the resisting Alex.

———

The cuffs snapped shut around his wrists and ankles, holding him spread-eagle and standing upright in the center of a large, wooden frame. The chains that connected the cuffs to the frame had barely any give and forced his body into a large x-shape, with no room to maneuver.

The combined groups of soldiers settled back for the show as Cora paced slowly around him. Under other circumstances, he might have found her an attractive-enough woman. Right now, he battled his own anger and frustration at his situation, and his worry over Bella, who'd been left up on the dais with the Wolf and Cora's right-hand man.

"Aren't you a pretty one?" Cora murmured, stepping closer to draw one of her nails down the center of Alex's chest, hard enough to leave a red mark but not so hard as to break skin. Alex kept his face impassive and stared down at her. She smiled up at him, tracing her nail over to his nipple and lightly circling it with her finger. "And so fierce. Trace wanted to play with the pretty Pet, you know. She seemed so sweet ... so submissive ... but I wanted something a little more entertaining today."

Her other hand gripped his balls and squeezed, hard enough that he gasped as sweat broke out on his fore-head. The pressure was painful and unexpected, and, if he hadn't been cuffed to the frame, his knees might have buckled. Cora stared up at him, watching his expression, and held on for a few moments before releasing him. When she did, he dragged in a much-needed deep breath of air, his lungs loosening along with her hold, and Alex sagged against the cuffs.

FUCK.

"Poor Moon Boy ..." she murmured, rubbing her hand over his chest in a soothing manner as he caught his breath. His balls were still cupped in her hand, cradled now. "No one ever teaches you how to deal with anything, much less pain."

Her fingers closed again, like a vise, and this time Alex couldn't help his half-strangled cry as his head fell back, his body trying to arch toward her and pull away at the same time, confused as to which would relieve the painful pressure on his sack. The crushing grip made him nauseous with how much it hurt.

This time, when she released, he opened his eyes to find her studying his expression, which he did his best to keep blank. She would still see the remnants of pain in the tightness of his jaw and the wrinkles on his brow he couldn't quite ease. Cora peered up at him with interest, her lips slightly parted, and leaning in toward him so her breasts brushed his chest. Her fingers cradled his balls again, gently massaging as if to make up for the pain she'd just put him through.

"If I let you go, would you fight me?" she asked, her voice husky with arousal.

"Yes," Alex grated out, fists clenching uselessly.

She laughed, sounding a bit breathless. "You'd lose, little boy."

The woman walked around behind him and dragged her nails along his torso, making him shiver and wince. It wasn't a tickling sensation and it wasn't painful, but an uncomfortable combination of both. He couldn't stop himself from writhing a bit, and he hated the involuntary reaction, but that was what she'd aimed for.

Her nails raked down his back, and he arched away,

the cuffs holding him in place as the painful scratches burned. The people sitting around the tables in front of him laughed; his movement had looked like he was thrusting forward. Something brushed against his back, lightly, and Alex tensed before he realized what she was doing.

Hot, open-mouthed, wet kisses trailed down the scratch marks, mimicking the way a mother might 'kiss' a scratch better. Except she'd made the wounds. Her nails trailed up and down his sides in a seductively teasing manner that made him want to squirm away, but she came at him from both sides, and her mouth was on his back, and there was nowhere for him to go. As her tongue licked over the upper swell of his ass, Alex's cock twitched, and he fought against the sensation.

Cora had moved from torturing to tormenting him. Even though his balls ached and the scratches down his chest and back burned, her gentler touch made his skin tingle with pleasure. Blood surged in his cock, and he could feel the traitorous organ begin to swell. The cock ring did its job, accelerating the engorgement of his penis as her teeth grazed gently over his buttocks and her fingers came down to tease the sensitive crease where his ass met his legs.

Alex gritted his teeth and ignored the laughter and murmurs around him as his cock came to a full, upright stand. Cora's nails trailed down the backs of his thighs and knees, making him jerk as the ticklish sensation caused spasms in his muscles.

When the sensations disappeared, he braced himself for whatever would come next. And waited.

And waited.

He looked over his shoulder and saw Cora rifling

through one of the chests of drawers that was available, looking for who knew what.

Straining his head over his shoulder like that hurt, so he turned back around and looked in the opposite direction: the dais where Bella was. The last time he'd looked up there, she'd been on the Wolf's lap; now she was over it, face down, her hands pressed against the floor to help balance. His fingers moved in and out of her body while his other hand held her in place. From the angle of his hand, Alex could only assume the Wolf was fingering her ass. Trace was beside them, avidly watching what the Wolf did to Bella rather than what Cora was doing to Alex.

Fury, some of which was toward his own inability to hold himself up and out of Bella's asshole when he'd been given the opportunity, swept through him ... but he didn't have time to dwell on it. Cora was already back in front of him, tiny silver clamps held open between the fingers of each hand.

"Ever tried nipple clamps before, Toy?"

Alex refused to answer and stared above her head. Fuck this. He didn't play this game with the Wolf, and he wouldn't play it with her, either.

Unlike the Wolf, Cora didn't seem to care about forcing an answer from Alex. She placed the clamps around the little pebbles of his nipples and let them close. Just as the pressure became painful, she opened them again. Alex's jaw tightened. And she did it again.

She played with him, letting him feel the pinch, making his nipples harden from the cool rubber grips and the stimulation, but drew out the anticipation. She let him get just a hint of how much it would hurt before drawing back from fully closing the clamps.

Alex wanted to growl at her to just do it, but he had a feeling she was waiting to see his reaction. He just his focus above her head, above the heads of the people behind her. Eventually, he might not be able to control his reaction, but, while he could, he would hold onto impassivity for as long as possible.

Apparently giving up, or possibly bored with his lack of response, Cora let the clamps fully close on his nipples to crush the tiny buds. Alex hissed in a breath through his teeth as he felt the full impact of the clamps. The pain blossomed in his chest, throbbing with his heartbeat as his blood was stymied, unable to push past the grip of the clamps. A throb answered in his cock as the cock ring seemed even tighter. His jaw ached as he clamped down against his verbal reaction.

Cora dragged her nails down his front, and he sucked in his stomach to try to relieve the painful scratches. His cock jerked as she neared it.

"You have a very nice cock, Toy," she said approvingly, encircling it with her fingers and squeezing. Reluctant pleasure washed over him as she began to pump the engorged shaft, rubbing her thumb over the head whenever her fingers came close enough. She watched him with slightly hooded eyes, a small smile curving her lips as she stroked him. "I'm going to enjoy riding it."

A shudder went through his body. Part pleasure, part revulsion, and part self-disgust because he knew, physically, he enjoyed the pleasure that she was giving him, even as parts of him burned and stung. The pressure building up in his balls needed release and relief, but he didn't want it like this and he sure as hell didn't want it from her.

Not that he got a choice.

She gave his cock a few more pumps, which made the cock ring feel even more restrictive around the base of the angry, red organ, before releasing him with a smirk. Alex breathed deeply as his dick throbbed. The painful pressure on his nipples had finally subsided and only flared when his upper body moved and accidentally made the clamps bounce.

Cora gave Alex a sultry look before she walked around behind him again and passed out of sight. It had been almost flirtatious. A mockery of the kind of look she might have given a man she was actually interested in.

A swishing noise reached Alex's ears just before thick strands of something thudded against his upper back. He jerked in reaction and groaned as the clamps bounced painfully on his chest, tightening around his poor nipples as they were jostled about. The actual blow to his shoulders wasn't overly painful, just a thudding impact and then a slight sting.

It came again, less of a surprise this time, and he was able to brace against it. The stinging increased. The next blow struck across his ass and made him jerk in surprise again before the strands hit back against his shoulders. They began to alternate—shoulders, upper back, his ass, and his thighs, following no discernible pattern that might help him anticipate where the next one would land.

She wasn't hitting him very hard—just hard enough for him to feel the snap of the strands against his skin— but the more blows that fell, the more sensitive his skin became until every slap of the strands was like hundreds of little bees stinging him all at once. The surface of his back, ass, and thighs felt like it was burning, prickling, and there was no way for him to twist away from it. His fists clenched and unclenched as he occasionally gasped and groaned when the strands would hit a sensitive spot. The underside of his ass became particularly painful.

It wasn't long before he couldn't contain his vocal reaction, and it came out through his clenched jaw as pain-grunts. The impact increased, and he tried to relax his muscles—tensing only increased the pain.

When she stopped and walked back around in front of him, Alex couldn't help sagging with relief. Now he could see the whip; it looked like it was made out of leather, with lots of long strands. In her other hand, she held a shorter, smaller version, but it had to have been the bigger one she'd been beating him with. His mind felt fuzzy as he wondered what the smaller version was for.

"Did you enjoy the flogger, Toy?" Her voice was a purr as she used the whip to rub his thighs and belly and let the strands knock gently against his cock, which bobbed angrily in front of him. Now that she'd stopped distracting him, Alex could feel the painful pressure of his dick again: achingly hard and without relief in sight. The tension radiated up his body from his groin and made it hard to breathe. Every brush of the leather strands against his cock was a tease he felt all the way to the back of his neck, where the little hairs stood straight up. "You certainly look as though you did."

Arguing would be pointless. If she wanted to pretend his erection had anything to do with the stinging abuse of his backside, it wasn't like Alex would be able to persuade her otherwise. The surface of his skin was still hot and sensitive; cool air trickled over him from somewhere— something he hadn't noticed before and probably wouldn't have if his skin hadn't felt so hot by comparison.

A swish of her wrist, and the strands snapped against his balls. Not hard, in relation to his backside, but the stinging against his sensitive sack was far worse than any of the other blows she'd landed. Alex arched as he gasped with pain; it radiated in sharp spikes through his groin. He might have shrieked if the shock hadn't paralyzed his vocal cords. Nothing he'd experienced before had ever felt anything quite like this, no matter how roughly his partners had played. Cora laughed and flicked her wrist again to snap the tiny flogger against his cock. It bounced backward, smacking his body as though it tried to flee the nasty whip.

Alex gasped with every snap of the whip against his cock and balls, unable to achieve a complete lack of reaction, and felt as though his head was beginning to splinter apart. Not just because of the pain, though it grew with every stinging snap of the leather against his most vulnerable parts, but because of his helplessness. A woman he didn't know was whipping his manhood in front of an audience, and he couldn't do anything to stop her. He wasn't even sacrificing himself for Bella this time —when he turned his head, he could see her bent over a bench with the Wolf thrusting behind her and Trace pushing his thick cock into her mouth.

There was nothing to help Alex hold onto his definition of reality, his sense of rightness, or to explain the pain that built up. His balls and cock were swelled under the lash, the pressure becoming immensely painful as the cock-ring trapped the blood in his dick. The erect organ turned a dark, angry red—he couldn't see his balls and he didn't want to. The building spikes of pain stabbed into his lower back and up the base of his spine.

No matter how Alex twisted or pulled away, the nasty

sting always found his groin, lashing his balls, his cock, and the sensitive skin around them. Tears stung his eyes and made his vision blurry, and he began to hope he might pass out if only to escape from the nightmare. Without the cock ring, his entire groin would be shriveled in and trying to hide; instead, his dick looked like a grotesque mockery of arousal.

The painful throbbing of his cock matched his heartbeat, which pounded in his ears to drown out every other noise.

When Cora finally dropped the whip and stepped forward to wrap her fingers around Alex's shaft, he couldn't stop the whimper that escaped past his lips. Even her deliberately gentle touch felt like it was chafing sandpaper against the sensitive skin of his cock.

"Take him down," Cora said, her voice filled with eagerness.

For once, Alex didn't consider fighting as the soldiers unshackled his wrists and ankles. He was too wrung out, too dazed, and too tender in too many places to risk it. Not to mention an escape attempt right now would be the height of stupidity.

They pulled him over to the bed and strapped him down, face up. Alex groaned as he realized why, but by that time it was too late to fight. His red, angry cock pointed straight up, and the cool breeze flowing across his skin did nothing to soothe it. The restraints were tight around his wrists and ankles, holding him in place. His back and ass stung and burned where his skin was touching the sheets, still sensitive from the lashing he'd received.

Cora crawled onto the bed, gloriously naked. She was a beautiful woman, there was no denying that. Her hazel eyes glinted with anticipation as she moved toward him, slight breasts jiggling beneath her body. Unlike the women on the Moon, her limbs were sleekly muscled, her body toned from the necessities of her position. She straddled him, light-brown nipples erect with her arousal.

She grasped his cock in her hand and smiled as he gasped and arched, unable to do anything to relieve the intense pressure and pain that came from being touched again.

"Fuck!"

The woman laughed as she lowered herself down so her sopping-wet pussy touched the tip of his cock. The heat of her body felt like molten lava, trickling over the tender crown. "That's exactly what we're going to do, Toy."

Alex choked off a scream as she pressed down and took his tortured cock into the tight sheath of her pussy. His cock felt like it would explode now, and not with orgasm. The heat was all around him, scalding him, her clenching muscles squeezing painfully as she settled herself on top of him. She moaned, arching her back and shuddering as her pussy lips pressed against his groin.

He'd never realized sex could be so painful.

Cora reached up to cup her breasts and pulled on the hard points of her nipples, and then began to ride him. His body jerked and shuddered beneath hers, trying to escape the overload of sensations. The painful rasp of her walls against his sensitized skin, the aching, throbbing of his balls and cock as they swelled and swelled inside of her—the pleasure that was so intense it felt like it might kill him.

And with every movement, the chafing of his back

and ass against the sheets added more stinging sensation so he was awash in flickers of pain from every side. Atop him, Cora moaned and bounced, playing with her breasts as she used him like the sex toy the Wolf had named him. Every time she settled on him, she swiveled her hips and ground her clit against his groin, clenching him inside her and making him want to howl with the pain that was drowning him.

The worst part was he could still feel his orgasm building. The steady stimulation and her slow pace coiled a much-needed release in his balls. His body started to have trouble deciphering the pleasure from the pain; his mind whirled in a chaotic vortex of sensation that overwhelmed his reactions and thinking.

Moaning, gyrating, Cora began to ride him harder, making his body arch as he gasped with pained pleasure.

"FUCK YES!" she cried out, grinding down on him, her fingers tightly pinched around his nipples. At that exact moment, the cock ring released, and Alex screamed as the most painful orgasm he'd ever experienced rocked him from his head to the tips of his toes.

With all the other sensations throughout his torture session, he hadn't noticed, the cock ring slowly tightening to ensure he would stay swollen and erect. Now that it had been released, he realized what had happened, but there was nothing he could do about it. The pent-up cum seared the inside of his cock as it spurted, and Cora's massaging cunt milked him in the most painful manner possible. His entire groin felt like it was on fire, and his lower body ached from his cock up the base of his spine and into his muscles.

And yet his orgasm flowed on, unabated.

Watching Alex being whipped by Cora had been harder than Bella could have ever imagined. She'd ended up closing her eyes while the Wolf played with her ass, inserting first one finger and then another, rather than watch Alex's body uselessly twist in the air and try to escape the long whip Cora used on him. Bella couldn't shut out the sounds of the leather slapping against his body or his low grunts of pain, but at least she didn't have to watch.

At some point the Wolf had his men bring up a padded leather bench that he bent her over. The next thing she knew, Trace stood in front of her, thick, brown cock pressing against her lips, and the Wolf pushed his cock into her ass at the same time. Bella gasped as her anus opened for its second cock, ever, the sharp, stabbing pain of first entry not entirely ameliorated by the prep-work the Wolf had done with his fingers. And Trace used that moment to shove his dick between her lips, muffling the sound of her pain.

He was thicker than either the Wolf or Alex, and her jaw ached as she struggled to open wide enough for him. With one hand in her hair, he held her head in place for him to thrust easily into her mouth and shove his cock directly down her throat. The thick crown forced its way past where her gag reflex would have been if it hadn't been for the gel. At the same time, the Wolf burrowed into her ass, stretching her with hard, fast strokes that went a little deeper each time—a sharp contrast to Trace's immediate dominance over her mouth.

The big man groaned with pleasure as he pressed her nose against his groin and filled her nostrils with the smell of his musk. She whimpered as the burning in her anus went deeper, her sphincter clenching uselessly around the Wolf's lubricated shaft as it tried to push him out. It made her stomach cramp as he forced his way into her tight hole, his fingers massaging her hips all the while.

The sounds of male pleasure filled her ears as they began to fuck her, one at each end, neither of them paying attention to the other's rhythm. Bella whimpered and clutched the bench, writhing between them. Trace reached down to pluck at her nipples, to cup her hanging breasts and squeeze them hard in his big hand as he slid his cock in and out of her mouth. Behind her, the Wolf angled his cock in just the right way to rub over an incredibly pleasurable spot deep inside her ass.

Her body quivered between the two men, her pussy clenching around nothing as they plowed into her. They both used her for their pleasure, but Trace's manipulation of her breasts and nipples, combined with the Wolf's gentle massage of her hips and buttocks as he fucked her ass, was surprisingly pleasurable. The swollen little nub was almost getting just the right amount of pleasure as her mound pressed against the bench and sent flares of arousal through her lower body, despite the circumstances.

It made her feel guilty when the sounds of Alex's torment changed. She couldn't see what had happened, but something was different. The higher pitch of his voice, the increased volume indicated Cora was doing something awful. As if in response, the Wolf's thrusts got harder, faster, and his fingers dug into her hips as he used her ass. The nearly virgin orifice tightened in protest, which only increased the burning friction as he fucked her hard.

Bella's gargled gasps and whimpers vibrated against Trace's cock as her sore jaw and throat struggled against biting down. She didn't want whatever punishment might follow such a transgression.

His fingers tightened in her hair as his thick rod began to grow even thicker and longer and it pressed against her tongue. Bella almost choked as his cum began to spurt; he was still thrusting rather than burying himself, and his jizz coated the inside of her mouth and throat, forcing her to actively swallow or risk inhaling the hot fluid. Her tongue and throat worked as he pumped, groaning above her head. The bitter taste of his sperm lingered, even after he stopped spurting it.

Trace kept his cock in her mouth as it began to soften but sighed with pleasure when he finally withdrew. Bella whimpered and braced herself more firmly on the bench. Without Trace's hard body in front of her, the Wolf's thrusts put her off balance, as if she might pitch forward at any moment.

She looked over at the platform and felt a shot of jealousy roll through her as she saw Cora riding Alex. Stupid jealousy, because it wasn't like Alex had a choice. But seeing another woman straddling him, having sex with him ... It made Bella want to tear Cora's hair out.

Trace's dark face blocked out her vision as he crouched down beside her, his lips quirked with amusement. "Don't worry about the kid, pretty girl, Cora will leave him in one piece."

He cupped her breasts with both hands and tweaked her nipples, and Bella gasped. Her eyes got big with surprise. This was the first time any of the men, other than Alex, had shown any interest in her after they'd gotten off. The taste Trace's cum was still in her mouth, and he wasn't aroused anymore, so why was he touching her?

He pinched her sensitive nipples, and she couldn't stop herself from moaning. Her ass clenched around the Wolf's cock in response, making her shudder as fire flared through her.

"I thought these seemed rather sensitive," Trace said, his deep voice sounding smug as he began to pull on the little buds. Bella whimpered, hating the bolts of pleasure that shot through her now that someone was paying such focused attention to her nipples. There wasn't as much to distract her now, either; she couldn't see Alex and Cora, and she wasn't struggling to breathe anymore.

The slick glide of the Wolf's cock in and out of her ass had stopped being truly painful; her muscles had adjusted, and she began to feel more pleasure than pain, as a whole. Especially with Trace's hands and fingers nimbly squeezing and tweaking her breasts and nipples. Bella arched slightly and tried to press her breasts more firmly into his hands as she reached for the pleasure that built up inside her.

Her mons pressed against the bench, and the Wolf's hard thrusts put more pressure on her swollen clit as Trace tugged at her nipples. The big man leaned forward and took one into his mouth to suckle and tease it with his tongue. Bella moaned, arching again, and thrust her ass up and her breasts down.

The Wolf grunted, his fingers splaying across her hip bones and digging in deep as he began to plow her, hard. From the dais, she could hear Cora's pleasure, Alex's howl, as her own body began to reach its critical point.

Trace's manipulation of her sensitive nipples tipped her over; Bella cried out as she shuddered with pleasure, and her pussy spasmed emptily as her ass clamped down on the Wolf's thrusting cock.

He plowed into her, harder and faster, and the burning friction of his cock against the sensitive walls of her ass made her ecstasy spin even higher as Trace's teeth bit down gently on her nipple. It was exactly what she needed to fly high; her orgasm shuddered through her more forcefully than any other since they'd been taken by the Wolf. Pleasure engulfed her, rode her, and she was buoyed along the top of it as it crested and fell.

Heat spurted inside her, her nipples blossomed with pleasure, and the front of her mound pressed so hard against the bench it was almost painful.

As the pleasure slowly wound down, her body shuddered and clenched over and over, spasming in the aftermath of her intense orgasm. She didn't realize she'd closed her eyes until they fluttered open again. Trace still gently tugged on her nipples—he'd been intently watching her while she came.

White teeth flashed as she blinked at him, dazed. "Beautiful girl."

One last tug on her nipples and then he stood up and moved away from her. Bella groaned as the Wolf pulled himself free, and her sore anus quivered as it was emptied of his cock.

———

That night neither Bella nor Alex spoke. They curled around each other, lost in their own thoughts.

Besides, what could they say?

17

The morning started like every morning since Trish had been taken. She was dreaming when she felt the first trickle of awareness; a touch skimming along her body that brought feelings of both arousal and anxiety. Before she was truly awake, her lips parted on a gasp, her nipples hardened, and she was wet and ready. It was a Pavlovian response.

She'd studied the history of psychology before she'd found a passion for art history, and she knew what was wrong with her. There was a name for what she was experiencing, but the knowledge didn't lessen the impact.

It was called Stockholm Syndrome.

And it didn't stop her from moaning, from spreading her legs even wider than the hard hands on her inner thighs pressed her to. Her eyelashes fluttered as her eyes adjusted to the light. The swipe of a tongue up the center of her pussy made her moan again as her hips rolled, her half-asleep body easily manipulated by a man who had spent quite a bit of time learning her responses.

"Open your eyes, little girl."

That was something he always insisted on. She obeyed and looked down the length of her body, past the small mounds of her breasts with their perky, pink nipples, to the man whose mouth hovered inches above the short, white-blonde hair of her pussy. His blue eyes seemed to glow as he met her gaze and held it as he lowered his lips to deliberately suck her clit into his mouth while she watched.

Trish shuddered and her hands clenched in the sheets. His tongue rasped over the tender bud, and her back arched as the pleasure washed over her. The steady sucking on her clit was almost too intense to bear, and she tried to close her legs, to protect the sensitive area, but his hard hands kept them wide open. Left her vulnerable.

"Please," she whimpered, and her fingers dug into the sheets again. She'd learned, after the first day, not to try to stop him with anything but words. Her ass still burned when she remembered the spanking he'd given after tying her hands behind her back. And, as always, when she remembered it, shame and sexual excitement poured through her in equal measure. "It's too much."

Jordan must have been feeling indulgent today; he gentled the suckling before he released her clit and began to lick up the center of her pussy, seeking out the wetness that trickled between her folds. Trish moaned and writhed some more for him while she watched the slight bob of his head, up and down, between her legs. Every so often, his eyes would flick up to meet hers, to ensure she was watching, to trap her with his gaze.

The slow, seductive laps of his tongue against her swollen flesh and the occasional nibble of her tender lips soon had her panting with need. She wanted him to suck her clit again, but didn't ask. That was one point of pride left with her: she never asked for the pleasure.

Jordan gave it to her anyway. When he was ready.

It felt like her body was burning up from the inside out, as her insides clenched and spasmed, empty and hungry for fulfillment. Trish moaned and moved her hips up and down, her eyelashes fluttering open and shut the way they did when she was became lost in the physical sensations. Her orgasm built, too slowly for her comfort, as Jordan tormented her with pleasure.

When he moved away from her pussy and began kissing his way up her stomach, she nearly screamed with frustration. The need to cum was overpowering, and her body moved to connect with him, her pussy trying to rub along the hard muscles of his body as he slid upward. When he sucked her nipples into his mouth, she let go of the sheets and clutched at his head, pushing her small breasts upwards to encourage him. One large hand completely covered her other breast and squeezed it just hard enough to make her gasp with pleasure.

The head of his cock nudged against her pussy, and she bucked and tried to position it at her entrance, needing more.

Jordan grinned wickedly and tugged on her nipple with his teeth before releasing it. His large body covered hers, and he grabbed her hands and placed them over her head as his cock nestled against her slick hole. Trish moaned. She was about to get what she wanted. Needed. Whenever they were alone, Jordan restrained her, either with his hands or actual restraints. If people watched, he preferred for her to have her hands free. Those were his two dominant kinks.

Her pussy stretched as he moved his hips forward.

"Open your eyes."

Trish moaned as she forced herself to look up at him. He always insisted on looking into her eyes as he entered her. That icy gaze took in every detail of her expression as his thick cock stretched her open. Whatever he saw, it always seemed to arouse him more. Sometimes Trish swore she could feel him get harder when she gazed up at him, helpless and trapped beneath his much larger, much stronger body.

And damn her own traitorous reaction: she became more aroused by it, as well.

She was so wet from his mouth, from being so close to orgasm, he could take her as roughly as he wanted. Which was probably his intent in waking her up the way he had. She cried out as his lips lifted in a soundless snarl, and he shoved in deep and fast, his cock splitting her open. She was wet, but she was always tight when he first entered her, and it would take several pounding strokes before her body would adjust to the length and girth of his dick as it split her open.

But the burning stretch felt as good as it did painful, and her body arched to rub her wet pussy lips against him. Trish wrapped her legs around his thighs and held onto him the only way she could, her hips canting up to meet him.

Before Jordan, she'd never had rough sex. Never known she would like it.

She'd never had sex in front of people. Or sex while restrained. Or sex with another woman.

Some of it she still didn't like, but this ... These mornings with just him teasing her body and then pounding her into submission beneath him ... These she could become addicted to. When he wasn't fucking her brains out, he treated her like a fragile flower. But in bed, he let loose with a savage dominance that left her pussy feeling bruised more often than not. Yet she orgasmed every time.

So hard … So hot inside her …

She came with a scream, ecstasy rolling over and through her as his dick rammed home. Her pussy became even more slick as she creamed herself on his cock and writhed beneath him in passionate bliss, her trapped wrists pushing uselessly at his hand. It was agony and rapture as he fucked her, just as hard, and forced her body to spasm as her pleasure-organs were overstimulated.

Trish's drawn-out cry was strangled, her eyes wide open and sightless as she came again and again beneath him, her pussy clamping down around the thick cock that continued to pierce her with savage thrusts. She sobbed out another plea … an entreaty … It was too much.

"My name …" Teeth bit down on her ear. "Say it."

"Jordan!"

She screamed again as he plowed into her, filling her completely before he went still. Her pussy throbbed so hard from her climaxes she almost didn't feel the pulse of his cock inside her, the thick jets of liquid that filled her. Everything was white light and shimmering passion, her body tingling from head to toe, and the final satisfying shudders of her orgasm.

———

When she woke again, it was exactly an hour later. Jordan had a morning routine that went like clockwork, no matter what.

"Come on, little girl, time to get up." His eyes flickered over the naked length of her body once he'd pulled the sheets away. For a moment, those eyes lingered on the dark, pink lips of her pussy, still looking battered from earlier. Trish didn't bother trying to get up because it didn't matter. He would do exactly what he always did. A heartbeat later she was scooped up in his arms, and he was carrying her to the private washroom attached to his bedroom.

Jordan scrubbed her down in the shower, intimately and thoroughly, which left her gasping and aroused again, and then he picked out what she'd wear for the day while Trish sat on the edge of the bed and waited. Patiently. Like a doll.

As long as she didn't move from the spot he'd put her in, she could do whatever she wanted. Swing her feet. Mess up the sheets. Ask him questions. He'd even answer. But move one inch from that spot and he wouldn't just spank her, he'd get out the paddle.

The first few days she'd been resentful of his constant ordering of her life. Now she was used to it. She almost found the routine soothing in some ways. Yeah, Stockholm at its best: that was her.

Jordan pulled a light-pink dress from the closet and turned to come toward her. He tended to put her in the lighter colors—the ones that went so well with her pale features. Sometimes Trish wondered if he liked her for herself a little bit or if he was still just obsessed with her hair color. Because he definitely was.

That's what came after getting dressed. He would sit her on his lap and brush her hair until it was almost dry. It was another part of the day she found soothing, although at least it made sense. It was also the part of the day she wished would last longer because once it was done, it was time to leave the room. Time to go out into the halls and the rooms where there were other men and women; where she would be exposed and played with and sometimes fucked in front of them.

At least none of them ever touched her. Not like Bella and Alex. Jordan liked to show her off, but he was wildly possessive.

Today was different, though. He only brushed her hair for about ten minutes before he put it into a braid. That made her nervous.

"What's going on?" she asked hesitantly as he led her out of their room. With one hand in his, looking up at him, she felt a bit like the little girl he called her when he led her everywhere by the hand. But it also made her feel safer.

He smiled down at her, reassuringly. "Sorry, little girl. We've got things to do today."

It amazed her how Jordan was allowed to bring her wherever he wanted around the compound. At first, he'd left her in the room for periods of time; now he almost always took her with him, and no one said a word. Eventually she'd realized it was because, for the most part, she'd been extremely well behaved after the first couple days. Even at the beginning she hadn't put up more than token resistance.

After all, what was the point? No one on the Moon cared if she was here—not like Bella and Alex. If they did care, it would only be as a novelty, and they'd probably lose interest once they realized the Wolf didn't have anything to do with her. Some other student would get her scholarship, but that was the most disturbance her disappearance would have caused anyone: a bit of paperwork. That was just how it was. There were people who were important—or, at least, the children of people who were important, like Alex and Bella—and people who weren't. Like Trish.

Strangely, in some ways, she was treated better here on Earth.

Cool air swirled around her thighs as they passed by people in the hallways. They were almost all soldiers. The entire compound was filled with them, and there were more around than usual because of Cora's visit. Those who knew the woman either nodded or smiled at her as she passed. At first, the soldiers' attitudes toward Cora had startled Trish, especially because none of them leered at her or made crude comments.

Not that Jordan would put up with that. As much as he enjoyed showing her off, it was always on his terms, and he never let anyone else touch her.

Well, with a few exceptions.

Laura, one of the women she could sort-of call a friend, waved at her from down the hall where she stood next to her man, Marek. Well, 'stood next to' … Really, tucked under his arm. Like Trish, she wore a dress, although hers was a deep purple that would have washed Trish out.

There were two kinds of women in the compound. The vast majority were soldiers—they were all shapes and sizes, all levels of attractiveness and they all had one thing in common: they were hard. They played hard, fought hard, and were treated by the men as equals. Trish had seen plenty of relationships between soldiers, and no one seemed to care.

But then there were a few men who had 'their' woman; one who wasn't a soldier but was allowed to stay in the compound, and those women always wore skirts. It was like a special uniform to let everyone else know that woman was off-limits.

Everyone respected the skirt.

Strangely, there didn't seem to be an equivalent for the men, though a few of the female soldiers had their own women in skirts, too. When she'd asked, Jordan had shrugged and said they weren't restricted from bringing a civilian male into the compound. But, for whatever reason, none of them had one.

"Morning Princess," Chevie said as he dished out Trish's usual eggs and potatoes. Jordan hovered protectively over her shoulder, although he didn't consider the friendly cook any kind of problem. His eyes watched over the newcomers.

"Morning Chevie." Trish took her plate. "How's Trix?" She didn't see the sunny redhead anywhere in the kitchen behind him, where there were quite a few people working.

"She's good," Chevie said cheerfully, but didn't expound further, and there were people behind her, so she had to keep moving. Jordan kept one hand on the small of her back while his other held his plate full of food. He ate nearly three times as much as she did.

Every morning, Jordan chose a different table to sit at and circulate among the Wolf's soldiers. It was probably part of his job as the Wolf's second-in-command. It certainly meant she got to see a lot of different aspects of the Wolf's operations, but no one seemed concerned about what she overheard.

Today, everyone talked about Cora, of course, but instead of talking about whatever was going on, they all discussed her torment of Alex the day before. With

Jordan's hard body next to her, his hard thigh pressed against hers, Trish sat quietly, eating and listening.

"Did you see how shocked Moon Boy was?" one of the women asked, laughing. "Bet he'd never felt anything like that on his nuts before!"

"At least he didn't cry and beg like the last one, or worse—wet himself."

"Couldn't wet himself with that hard-on anyway."

"Did you see the way Trace was eyeing Pet? Bet you that Cora asks for her next time."

"Ha, not after the way she enjoyed Toy! She actually got to have some fun with a Moon Boy for once!"

"Ten credits she gives in to Trace and takes Pet."

"Done!"

The happy banter and cheerful betting felt incongruous with the events of the day before. Trish shivered. Sometimes she wondered about the people of Earth.

Everyone was nice to her. They enjoyed watching Bella and Alex's debasement, but they seemed to see some difference between Trish and the other two captives. Was it because she was with Jordan and not the Wolf? Or because it was well known Trish was an orphan and not part of the privileged classes who lived on the Moon?

The soldiers were all derisive of the Moon families; contemptuous, even. Alex had garnered some small amount of respect and fascination, although he probably wouldn't be overjoyed to hear that since the reaction was a group desire to see more of his debasement, to try to predict his reactions. She'd seen more than one bet being settled over his behavior.

Bella's behavior was less interesting to them. Her reactions were similar to those they'd seen before, although more than one person had commented that if Alex hadn't been taking up so much attention, then Bella might have been more of a standout. She had a grace under pressure; a steady bravery that kept her going.

Trish had started trying to emulate her in some ways.

When she'd first been taken, Trish had been nearly hysterical, and her first few days had been hard. But she'd seen how Bella had stayed calm and done whatever she'd needed to do. She hadn't seemed to dwell on the things that were done to her; she'd held herself together and hadn't fallen apart, no matter what the provocation.

Trish had the unfortunate suspicion that her trying to do the same was feeding into her own problem—she'd become so accustomed to this life she had trouble imagining leaving it. It should have been terrifying, but what was really scary was it *didn't* terrify her.

What did she have to go back to, after all? At least here, she felt wanted. Cherished. Desired.

Yeah ... She was definitely losing it.

"Here, Trish." A pancake was dumped onto her plate by one of the women across the table—a hard-edged brunette whose name Trish couldn't remember, although she'd seen her around often enough. The woman frowned at Jordan. "You need to take better care of her, Jordan She's barely touched her food and she hardly weighs anything as it is."

Oh shoot.

The big blond turned away from the man he'd been talking to and frowned down at Trish.

"Sorry." She blinked up at him. "I'm eating." Trish shoveled a forkful of eggs into her mouth and then began cutting up the pancake.

Jordan stroked his hand over her head before letting it

come to rest on the back of her neck, a steady reminder of his presence. And to eat. Trish was exasperated, but there was no point. The brunette went back to her own conversation, but kept one eye on Trish. It was unsettling, after years where no one cared what she did or how she was, to be so constantly under everyone's scrutiny. Strangely caring scrutiny, sometimes.

After breakfast, Jordan picked up the food he always brought to Bella and Alex. He was leading Trish out of the cafeteria when he got a call on his com-unit. He put one hand to his ear and then pulled her to the side of the hallway while he answered it.

"Yes ... Yes ... No ... Yes, Sir."

Jordan grabbed Trish's hand and pulled her down the hall.

The wrong hall.

"Where are we going?" The change in routine made her uneasy.

A smile flickered across his face. "You're going to see a secret, little girl."

The small hallway he took her into was empty, and they were about a third of the way through it when he stopped and faced the wall, which had a marking on it that looked a bit like an s with a horizontal line through the top curve. The marking was all over the compound; Trish had seen it a million times. It was in hallways, rooms ... There were three of them in Jordan's room, and at least a dozen in the cafeteria. It was the kind of innocuous wall decoration that went unnoticed because of its commonness.

Jordan pressed his fingers across the shape quickly; the right end of the bar, the left end, the bottom curve, the top curve, and then on each place where the s intersected the horizontal bar. The wall sank inward and then slid silently to the side.

Trish's jaw dropped as she stared into the dimly lit hallway beyond, barely hearing Jordan's chuckle at her shocked reaction. He grabbed her hand in his again and pulled her into the hall. When she glanced back over her shoulder, she saw the door had slid smoothly shut behind them. The same decorative symbol was on this side of the wall.

"Are all of them like that?" she asked. If there were … Good grief, how many secret passageways would be around the compound?

"No. All the passageways are behind symbols, but not all the symbols have passageways," Jordan said, walking quickly enough that Trish had to trot to keep up with him. His legs were so much longer than hers, but he expected her to make up for it. "The entrances are not commonly known, nor are the way through the passages, although everyone knows they're there. You could get lost in them if you don't know where you're going."

As if to emphasize his point, they had already reached an intersection that branched off into four other passage-ways—five, including the one they had just come from—and nothing to differentiate one from another. Jordan took the second to the left without hesitating.

"But what are we doing in here?" Trish looked around for any sign of where they were within the compound. They passed more symbols, so she assumed they were passing exits from the tunnel, but where would they open up?

"There was a … disturbance on our usual route," he said, unperturbed by both her questions and whatever the disturbance had been. Trish sighed and hoped it wasn't something too awful. Maybe Cora's men and the Wolf's men were fighting?

It might be easier to escape with the two sides fighting each other ... but escape to what? Where? Plus, how would she find Bella and Alex? Could she live with leaving them behind? And what would happen to Jordan if there was fighting?

Dammit ... She shouldn't be worried about him, but she didn't like the idea of him being in real danger. Even though, by all rights, she should have wanted to see him hung out to dry, the idea of his admittedly beautiful body being ripped open by violence made her insides clench in a kind of anguish.

Her suffering from a psychological condition didn't dissipate the effects of it.

Trish fell silent, disturbed by her own thoughts, and wondered about the passageways behind the compound's walls. Where did they all lead to?

They went through two more intersections before Jordan stopped in front of another symbol and pressed his fingers in the same pattern as before. The right end of the bar, the left end, the bottom curve, the top curve, and then on each place where the s intersected the horizontal bar. As he did it, Trish stood behind him and watched, silently mouthing the pattern and trying to commit it to memory.

As soon as the new passageway opened and they stepped out into the hall, Trish recognized where they were: steps away from the room where Alex and Bella were kept. Trish was willing to bet she and Jordan had barely lost any time from their detour. One look back at the wall, with its distinctive-but-common decoration, and then Jordan was pulling her along again.

———

"Secret passageways?" Bella repeated, her mind whirling around the possibilities.

Trish nodded, nervously glancing over her shoulder at Jordan, who stood talking to a small group of soldiers, a mix of Cora and the Wolf's men. The blonde wasn't a very good actress—she was obviously agitated as she passed the information on to Bella and quickly whispered the way to open the panels while Bella tried to memorize it.

As usual, Alex was swimming his laps, frustration and anger written in every line of his body. Bella was pretty sure he still felt the effects of Cora's torment, both physically and mentally. Last night they had slept wrapped around each other, but neither of them had known what to say.

Bella carefully committed everything Trish said to memory and tried to dampen her excitement. This was something Alex would want to know. He would hope the passageways could find them a way out of the compound. Bella wondered what else they might be able to learn inside the compound. A lot of questions had arisen in the past few days—not just about Earth and the Wolf, but about the Moon's government.

Now she just had to figure out how to pass the information along to Alex.

———

By the time Alex pulled himself out of the pool, every part of his body ached. He'd been swimming for at least an hour, he'd scrubbed himself clean in the shower before that, but he still felt like there was a layer of dirt on his skin that wouldn't come off.

There was a small group of three soldiers nearby, talking and joking. Two were the Wolf's; one was Cora's. Tidbits of their conversation floated on the breeze, but he wasn't interested in listening. At least they weren't talking about him. Then a tingle went down his spine as he heard something more relevant.

"… the Wolf and Cora …"

"… think they'll run into any trouble?"

"… Jordan and Trace are still here …"

"Guess we'll find out tomorrow."

Did that mean the Wolf and Cora were out of the compound, personally leading whatever mission they were on, while their seconds-in-command stayed behind?

Alex looked across the pool, past where Trish and Bella were deep in conversation, and over at the big blond. It wasn't often that Jordan allowed Trish out of arm's reach, but it looked like his attention was divided today. Soldiers would come into the outdoor area and head straight to Jordan and, as soon as he finished talking to them, would walk purposefully back out. Which was very different from the usual day, where Jordan would walk Trish around the gardens and watch over her exercise.

Now that he thought of it, Bella or Trish hadn't gotten anywhere near the pool, and no one seemed to care. Something was definitely going on.

It became even clearer after he and Bella were fed and exercised and escorted immediately back to their room by some more soldiers. Jordan had already gone off, Trish in tow, and Alex hadn't seen the big blond molesting her even once. She'd also looked incredibly nervous and had given Bella a little glance as she'd been pulled away. What had the two of them had been talking about?

When they got into their room, which was empty as usual, Bella looked over at him. He could almost see her thoughts churning inside her head as she chewed on her lower lip. There was something she wanted to tell him.

Alex glanced around the near-empty room and inwardly sighed before going over to the bed. His cock still felt a bit sore, his balls tight and achy, but there was no other way to get any kind of privacy. If they were observed whispering to each other, they wouldn't be left alone for long. Even if the Wolf was out of the compound, they couldn't be sure no one was watching.

He walked over to the bed and sat down, and looked over at Bella, who shifted nervously back and forth on the balls of her feet as she watched him. His cock and balls had been tortured yesterday, but Alex still felt the familiar stirring of arousal as he looked at her feminine curves, the tight, pink nipples tipping her breasts, and the puffy lips between her legs. It didn't matter that he saw her naked all day or that it wasn't by choice—whenever he focused on Bella, his cock got a little jolt of excitement.

He patted the bed next to him.

"Come sit down," he said in a low voice, giving her what he hoped was a significant look.

Bella's eyes widened, but she came toward him. Was it his imagination, or did her nipples get a little bit harder?

To his surprise, she didn't sit next to him and instead crawled onto the bed, going behind him to force him to turn and follow her. Not that he minded. She lay down on her side, facing him. This would be easier to get close enough for them to whisper in each other's ears while making it look like they had another reason for their closeness. He lay on his side, facing her, so close he could feel the heat of her body against his, though they weren't quite touching.

Her cheeks pinked a bit as he leaned slightly over her.

The movement was deliberate: he crowded her and took charge of their interaction. Alex needed the return to control, the dominance, after yesterday with Cora. And Bella was definitely sexually submissive. It was like a soothing balm to his psyche; one he hadn't known he desperately needed until this moment. His arousal stirred more as he looked down at her and saw her reaction to him.

It made his cock and balls tingle, in a not entirely pleasant way, as the remnant of yesterday's torture still lingered, but he couldn't help his physical reaction to those wide, brown eyes and the slightly parted, pink lips.

Alex swept her hair back off her shoulder and leaned forward to give her neck a kiss, his cock hardening as a shiver went down her body and her nipples lightly brushed against his chest hair. She shifted, giving him more access to her neck, making herself more vulnerable and arousing him further.

"I think the Wolf and Cora are gone today," he whispered in her ear as he moved his lips up her neck. "And Jordan and Trace have been left in charge." Alex brought his hand up to rest lightly on her hip. His fingers drew little patterns on the side of her buttock, eliciting more small shudders for him to enjoy. His cock began to swell and reach for her, uncomfortable as the skin stretched, but even without the cock ring, that tiny bit of discomfort wouldn't be enough to deflate him.

One of Bella's hands pressed against his chest, trying to push him back. He was pretty sure she wanted to be able to speak back to him and couldn't because right now her face pressed against his arm and shoulder. But Alex didn't want to lean back and let her on top, so instead, he relinquished his resting spot on her hip and grasped her wrist in his to push her onto her back.

Bella gasped as he leaned over her, half-covering her soft body with his harder one. He pressed her hand down next to her head and continued to explore her throat and collarbone with his lips, inserting his thigh between her legs as he felt her hips lift in response.

"The sheets!" Bella whispered urgently in his ear. Alex growled at the reminder that they couldn't touch each other freely but released her wrist to reach down and grab the sheets and pull them up to cover the two of them.

With any luck, if the cameras in the room were on, whoever was watching wouldn't realize anything more than sex was happening. Although, the last time they'd touched each other, no one had been watching. Maybe the cameras had only been turned on because the Wolf had known there would be a show after injecting Bella with the aphrodisiac.

Not that they needed extra help right now. Alex's cock was hard and pressing against Bella's hip, and, from the way she wriggled underneath him, he could tell she was just as aroused as he was. Her silky skin felt almost too intense against the sensitive surface of his dick, but it wasn't nearly as painful as it had been yesterday.

When he moved back into position, he found Bella hadn't moved her arm an inch from where he'd placed it, and he groaned as he buried his face into the crook of her neck to find the sensitive spot where her neck met her shoulder. She gasped, her other hand sliding between their bodies to come up and wrap around the back of his neck, to hold him in place as she arched beneath him.

Bella twisted slightly and her lips found his earlobe. "This morning Trish and Jordan used a secret passageway."

That got his attention, even as Bella sucked his earlobe into her mouth and nibbled on it. The suction went straight to his cock, and he pressed it harder against her hip, bringing his thigh up more to find the wet heat between her legs. She gasped and rubbed herself against his leg, as if she were riding his thigh, and her fingers tightened around his neck.

"Tell me."

And she did. It was hard to concentrate while they caressed and moved against each other, her whispering words filling his ears even as erotic need filled the rest of his body. Bella was so soft, so willing beneath him ... It was an incredible gift for her to be so willing, considering their situation. It was also hot as hell. Not being able to move away from kissing her neck and shoulders so she could whisper in his ear was slow torment, especially because Alex's ears were on a direct line to his groin.

He slid between her legs and rubbed his cock against her pussy while she repeated the directions to open the passageways and tried to concentrate while pleasure and a slight amount of pain shot through him. There was soft, wet heat, but it was almost too much to bear. He cupped her breast and squeezed, and her nipple pressed against the palm of his hand as Alex enjoyed the way she writhed beneath him.

Her repeated words became breathless, ragged, as he aroused her.

Being on top of her felt right. It felt good.

It was easy to forget it wasn't a necessity of their situation. As a gentleman, he should stop. Pull away. Stop trying to make her as horny as he was. Just because they'd touched each other, had an intimate moment, didn't mean she would necessarily consent to sex. But he didn't want to stop. He pinched her nipple and tugged on it, knowing how sensitive those little buds were.

Bella arched beneath him, her legs wrapped around the backs of his thighs, her heels digging in just above his knees as she tried to pull him into her.

"Please," she whispered in his ear, interrupting her recitation of the sequence to press on the s-shape. It didn't matter—he had it as committed-to-memory as it was going to get. He couldn't concentrate anymore because all his focus was on not plunging his cock into her. But then she moved her hips and brought it up to him, rubbing her juices over the length of his cock.

Alex drew back just enough to angle himself correctly, pressed forward ... and hissed between his teeth as her molten core gave way for him. It didn't hurt like it had yesterday, but it wasn't pure pleasure, either. She was incredibly wet, which helped, because her tight walls provided a lot of friction over the sensitive surface of his cock, and her muscles gripped him as he slid into her.

"Yes, yes, yes, yes, yes," she chanted under her breath, and, as Alex pulled his head back to look down, her cheeks were flushed a bright pink, and her eyes were closed.

"Look at me," he growled, curling his hands under her

shoulders to hold her in place as his cock nestled home inside her.

Eyelashes fluttered, and she looked up at him, her gaze hot and feverish, clashing against his as he shoved the last inch of his cock into her heated tunnel. Her lips made a small 'o,' and her eyes widened as he ground his body against her pussy lips and clit and she jerked beneath him in reaction.

Fuck ...

This was exactly what Alex needed. Bella, wet and willing, not just allowing him to be on top, but wanting him there. Being turned on by his control. Her pupils dilated as he stared down into her eyes, and his hips flexed to pull out halfway and then thrust deep. She whimpered, but kept looking up at him, still obeying his order. Giving him that small amount of control in his life.

Something dark and needy unfurled inside him, and he growled again, low in his throat, as he slid his hands up her body and forced her arms above her head. His fingers intertwined with hers to make her stretch out beneath him and to hold her in place on the mattress. Bella moaned, bucking as her pussy clamped down in visceral reaction to his dominance.

"You would tell me to stop if you didn't want me, wouldn't you?"

It wasn't really a question as he pulled back and thrust hard into her, but more a demand for her to acknowledge she wanted him, she wanted this. Bella's eyes burned into his, shining up at him, as her body welcomed him in.

"Yes," she whispered, and tightened her legs around him. Alex pulled out again before shoving back in, hard and deep. She made a sexy sound, low in her throat, as he filled her. It felt like her pussy was made of hot, wet, nubby silk, wrapping around him, rubbing against him.

"And you want me, don't you? Tell me you want me."

"Yes ... Alex, please, yes!"

Bella shuddered and arched beneath him as he began to pound into her, hard and fast, fulfilling his need to claim her. Images of the Wolf and Trace double-teaming her ran through the back of his mind—images he wanted to erase from her memory and replace with himself. He pressed down on her hands and leveraged himself up to take her hard, sending slices of pain through their pleasure as he pummeled her with his sensitive cock. It only made the ecstasy stroke higher.

"Yes, yes, yes yesyesyes!" Bella chanted the word as if her life depended on it, her throaty affirmative voicing her desire, her joy in choosing him, choosing this.

And Alex reveled in it; wallowed in her passion the way he wallowed in her body, wrapping himself in her sexual need and allowing it to fulfill him in a way he'd never felt.

He'd never so badly needed a woman to say 'yes' to him. Never so badly needed to have control over both himself and someone else, or needed the peace that kind of trust could bring. He'd never been so out of control, never been sexually tortured, and never been so aware of the privilege of receiving that 'yes' before they'd been taken by the Wolf.

When Bella came, pulsing around him, writhing beneath him, the ecstasy was so great Alex felt it all through his body and in the air around him, as if their orgasms were too large to be contained by their physical bodies. It reached into his brain and touched his soul, his inner self, in a way none of the Wolf's depravities or torments ever could. The pleasure, the connection, was pure ... beautiful ... and real.

Alex gripped her hands tightly as his cock throbbed inside her and shot jets of cum into her pussy with the same rhythm she clenched around him, as if she were pulling every pulse of pleasure from him.

Fuck ...

Completely spent, he nearly collapsed on top of her. His body and head whirled with the combined effects of their passion and the information about the secret passageways.

Alex groaned as he turned and brought her with him so they were still connected as he pulled her on top of him. She was a soft weight, like a blanket over his body. With a sigh and a small wriggle, she settled in, her cheek resting on his shoulder.

A tender care stole through him as he stroked her hair away from her face and turned to place a kiss on her forehead. As much as Bella aroused him, she elicited much softer emotions from him, as well. Protective emotions that were all the more frustrating because of his inability to provide her with any kind of protection or care.

What he could give her was this: a gentle touch, a sweet caress, and soft kisses while she hummed with pleasure. A stolen moment to pretend they were just two lovers, cuddled together after their passion.

But even as he blinked and looked across the room, his eyes focused on the s-shape, his mind already moving away from the moment and toward the possibility of their freedom.

The End

THE STORY CONTINUES...

Toy, Pet, and the Wolf return in the stunning conclusion to The Warlord's Duet, His Pet.

Escape. Survive. Rebel.

When Alex and I were taken by the Wolf, I never expected to see our home again.

But we had no idea how devious Earth's most dangerous warlord really was.

Or how deep the corruption of our own government ran.

The Wolf continues to mess with our memories, for reasons we haven't yet figured out, even as he uses us for his pleasure, sharing us with whoever he pleases. In between, we plan our escape, determined to return home.

And when a group of the Moon's most important government officials visit us, we finally have our chance.

We'll return. Then we'll do everything in our power to free our people from the corruption and oppression happening right beneath their noses.

Because I would rather die than live the rest of my days in another cage. No matter how gilded it may be.

Grab His Pet on Amazon!

ABOUT SINISTRE ANGE

Sinister Ange is a *USA Today* best-selling author and the alternate pen name for Golden Angel. She is happily married, old enough to know better but still too young to care, and a big fan of happily-ever-afters, strong heroes and heroines, and sizzling chemistry.

She believes the world is a better place when there's a little magic in it.

www.sinistreange.com

ABOUT GOLDEN ANGEL

Golden Angel is a USA Today best-selling author of heart and bottom warming romance.

She is happily married, old enough to know better but still too young to care, and a big fan of happily-ever-afters, strong heroes and heroines, and sizzling chemistry.

When she's not writing, she can often be found on the couch reading, in front of her sewing machine making a new cosplay, hanging out with her friends, or wandering the Maryland Renaissance Fair.

www.goldenangelromance.com

bookbub.com/authors/golden-angel

goodreads.com/goldeniangel

facebook.com/GoldenAngelAuthor

instagram.com/goldeniangel

After years of working in different aspects of the publishing industry, Niki Roge and Rayanna Jamison came together to form Get That Book Publishing, known as GTB Publishing. GTB Publishing is a small press publishing house with a focus on anthologies and indie authors.

Within GTB Publishing, we have designed 4 specific publishing brands for readers and authors alike to easily find the tropes and books that fit them best.

GTB Publishing focuses on dark romance. From gray to pitch black, dark romance lovers everywhere are going to find something to satisfy their desires.

Dirty Daddies Publishing focuses on Daddy Dom, age play, DDlg, and all aspects of Daddy romance. This brand was established in 2018 and has many USA Today and bestselling anthologies already and is now being expanded to accept Daddy books of all kinds!

Passionate Pages Publishing focuses on all aspects of romance that doesn't fit into the above categories. From contemporary to sci-fi to everything in between, you'll find something passionate in the pages!

Red Hot Romance focuses on newer authors, shorter stories, high spice and lots of power exchange!

Find more information about us:

Website: https://gtbpublishing.com/

Newsletter: https://gtbpublishing.com/newsletter/

Facebook: https://www.facebook.com/gtbpublishing